# WHEN EVIL CHANGES FACE

A MOTOR CITY THRILLER

BY
## THERESE SZYMANSKI

## Bella BOOKS

Ferndale, Michigan
2000

**Bella Books, Inc.**
P.O. Box 201007
Ferndale, MI 48220

Printed in the United States of America on acid-free paper
First Edition

Editor: Lila Empson
Cover designer: Bonnie Liss (Phoenix Graphics)


ISBN 0-9677753-3-7

*To my beautiful Swan.*
*I wish all love could be so simple.*
*I cannot imagine my life*
*without you in it.*

## Acknowledgments

I'd like to thank Kelly Smith for liking Brett enough to continue her — and for letting her be as bad as she really is. Of course I'd like to thank Barbara Grier and Donna McBride, for first taking a chance on a Polish baby dyke from the Motor City.

A big thanks to Julia Watts and her friends for telling me to submit this book, which was hidden in a desk drawer for several years, instead of the previously planned fourth Brett. Also thank you to Marianne Martin for checking over my high school facts.

Thank you to Bella's staff — Bonnie for the fabulous jacket and Kathleen for her always fun over-the-top jacket copy — but most especially to Lila Empson for pinpointing exactly what needed to be done to this novel to make it so much better, for her wonderful reality checks and fact findings, for opening my eyes to more than a few things, and most important of all, for her incredibly insightful editing overall.

I'd also like to thank my DFBs, Fred and Martin, for the fun, drinks, and random acts of silliness. (Alas, poor Astro, Fred's yellow lab, passed away in 1999.) I'd also like to thank my DSB (Designated Straight Boy), my brother, Bruce Szymanski. Thank you for the late-night phone calls about deadly firearms, pipes, cigars, and other things that have added to Brett.

Finally, and definitely most important, a big hug and butch-bonding arm wrestle to Kathleen for all the laughs, and a big hug and kiss to Barbara, without whom this novel would not be as good as it is, for listening, inspiring, and making me laugh and think.

## About the Author

Therese Szymanski has done quite a number of things to keep a roof over her head. Because she has had remarks made in the past about the suspension of disbelief in her novels (something that causes her friends to collapse in gales of laughter), she would like her readers to know that, sitting on the "wrong" side of thirty, she still frequently gets carded — even for smokes. (Waiters and cashiers have been known to laugh in her face when she attempts to purchase alcohol.)

She maintains that she is not on the "wrong" side of thirty because she's never had a better time with the ladies and never wants to see eighteen, or high school, again.

*When Evil Changes Face* is her fourth novel. The first three in the Brett Higgins series, *When the Dancing Stops*, *When the Dead Speak*, and *When Some Body Disappears*, are published by Naiad. She also has short stories in the Naiad anthologies *The Touch of Your Hand* and *The Very Thought of You*, the latter of which includes a short story she cowrote with Barbara Johnson, "Double Fantasy" in which Brett Higgins meets an attractive femme in an elevator that conveniently breaks down.

# Prologue

It was a night like so many other nights.

He pulled his car up into the driveway. It was late, and snow was beginning to lightly trickle down from the sky.

"That was one helluva party," his friend said, climbing out of the backseat.

Half slumped in the front seat, she slurred, "Party . . ."

"C'mon babe," he said, going around the car to help her out. His parents weren't home, so he planned on continuing the party at his place.

She was wearing only the Tinkerbell costume he had talked her into donning for the Halloween party. He liked how short the skirt was, how much he could see of her ripe body. He liked it that others looked at her lustfully. And he liked what he knew was going to happen in just a few more minutes.

"You comin'?" his friend called from the front door.

"Yeah, 'course." She was nearly deadweight, and he had to half carry, half drag her to the house. "You think we gave her too much of that crap?"

"Nah, man. This is gonna be fuckin' great! Roofies rock, man!"

He laid her out on the couch while his friend found the video camera and set up the tripod. He turned the camera on, focusing it so that it would pick up the entire couch area.

Driven by hormones and overpowered by greed, he reveled in the task at hand and didn't look back. He would learn way too late that he should have.

# 1

"I'm home!" Brett Higgins called as she entered the hotel suite that was home while she and Allie house hunted in the Detroit Metro area. Her meeting with Frankie had lasted all afternoon. And now she was so hungry even an all-you-can-eat buffet wouldn't satisfy her, but she was still surprised when not only did she see Allie and Madeline, but also another woman in the sitting area of their suite.

"Hey, honey," Allie said, tossing her long blond hair over her shoulder while a small seductive smile spread across her aristocratic features. "I hope you don't mind if a friend of Madeline's joins us."

Brett glanced at Madeline, who was watching intently. From another person, this might've perturbed Brett, but she was accustomed to such strange behavior from her old next-door neighbor. Before Brett could speculate further, the stranger stood and approached her.

"Hi, I'm Leisa Kraft," the woman said with a slight smile. She was tall, a smidgen taller than Brett in fact — probably around five-eleven — with hair the color of molten gold. Although Brett normally preferred her women to be slender, like Allie, Leisa, who had a bit more of a build to her, was still quite attractive. An obvious added perk to this, even though Leisa tried to cover it with a rather loose, baby blue polo shirt, was that she probably wore at least a D cup.

"Pleasure to meet you," Brett finally said, after running her eyes up and down Leisa's body but stopping before Leisa faltered from Brett's assessment. Brett met her eyes and was immediately arrested by the most startlingly intense green eyes — a shocking sea green — she had ever seen. Leisa's hand was warm in hers, and Allie sat just a few feet away.

Brett dropped the hand. "Madeline, is there somethin' you haven't told us?"

Madeline finally smiled. "Yes, but not what you are thinking."

"I'm starving. Let's eat," Allie said, standing.

Leisa and Madeline preceded Brett and Allie out the door and down the hall.

"What's goin' on?" Brett whispered as she locked the room.

"I don't know," Allie answered. "Madeline wanted to wait for both of us before she'd tell me anything. She got here earlier. We had brunch, looked at houses, and came back here. Then Leisa showed up." Allie shrugged to display her lack of knowledge in the matter. "She seems nice enough. I'm guessing she's from Alma."

Leisa and Madeline paused at the elevator, waiting for them.


In the restaurant, the waiter led them to their table. "Can I bring you anything to drink?"

"I would like a glass of white wine," Madeline said, and Leisa and Allie ordered the same.

"I'll take a Glenfiddich on the rocks," Brett said, thinking she needed something stronger, considering Madeline's secretive mood.

The waiter looked at Allie and Brett. "Can I see some ID?" he asked.

Allie smiled and handed it over, but Brett grimaced. Once the waiter had left, she looked across at Madeline and Leisa. "So what's this about?"

Madeline turned to Leisa. "She is not known for outstanding patience or waiting until after a peaceful meal and conversation. You might as well tell them now."

Leisa smiled slightly at Madeline before turning to face Brett and Allie. "I live in St. Louis, a small town near Alma, and I teach at Alma High School." She paused, as if trying to find the right words. "And lately we've been having some problems there," she continued with a sigh. Brett watched those amazing green eyes cloud over.

"What sort of problems?" Allie prompted.

"I'm not really sure. Kids who have always been perfect are now late and absent a lot. They are acting up across the board. I don't have any proof or anything, but I think maybe drugs are involved."

"What sort of drugs?" Brett asked.

Leisa shrugged. "Marijuana. Cocaine. I don't really know. I don't want it getting out of hand. Nobody does."

"Of course not," Allie said. "Nobody ever does."

"There're just a few of us who suspect anything, and the police won't get involved because we don't have any hard evidence."

Brett took a sip of her drink, laid it on the table, lit a cigarette, and sat back in the booth, studying the women across from her. There had to be a damn good reason why Madeline had brought Leisa all this way to tell them this rather mundane story. Madeline always had her reasons for everything she did, no matter how strange those reasons sometimes were. There had to be more to the story.

"I've lived in the area my entire life, and I've never before witnessed anything like this. I mean, I know there've been drugs — hell, no place is safe from them anymore, and we do have the college in town — but it upsets me. I'm concerned about the kids, and I don't want whoever is causing this to get the idea to move on to bigger things."

Madeline reached over and put a hand on Leisa's shoulder. Leisa turned to her and slightly bowed her head.

The intensity of that private moment was broken when the waiter brought their food. He spent a few minutes arranging their plates in front of them, after which Brett cut up her steak, medium rare of course, and buttered, salted, and cut up her baked potato as well. The steak practically melted in her mouth. She enjoyed good food like she enjoyed good women. She slipped her hand onto Allie's slender, muscular thigh.

Leisa looked up from her chicken Kiev. "There're just a few of us who feel this way. Most of the teachers think it's a case of kids being kids, but three of us want to do something and we don't know what we can do."

Brett nodded. That was it then; they wanted to bring Allie in as a detective, which made perfect sense. After all, she had done that sort of thing for the police before.

"I care about these kids, and I don't want happening in Alma what's been happening all over the country." The passion blazed in Leisa's eyes.

"Do ya mean the drug abuse and crime, the way kids get started younger and younger," Brett said harshly, "or the violence, the goin' postal and shooting classmates down in the library?"

Leisa swallowed, staring at Brett over the table. There was a long pause, but Brett knew what they were thinking — Paducah, Jonesboro, Columbine. Six-year-old murderers.

Allie broke the silence. "Brett, I can tell when you've spent too much time with Frankie — you start talking like him."

Brett suddenly realized what Allie said was true. She was an educated woman, yet she often changed her vocabulary, enunciation, and sentence structure to whatever was appropriate for the situation. But obviously she hadn't done so today. Why was that?

She affected the proper accent. "Please excuse me," she said to Leisa. "I do often blend into my environment, play a role if you will, so I become part of that environment. However, in this instance, I have continued my prior role when another was suggested."

Leisa paused, then broke into a smile. "Thanks, I needed that."

6

"I told you that these two could do whatever is required," Madeline said.

" 'These two?' " Brett said. "Hold on, I was thinking you wanted Allie to do something —"

"Brett, dear, lower your voice," Allie prompted.

"We actually require the services of both of you," Madeline said.

"Both of us?"

"Yes. That is the only way to sufficiently cover all the required areas."

"What do you have in mind?" Allie asked.

Leisa and Madeline exchanged a glance. "Perhaps we should wait until after dinner to discuss that," Madeline finally said.

"Oh no, don't go bringing up something like that and then trying to drop it," Brett said.

Leisa met her eyes over the table. "I'm desperate. I don't want things to change, at least not like this. I love my kids and don't want anything to happen. I'm already having trouble sleeping. I don't know how I'll ever sleep again if I find out that something's happened that I could've helped avoid."

Brett looked into her green eyes for a moment, then turned to the blue-eyed Allie and put an arm around her. "Damn you, Madeline, you know my weak spot for blondes," she said, looking right at Leisa. She planted a brief kiss on Allie's lips and felt the silkiness of Allie's long, blond hair caress her fingers.

During the drive home, Allison Sullivan looked over at her very butch lover. When she had first come out, she never could've imagined that such a woman would do to her what Brett did. But then Brett came along and did it. Allie had started off preferring femmes, but now she realized that she relished Brett's strength and power. Brett's way was to do the unexpected, to be who she was no matter what. Allie loved that about her. The seventeen-year-old Allie had known that from the moment she met the tough twenty-three-year-old Brett. However, no matter what anybody ever thought about Brett Higgins, it was she, Allie, who had to first kiss Brett, who had to first seduce Brett.

Brett thought she was some sort of a big, badass butch, and she fit that image with her imposingly tall five-foot, ten-inch well-muscled body; her head of thick, short hair black as night; and her wild, wicked past full of exotic dancers and illegal dealings that Allie knew she would probably never know the full extent of. Brett was like a big, dangerous, powerful black panther.

But Brett was charming and good-looking, and she exuded the excitement Allie lacked. Brett took Allie the way Allie had always fantasized. Brett knew exactly what Allie wanted and how far to push her. Allie trusted her. Bret teased Allie — hell, she would openly flirt with other women, like she had with Leisa tonight — but she would make sure that Allie and everybody else knew that Allie was the one she was going home with. Brett made Allie feel special, knowing she was always the winner every time. The others could hope Brett would follow through on her flirtations, but she never would.

Allie never understood why someone like Brett, who could obviously have her choice of a great many women, would want her. Brett was so handsome and exciting. Allie was good-looking and attractive, but was what most people would call rather vanilla. Other than with her parents, and they weren't around anymore, it was only with Brett that she felt special and wanted. Allie's first female lovers had all cheated on her — sometimes with each other — and even though Brett had done the same, she had dumped the other women for Allie.

Allie had to admit to herself, though she'd never tell anybody else, least of all Brett, that she enjoyed knowing that other women looked at her woman. But she knew Brett was hers. She knew it every time she looked into those exciting eyes that varied from almost brown to almost green, depending on Brett's feelings and intentions. And it was only because of Brett that Allie had become aware that other women were looking at her, at Allie. That was a part of Brett that most others had no idea about, that Brett would point out when other women were looking and would make Allie feel even more special and wanted.

Above and beyond all that was the fact that while other women would make remarks about how much they loved their girlfriends, Brett had proven to Allie that she would quite literally die for her. That was one hell of a thing to live up to.

Allie was especially excited that Madeline and Leisa wanted

Brett and her to work together on whatever scheme they had in mind. She wanted to work with her lover, wanted to show Brett her world, since she had already learned quite a bit about Brett's world.

Throughout dinner and the drive home, Leisa and Madeline stubbornly refused to discuss their plan, but the minute they entered the hotel room, Brett shut the door and looked at them. "Okay, now, what the fuck's on your scheming little brains?"

"Alma, St. Louis — all the towns near there — are all small. The residents know or know of one another," Madeline began, sitting calmly on the sofa. "You two are not originally from that area, only lived there a short time, and managed to remain anonymous."

"One does try to do that while on the lam, y'know," Brett said, walking to the bar to pour herself a scotch.

"You better make me one too, hon," Allie said, coming up behind her. "I have a feeling I'm going to need it." She looked at Madeline and Leisa. "Anything for you two?"

"You know, neither of you really needs a drink, for what we are about to request is actually quite simple and will come naturally to both of you."

"Then tell us what it is, already!" Brett said, downing her scotch and pouring another.

"We want you two to come to the school and check things out," Leisa finally blurted. She took Brett's drink from her hand and claimed it as her own, downing half of it in a single gulp.

"Check things out?" Brett asked.

"Yes, we want you to investigate the situation, discover what is really going on," Madeline said.

"And just how do you suggest we do that?" Brett wasn't liking this one bit and definitely still needed that drink. So she poured herself another one that no one was about to take from her.

"We want you to go undercover as students," Leisa answered. "As teenaged brother and sister." Her eyes were wide, as if all of Madeline's toying with them was driving her as nuts as it had Brett.

Leisa's actual words hit Brett when as she heard Allie say, "What? You've got to be kidding!"

"You want us to what?" Brett echoed.

9

"Pretend to be students so you can figure out exactly what's going on," Leisa said.

"It is a sensible idea; it makes perfect sense," Madeline stated in her perfectly logical and sensible way.

"C'mon, for crissake," Brett protested. "There's no way we can possibly pass as high school students." She took off her jacket and loosened her tie.

"I hate to say it," Allie said, "but Brett's right. There's no way this can work."

"But it's got to!" Leisa said.

"Brett, dear heart," Madeline cajoled with a smile. "We're hoping to settle this all peacefully before anything goes truly awry."

"Maddy, honey," Brett argued, running her hand through her short hair. "You see this gray in my hair? It's caused by shit like this."

"Some Grecian Formula should take care of that," Madeline replied matter-of-factly. "Things are known to happen for a reason, and I believe that this is one of those times. Perhaps you two have some unresolved issues that such a task might help you to better face and thus deal with as you build your future together."

Sometimes Madeline talked in a way that made it tough for Brett to keep up with her, and this was one of those times. "Yeah, right, in your dreams!" Brett barked, once she had worked her way through Madeline's riddle and realized that she was insisting that they needed to do this. "There's no way in hell I'm going back to high school!"

"Besides," Allie added, laying a calming hand on Brett's arm, "as I said, no one would ever believe we're teenagers."

"They don't want to do it, Maddy," Leisa said, slouching on the couch, her disappointment apparent.

"I disagree," Madeline said. "As I said, with some Grecian Formula and the appropriate crotch-scratching, Brett could quite easily pass as an adolescent male —"

"Madeline, I'm thirty-three and she's twenty-seven," Brett said, pointing to Allie. "Besides, we've got way too much to do — like house hunting." She looked at Leisa, who looked forlorn. Lost. Brett felt a pang of guilt. Leisa really cared about those kids.

"So you want us to be narcs?" Allie questioned, apparently becoming intrigued with the idea.

Their recent success at helping to apprehend several criminals was obviously bringing back her love of truth and justice, Brett thought. It was bringing back the woman who had grown up to be a cop. Brett wasn't sure she liked that idea. After all, it was that same woman who had shot at Brett and thought she had killed her.

"*Narc*," Leisa replied as Brett refilled her glass. "That's such an ugly word, isn't it? A word I never thought I'd hear in relation to Alma." Her eyes took on a glassy, faraway look. Brett wasn't sure what Leisa's tolerance for alcohol was, but Leisa was already beyond that limit. Brett knew that she was going to have to insist that Madeline and Leisa spend the night with them.

"That is what needs to be done," Madeline replied. "It is the perfect way to get inside the circle, to find out what is really happening."

"It's probably just the same old crap," Brett said, trying not to stare at Leisa. She was an attractive woman, and her glazed eyes made Brett think of the first startlingly attractive blonde in her life, her cousin Marie, the first woman Brett had ever really loved.


Brett's sweet Marie was her first cousin, and Brett's own age. Brett remembered dear Merry with her long, blond hair and soft, loving touch. She always thought of herself as Marie's evil twin, her exact opposite, but Brett knew they had a great deal in common — like the physical, emotional, mental, and sexual abuse they had each shared at the hands of their families.

From their earliest days, the two had planned on escaping from their grim lives, but starting at the age of fifteen Brett saw Marie decline into a world of drugs and prostitution, a world of easy money and total escapism.

Brett remembered well Marie's glazed eyes the last time they had met. Brett had yearned for her, had looked forward to the meeting, but Marie was no longer the same woman. Actually, she had seen Marie one more time after that, when her dear cousin had unknowingly gone looking for a job at the adult theater Brett managed. Brett couldn't stand seeing what had happened to the intelligent, beautiful, and sweet young woman she had first fallen in love with. She was now unnaturally slender, emaciated even, and her once gorgeous hair, now hanging limply around her face, had lost its rich sheen and luster.

Brett had found Storm and told her to take the young woman out for dinner, to make sure she ate a good, healthy meal. She also gave Storm money to give to Marie, and told Storm to try to talk Marie into using it for food and shelter instead of drugs.

She never saw Marie again after that.

She wondered if she was still even alive.

She wondered if any of her family was still alive.

Brett had lost the first person she had ever loved to drugs, and drugs had always played a role in her life through others. For fuck's sake, she had even sold them at one point!

Madeline apparently saw her opening and moved in for the kill. "This idea first started to form when I realized I had never seen either of your pictures in the news with regard to your recent escapades."

"We like our privacy," Brett said.

"Whatever," Madeline replied with a wave of her hand. "I know you two have a lot of experience in this sort of matter, which, with your relative anonymity, is exactly what we need."

"It doesn't matter, Maddy," Brett said. "You see, I'm a bad guy. If I lived in the Old West I'd be riding around in a black hat. I am not a good guy, I don't do good things, and I don't help damsels in distress. I am a bad guy."

Allie leveled an even glare at her lover. "So this is your penance for your years of troublemaking?"

"Are you telling me you want to go back to high school?"

"No, but I think we should at least listen to what Madeline has to say." With that Allie turned back to Madeline. Brett glanced at Leisa, who now looked hopeful.

"I have it all figured out," Madeline began. "You two will pose as brother and sister — fraternal twins. Your father, my brother, recently passed away. Your mother has sent you to live with me because you were getting into too much trouble in your Detroit neighborhood."

"So we would have to live with you?" Brett asked. When

Madeline nodded her head, Brett added, "But we were living with you not too long ago. What if someone recognizes us?"

"They probably won't. Now you will be teenaged sister and brother, my niece and nephew. They will see you as different people because they will see what we want them to see, which is what we'll tell them. But if they do remember you, we can say you came out on vacation, and they will accept that."

"And Brett," Allie added, thinking out loud, "you can still be bad. You'll be the bad boy and I'll be the goody-two-shoes girl — that way we can fit into most of the school."

"Wonderful idea, Allie!" Madeline exclaimed, while Brett shook her head.

Brett wrapped her arms around Allie. "Allison," she whispered in her ear, "do you really want me to pose as your brother?"

"Think of it this way," Allie whispered back. "The sooner we get to the bottom of things, the sooner we'll be done."

"But how do you know there's a bottom to things, that it's not just a case of kids acting up?"

"I have a feeling," Madeline said.

Brett was beginning to hate Madeline's feelings and the fact that she could overhear everything. "There's no way I can pass as a teenage boy."

Allie looked at Brett, as if analyzing her appearance. "You're tall, and if you were a boy, you'd be considered lanky. You're not heavy enough to be a man."

"What about these gray hairs?"

Leisa ran her hand through Brett's hair. "Grecian Formula or hair dye should take care of it."

Thinking that Leisa's fingers felt too good, Brett moved away. "It ain't gonna work."

"People have a tendency to see only what they want to see," Madeline said. "The last thing they would be looking for in you is a thirty-three-year-old woman."

Leisa was intently gazing at Brett. "How often do you get ID'd for alcohol?"

Brett shook her head and turned away, but Allie chimed in. "A lot. And she gets called *sir* a lot as well."

"People are idiots," Brett said. "I think they mostly do it when they think —" she broke off, knowing what her line usually was.

But of course Allie knew it. "You think they do it when they think you're a twelve-year-old boy."

Leisa grinned. "I thought so." Before Brett could voice another objection, she added, "And if you're supposed to be the bad boy, you could have flunked a grade or two, so that you're nineteen or twenty."

"This ain't gonna work."

"It's got to," Leisa said firmly. "I can't stand not doing anything while these kids destroy their lives."

Brett thought again about her cousin Marie, the only family member she had ever really cared about. She hadn't had a lot of choices about where to turn. But Brett couldn't understand other people, people who had real choices and good lives, who turned to drugs. People like those kids, who probably had pretty decent lives overall.

"I think we should do this, Brett," Allie said, sitting next to her.

"You do?" Leisa asked Allie.

"I told you, my dear. These two women have the ability and morality to handle such an assignment," Madeline said.

"What the hell's going on?" Brett grumbled. "Are you guys just assuming I'm gonna do this?"

Allie grinned. "You know, Brett, you're really not a very good butch."

"Huh? What the hell do you mean by that?"

"I always thought the two most important phrases in any good butch's vocabulary were *yes dear* and *how high?*" Allie winked at her.

"You guys are fuckin' with me," Brett said. "I don't see how you can even expect such a stupid thing to work."

"It will," Madeline said, "because it will."

"Please, Brett, we've got to at least try," Leisa said. "I don't know what'll happen if it doesn't."

"Why the hell do you even think I'll know what the fuck to do?" Brett said.

"You will do what you need to do," Madeline said.

"You definitely have the linguistics of the role down," Leisa said.

"This won't work," Brett insisted.

"Yes, it will," Allie said. "You want to do it, and you know it."

~ ~ ~ ~ ~

Elsewhere in town a man was speaking on the phone, ending an hour-long conversation.

"Okay, sis, we're all set then?"

"Yeah, I'll leave first thing Saturday morning."

"You know, I really hate to ask you to do this on your vacation and all."

"Listen, he's my nephew. I don't want him getting mixed up in any of this crap any more than you do."

"For all I know, I could just be imagining things."

"Don't worry about it. If you are, then I get a vacation, and, if you're not . . ."

"I'll see you in about a week, Randi."

"Okay. Give my love to Pat and Jake," Randi McMartin said as she hung up the phone with her brother, who lived about two and a half hours north of her in Alma.

Randi picked up the picture she kept near the phone. It was the last picture taken of the entire family before . . . before . . .

She wouldn't think about it. She wouldn't remember it. She couldn't go back through that again.

Anyway, the picture included a young Jake of maybe two.

Randi McMartin stared at the photo for what seemed like an hour, remembering when her family was whole. She wouldn't let another one get away from her.

# 2

As Leisa and Madeline slept soundly on the foldout bed in the living room of the hotel suite, Brett and Allie discussed the matter in the bedroom.

They had agreed to do the job, even though it wouldn't pay. Money wasn't an issue, not only because they had Allie's inheritance, but because they also had all the money accumulated from Brett's career in organized crime. They would do it for the kids, for the lives they could help. This had never before been Brett's MO, but she would do it for her dear, sweet Marie.

Allie was looking through Brett's and her clothes while Brett spoke on the phone.

"Okay, Frankie," Brett said. "That sounds great. Just overnight them to Madeline the moment you have them done." She listened a few more moments, said her farewell, and hung up.

"All set with the IDs?" Allie asked, looking up from the drawer she was digging through.

"Yeah," Brett said, wrapping her arms around Allie's waist and burying her face in the long stream of blond hair. "He says it won't be any problem. Especially since they'll be Michigan IDs. No one should notice they're fake 'cause he's got lots of experience with them."

"Was he able to do anything else?"

Brett grinned. "You know Frankie. He's got contacts everywhere."

"Even in the high schools?"

"He makes friends easily. And no one ever forgets Frankie. They like to do favors for him because they know he'll pay them back. Anyway, he's got some contacts at Pershing High School who'll set up some phony records for us in case anyone tries to look into our past." Frankie used to work with Brett when she was a criminal, but unlike Brett, he was still in the business.

"Everything else okay with Frankie?"

"Yeah. He's thinking about curtailing activities to just porn. Y'know, the theater and bookstores, et cetera."

"The legal stuff," Allie said with a laugh.

"Yeah, the legal stuff. I think he's realizing just how tiring it all can be. But I am still tempted . . ."

"You know, I always did kind of like him — even when he was just a paid thug."

"I was once too."

"I know," Allie admitted. "But now you're one of the good guys."

"Don't remind me."

They kissed lightly, and then Allie continued looking through their clothing as Brett lay back on the bed, admiring Allie's long, lean body and her mane of gorgeous hair. She wondered once again how she had lucked out to have such a woman love her. It was a fantasy come to life.

"You gotta move," Allie said. "I want to put clothes there."

"Oh, c'mon. Can't we do this tomorrow?" Brett pleaded.

17

"We don't have very long to get ready. The sooner we begin, the sooner it'll be over."

"But we're getting the car in Detroit on Monday, and we're not moving in until Wednesday to start classes on Thursday." That was the quickest time line they thought possible.

"So we have to shop tomorrow because we both need clothes for this."

"A lot of my stuff should be okay."

"But you're still gonna need some new clothes to cover those gorgeous curves of yours," Allie replied with a grin.

Brett felt her face get hot. She mostly wore baggy clothes to conceal her feminine form, but Allie enjoyed pointing out any of Brett's more feminine points. And, according to Allie, she had quite a few of them. But she knew, in this case, that what Allie said was true. Even though all her jeans were men's, they fit well enough to show some curves, albeit not a lot. But Allie took every opportunity to make Brett blush, even now, after all their years together.

"But we don't have all our clothes here," Allie continued. "Maybe Madeline can pack some of what we left at the house. But still, not a lot of the clothes I have would be appropriate for a teenage girl today."

"So," Brett said, pulling Allie onto the bed. "We shop tomorrow and pack on Sunday. We've got time."

No matter how many times or how long they were together, Brett would never get over just how it always was with Allie. They had a chemistry together that was beyond anything Brett had ever dreamed was possible. Other woman had been incredible lays, but with Allie . . . Throwing a match into an open well of gas at the corner station couldn't even be called a spark next to what they shared.

"So you want me to pack, eh?" Brett said, lying on top of Allie.

It could start in any way — a smoldering look in Allie's deep blue eyes, a glance at Allie's incredibly beautiful, long, slender fingers, a glimpse of her curvaceous figure or long, long legs, a whisper, a touch, a look, a smell . . . There was never any telling what would ignite the flame deep inside Brett, making her know that she needed Allie, needed her right then.

Their bodies entwined on the bed, fitting together perfectly with

Brett lying on top of Allie, a thigh between Allie's legs, her hipbone pressing into Allie, making Allie groan and squirm beneath her. Their tongues danced in each other's mouth, taking turns dodging in and out. Brett slowly moved down, gently sucking and nibbling Allie's sensitive neck, her tongue tasting Allie's soft skin, her hands roaming Allie's sides. Brett enjoyed the buildup; she liked teasing Allie, making her want her. She loved Allie's low groans and murmurs.

"Oh baby," Allie said.

"I think you're overdressed for this occasion," Brett said, helping Allie to sit up so that she could strip off her shirt and bra, deftly undoing the latter with a quick flick of her fingers. Brett gasped as she always did when she saw Allie's beautiful naked body. The sight of her full breasts, well-defined collarbone, and smooth skin always aroused something deep within Brett.

They lay back with Brett on top. Again Brett began to work her way down Allie's long body, tasting her with her mouth while her hands explored her curves. Her body never left any doubt in Brett's mind that Allie was all luscious, delightful woman.

Brett suckled one breast, pulling the hardened nipple into her mouth, and gently nibbled on it, teasing with her teeth as her tongue whipped back and forth against its tender tip. Allie moaned her appreciation and pushed herself up into Brett's mouth. Brett held her tight, enjoying the way she squirmed in her arms.

Allie's moans became more intense, and her hands cupped Brett's head, gently suggesting that Brett go to the other breast. Brett brought one hand from around Allie so that she could feel the hardened nipple with her palm and fingers while she began to roughly use her teeth on the other nipple. She sometimes thought she could make Allie come just by biting her nipples long enough and hard enough.

Brett was now lying between Allie's spread legs, and Allie pushed herself up into her. Brett tightened her stomach muscles and pressed down against her lover, grinding her hip between Allie's legs.

"Oh god, Brett, are you trying to drive me crazy?"

Brett sat up and unzipped Allie's jeans, keeping eye contact the entire time. She pulled off Allie's jeans and underwear simultaneously, grabbing the socks at the end of the long legs as well. She knelt for a moment between Allie's legs, looking down at her.

Brett really appreciated the gift a woman gave when she gave herself. Allie's beautiful body always took Brett's breath away, and Brett wanted to touch her, taste her, please her. She wanted to make love to her. She wanted to pull her so close that they fused together as one.

Brett ran her hands up Allie's inner thighs, and Allie pulled Brett's mouth down to her own. They sucked greedily on each other's mouth while Brett ran her hands all over Allie's nakedness. Allie wrapped her legs around Brett's legs, pulling Brett ever closer to her.

Brett worked her way down Allie's body while Allie twined her fingers through Brett's hair. Sometimes she would guide Brett like this, tell Brett what she wanted, needed, through her hands. A little pressure, a tightened grasp, and the music of Allie's moans were all Brett needed.

By the time Brett lay between Allie's long legs, inhaling the intoxicating scent, Allie was breathing heavily. Brett rubbed her cheek, then her lips over the swollen flesh, toying with Allie.

Allie moaned even louder, giving audible vent to her pleasure with what Brett was doing. When Brett finally brought her tongue to Allie's wet and swollen cunt, tasting her, Allie gasped and pulled at Brett's hair.

Brett began to lap at her, slowly, up and down, putting her tongue inside her lover, before following the swollen flesh to the very top, just under the hood. Allie's long legs were resting on Brett's arms, and Brett's hands wandered over Allie's breasts and stomach and hips. Allie reached down and grabbed Brett's hands, digging her nails into Brett's palms as Brett increased her pace.

"Oh baby, oh baby," Allie moaned as she tossed across the mattress.

Allie filled Brett's mouth, and Brett began to lose her control. She wanted this woman, wanted her to come in her mouth, to fill her. Her taste and smell filled Brett's head. Brett's tongue slid up and down on Allie, then back and forth across the swollen head of Allie's clit.

Allie pushed and pulled Brett's hands, squeezing them almost tightly enough to break them, digging her nails into Brett's palms, rearranging them in her frenetic flight. She pulled at Brett's hair, grabbed the headboard, arched, and bucked across the bed so that Brett had to hold on or else lose her connection with that incredible place.

"Oh baby, oh baby . . ."

Brett, aroused so much by Allie's movements, was soaked. Allie jerked against her, her hands clutching at the headboard until she suddenly brought them down to rip and tear at the hair on Brett's head.

"Oh my fucking god!"


In the other room, Leisa rolled over uneasily in bed. She knew Brett and Allie were trying to be quiet, but she could still hear their muffled cries. This usually wouldn't disturb her, for she was usually a sound sleeper, but tonight it did. She tried to focus on the steady sound of Maddy's breathing beside her, had rolled over to look at her, in fact. Maddy appeared to be sound asleep, oblivious to the sounds from the next room.

Leisa felt the awakening of desire within her. She tried to concentrate on something else to dissipate the feelings, a tactic that had worked before on numerous occasions — so much so that she really didn't have such feelings anymore. She decided it must just be the noises from the next room that were getting to her tonight.

Instead she thought about the role she was to play in the entire scheme — Brett and Allie would both have her for a class, and she was to help them in whatever way they needed to resolve the entire situation.

A part of her didn't like Brett being a part of the scheme. She seemed almost to be the sort of element Leisa didn't like the children being around, but she was sure Allie would make certain that part stayed tightly restrained. She knew she could trust Allie. After all, Allie had been a policewoman, a detective at that.

The plan would work because it had to.

The sounds finally ceased. She imagined Brett taking Allie into her arms and cooing soothing sounds of love to her. It was obvious from the way they looked at each other that the two women were very much in love, and it was almost a relief to know they still had a good sex life. Leisa had known too many regular couples whose relationships had ended when they stopped being attracted to and wanting each other. Brett and Allie's relationship was obviously strong, no matter how much Brett flirted with other women — like she had briefly tonight with Leisa. Leisa was flattered by the attention, but Brett really wasn't her type.

In the next room, Brett released Allie and pulled her into her arms. "I love you so very much, baby."

Allie curled up against Brett. "I love you, too." She reached down to find the sheet, but Brett stood, covered Allie, turned off the lights, undressed, and climbed into bed under the covers to hold Allie tight. Allie loved the way Brett would hold her the entire night, and she loved waking up in her arms. No matter what happened, they never went to bed upset with each other, and Brett always held her.

Those strong arms around her always made Allie feel safe and protected from anything that ever happened.

It was late. Very late. Probably too late for either of them to be up.

He sat in his car with the windows down, listening to the sound of the distant river. He saw headlights in the distance, but they winked out as the car neared his location. The other driver pulled up alongside his vehicle so that their windows were mere inches apart.

"You have something for me?" he asked.

"Yeah, I do, plus something else I think you'll enjoy. Think of it as my thanks for getting me that GHB. I thought you might like to see how useful it was."

The two exchanged packages, the other drove off, and the man waited fifteen minutes before he, too, left to go home. He was looking forward to a peaceful sleep.

~ ~ ~ ~ ~

Beth Bradley was stretched across the worn armchair in Scott Campbell's living room. Jerry Johnson and Jake McMartin were sprawled across the couch a few feet from her, and Scott was banging her twin sister, Becky, in his bedroom. Beth could hear the screams and moans from where she sat. Scott liked Becky to be loud.

"Want 'nother beer?" Jake asked, staggering toward the kitchen.

"Yeah, hit me with one," Beth said, downing the last of her Altes in a single swallow.

"Brewski, dude," Jerry said, raising his empty bottle.

"Want some real stuff, man?" Scott said, coming from the bedroom, zipping his jeans en route. He pulled a small plastic bag from his back pocket. "Now this'll really do ya in, man."

"Oh god, Scott, you rule dude," Jerry said, getting up. "Is that what I think it is?"

"It's the real shit."

The boys quickly prepared the works, grabbing a spoon from the dishes piled in the sink to be washed. Beth sat up as they heated the first bit into a liquid.

First Jerry, then Jake, and then Scott shot up. Becky came into the room, buttoning up Scott's dad's shirt, which was the only thing she wore. Beth had seen more of her sister's body since they had started hanging with this bunch than she had ever seen the entire time they grew up together. She had to admit that her sister had a nice body.

"Ya ready for the real thing, Bethie girl?" Scott said, dancing toward her in what he probably thought was a sexy manner.

"Nah, Scott, I think I'm high enough already."

"Ah, ya wimp. Bet your sister's up to it, ain'tcha, baby?"

Beth met Becky's eyes and shook her head slightly. Becky saw the gesture, grinned, and rolled up her shirt sleeve.


Brett was leaving school, going to work directly from class. Her books and work uniform were in a drawstring bag. She would've liked a backpack, but figured this made her arms work more each day. And practically every penny she made went to the bank account no one in her family knew about. She was going to go to college, somehow, someday. She would do whatever it took.

She pulled her ratty cloth jacket tighter around her. It had been handed down through several of her brothers before it got to her, and there really wasn't much left to it, definitely not enough to help against a cold, windy Michigan winter.

Half her clothes were way too baggy for her, others were too tight, depending on who and when it was left over from. Only when she was lucky did she get something that was in anything like decent condition.

"Yo! Girlie-girl, you gonna go flip those burgers for me?" Jaime said, coming up beside her before she got in front of the school's parking lot.

"Bro, da bitches have gotta be ready to feed us when we get back all hungry and shit after a hard night's work, ya hear what I'm sayin'?" Derek said, coming up on the other side of Brett and putting an arm around her.

She slouched down into herself more. She didn't know why Jaime and Derek always had to do things like this to her.

Suddenly, she heard the squeal of tires ripping around the corner.

"Fuck man!" Jaime screamed, turning around with a look of raw terror on his face.

Brett dove to the ground and rolled, knowing just what was happening. Guns were already pointed out from the car that raced toward them.

Jaime and Derek barely knew what hit them, but Brett did. Her one jacket was now covered with their blood.

Just another day on the streets of Detroit by her high school. Another nightmare to wake her up seventeen years later, covered in a cold sweat.

# 3

Madeline was helping them unload the nearly packed Jimmy they had purchased in the city of Warren the day before. They had decided they needed a vehicle different from the one they had previously used in Alma so that there would be no chance of being recognized. Also, their almost new Explorer would be too ostentatious for a couple of teenagers. Even though they had bought the Jimmy used, they worried that it was too nice for kids whose dad had recently died, until they decided he may have had credit life on his vehicle and their mom would've had her own car. They wanted a vehicle they'd still like after the assignment was over, and Allie liked the Jimmy.

Brett would have preferred a Subaru. She liked foreign cars

better than American ones. Not only because she thought they were better built, so that they lasted longer with fewer problems, but also because she had known folks who worked on the lines at the big three and didn't like much of the stuff she heard went on there.

"What have you got in this box?" Brett asked as she carried a fairly large heavy container into the house.

"We have to look like we're real teenagers," Allie explained. "So I had to bring a lot of shit we're never gonna actually use."

"Should I even ask?" Brett grunted and put the box down in the back bedroom they had used while they were renting from Madeline.

Madeline followed her into the room. "I am quite sure you probably do not wish to know that."

Brett opened the box and looked into it. "Please tell me that this two-hundred-pound box really isn't totally filled with makeup."

"You two will have to decide on the bedrooms," Madeline said. "I cleared out my office and borrowed a bed from a friend."

"I have always wondered what the hell these things are," Brett said, her voice filled with fear and apprehension as she extracted a metal handle with a curved, padded top from the box.

"Why'd you do that?" Allie asked Madeline about the bed.

"I bet it's a secret thing, passed down from the ancient Japanese torturers," Brett said, holding the implement like a weapon.

"To hold up your cover in case any of your little friends come over," Madeline replied.

"It's an eyelash curler, already, Brett!" Allie cried. "Now put it away and pay attention. This is important!"

Brett suddenly looked at Madeline. "Tell me you didn't just say 'little friends'? Because you're gonna pay for it if you did, Maddy," Brett growled. She never had 'little friends' even when she was little herself.

"Don't worry, dear," Allie said, putting her arms around Brett's neck. "As long as we're alone, we'll just be using one bed."

"Good." Brett hadn't been happy about this from the get-go, but sleeping in separate beds was simply beyond anything else. She could not deal with that. "Why does anyone need to curl her eyelashes?"

~ ~ ~ ~ ~

Allie was almost having fun. She had been working toward achieving detective status when she left the police force, and she had only worked one undercover job during her career — and that was in conjunction with the Detroit Police, working with Randi McMartin against Brett. They had chosen Allie because of her prior history with Brett, even though they hadn't had any contact in years, so it was a strange sort of undercover operation for a cop to be working on.

But this was real, this was something Allie could believe in, something she knew was right and could make a difference with.

Of course, going back to high school hadn't been on Allie's list of things to do this lifetime. She hadn't enjoyed it that much the first time around. Although it had started off nicely enough, with Allie getting decent grades and being fairly popular, it had ended with ostracism and harassment.

She had had a fairly normal life — good friends, a loving family — and she was considered good-looking and popular. She had been an only child, and her parents were significantly older than all her friends' parents, and now they were long gone. And her best friend from high school was dead as well — killed at the hand of some psycho bitch.

Now she'd be going into a new high school knowing no one. But no one would know her either, and she no longer had any of the insecurities she had had when she was a teenager.

She would have the advantage this time around, though. She had the confidence of her many years of experience, and she didn't have their self-doubts. Well, maybe she had some, but certainly not like she'd had during her high-school years. And this time she had a lover and her self-identity as a lesbian. She had no reason to come out to these people.

It was so much easier to deal with a situation when it would only last awhile and then disappear like a bad dream.

She was almost glad Brett would be portraying a teen boy. Brett hadn't had a good time when she really went through high school, and so she might actually have some fun with it, even though she wouldn't have as easy time passing as Allie would.

The major problem would be that Brett had come to a point in her life when she was far less likely to take mindless crap than she had been when she went through high school for real. Allie could remember the day that Brett came to her school to pick her up and had found Allie being harassed. She had pulled her gun and beat up Allie's harassers.

Brett wouldn't do such a thing now, but Allie wondered what exactly Brett would get herself into. Lord knew she was such a butch; she could always find some sort of trouble.


At least this time there wouldn't be any assholes calling her *dyke, queer,* and *lesbo.* The worst time she could have now would be being called *fag,* which would just be funny.

Now she would be in charge. She didn't have to worry about teachers harassing her, didn't have to kiss up to them so she could get a college scholarship and get into the right school to escape her life of hell. She didn't have to try to keep a low profile just to survive and live.

Back in the Detroit high school she had gone to she'd had to worry about her life on a daily basis, about being killed in her own school or on the street or in her home. Going to high school in Alma would not be the life-or-death situation she'd had growing up.

Allie never really understood the daily torture Brett had endured during those years. Allie had experienced normal peer harassment, a few bangs and scrapes, but she hadn't lived through what Brett had: people running around on drugs, hopping up on shit and needing money to keep hopping up on it. Willing to rob just about anybody or anywhere to support their habit. The gangs, teens so out of control that they banded together to take control in any way they could, constantly proving their power of life and death over those around them.

Drugs, gangs, poverty, abuse. It was all an ugly circle, a Catch-22 that kept it all alive. There had to be a way out, and the easier that way, the better. Politicians could spout off all they wanted to about the war on drugs, but that was only treating the symptoms of the problems. In Brett's old neighborhood, kids had taken drugs to escape. Teenagers would always try to escape from whatever problems, real or imagined, they had. The same held true for adults.

At least for some the ugly circle ended with the relief that comes with death. No more worries.

Brett went out back for a smoke.

She had been involved with it all — she had sold drugs herself — but not during high school. Then she had been concerned with keeping her nose clean. But after college, when she had such trouble finding a job, she had become involved with Rick DeSilva, who trafficked in illegal drugs.

People stupid enough to do drugs were too low, far below her notice. She had regarded the druggies as cow manure, and if she didn't make a couple of bucks off them, then someone else would.

At the same time, she had nothing to do with anything that even resembled child porn. She had had her own morality and judgments, and that was too disgusting for her.

Now she knew that drugs and porn were almost the same. Addiction could cause the proliferation of child porn — the kids needed some way to subsidize their habits. And she had sold those drugs. Not directly, but she had enough to do with it.

She didn't want to go back to high school, but she was going to do this for Marie and for all those nameless faces she had helped enmesh in the entire drug culture. She could still see Marie's glassed-over eyes in her mind, in her memory.

And like Allie had said, she had to atone for her sins. She needed to help some of those whom she had helped to degrade and bring down.

Brett Higgins was now all grown up, and she was gonna kick butt.


Later that evening, Brett and Allie were modeling some of their clothes and attitudes for Madeline and Leisa, who had come over to eat dinner with them and to help them prepare for the next day.

"It's a good thing lots of clothes come washed out," Madeline said, examining Brett's jeans. "You can't tell so easily that they're new."

"I think we still need to run them through the washer a bit more," Allie said. "To get rid of the new clothes smell, texture, and look."

"Though it would make sense that we'd have some new clothes," Brett argued.

"Yeah, some," Allie conceded. "Especially you, since you're a growing boy," she added, hugging Brett.

"Better believe it," Brett said, scratching her crotch.

"But you two had better watch it," Madeline said.

"Watch what?" Brett asked, her arm around Allie's waist.

"I can't remember a time since I've known you that you haven't looked like a couple."

"Ooh!" Allie smirked. "Incest is best, relatively speaking," she joked as she gave Brett a long kiss.

"Keep it in the family," Brett added, rubbing her thigh against Allie's crotch.

"Okay, Brett," Madeline said when Brett and Allie finally broke off the kiss a few minutes later. "Let's see the walk again."

Brett strode across the room with all three women watching her. "It's been awhile since me just walking has gotten this much attention." She sat on the couch, putting an ankle on the opposite knee. She then reached down and adjusted herself.

Leisa slowly nodded. "I think she's got it."

Allie sat next to Brett and grabbed her crotch.

"Oh, baby . . ."

"Mr. Softie?" Allie asked as Brett grabbed her hand and held it firmly on her crotch.

"Yeah, I thought it might work better than a double-condom filled with lube."

"And now you're ready for action as well, huh?"

Leisa was staring at them wide-eyed. Brett looked right at her and said, "No, Mr. Softie's just for packing. It really wouldn't hold up to any real use."

"Look at your fingernails," Madeline instructed Brett.

"Huh?"

"You do not need to question everything; sometimes you just need to react."

"Whatever," Brett said, lifting her right hand, palm side up with the fingers curled in, and looking at her fingernails.

Madeline slowly nodded, approaching Brett. "Yes, you are a butch. A butch but not a man or a boy." She took Brett's face in her hand. "You need to shave."

Brett reached up to feel her chin. "Damn, the five o'clock shadow setting in already?"

"A boy of nineteen or twenty would need to shave. Thus he would not possess the baby fine hair on his chin and upper lip that you do."

"Now wait a minute there, Maddy," Allie said. "If she shaves that hair it'll come back coarser, darker, and thicker."

"My dear, I know you like your butch just the way she is. That the hair comes back in such a way is merely an old wives' tale. It will originally seem coarser, but that is merely because it is new growth."

Leisa stared thoughtfully at Brett. "Can you walk across the room and stand over there?" she asked, indicating an empty space a few feet away from her.

"Here we go with the walking thing again," Brett said, standing and striding across the room. She stopped in the indicated spot, turned, crossed her arms over her chest, and looked at Leisa.

"What're you thinking?" Allie asked.

"She's not taking up enough room." Leisa walked up to Brett, knelt in front of her and moved one leg farther apart from the other.

"In another situation I might find this erotic," Brett said, looking down at Leisa.

"Guys think they own the world," Leisa said, standing back to study Brett. "They take up a lot of room. They sit on a couch, and they take it all up. Nobody can sit next to them. They walk down the hall and they fill the space. They want to be noticed, and they can only do that if they're alone without anybody near them. So they take up the entire road, hall, world. And that's the attitude you need."

"Have a few issues, do we?" Brett asked.

"It's just the truth." She looked around nervously. "Well it is."

Allie looked at Leisa, then turned to Brett. "How's the breathing?"

Brett grinned and felt her chest. "It's not bad, but I know my tits are gonna be so happy once I take these Ace bandages off."

"If anybody notices," Allie explained to Madeline and Leisa, "she's going to say that she was in a brawl just before she left Detroit and that they had to tape her ribs."

"This just might work," Leisa said, "just so long as you can get the speech down right."

"How is your monotone, Brett?" Madeline asked.

"Well, y'know, I guess it's okay," Brett said in a monotone before laughing and turning to assess herself in the mirror. She ran a quick hand through her even shorter, newly dyed, hair. It seemed strange not to see all the gray hairs. She had started getting them in her early twenties, almost as soon as she had graduated from college. Without them, and with the new clothes and haircut, she had to admit, she did look like a guy. Not a bad looking guy, either.

"Let's go over your class schedules," Leisa said, pulling out a sheaf of papers, which included their class listings as well as a map of the school. She spread the papers out on the table, and Brett, Allie, and Madeline gathered to look.

| Hour | Brett | Allie |
|---|---|---|
| 1 | Algebra I (*Fred Marin*) | Physics (*Burt Jones*) |
| 2 | Intro to Chem (*Lucy McNeil*) | Am Gov (*Caroline Thatcher*) |
| 3 | CP English (*Leisa Kraft*) | CP English (*Leisa Kraft*) |
| 4 | Am Gov (*Caroline Thatcher*) | Calculus (*Fred Marin*) |
| 5 | Shop (*Carl Rogers*) | Gym (*Kelly Green*) |

"Shit," Brett mumbled. "We got old lady Kraft for English."

"Leisa and I decided it may be a good idea to get all three of you in the same class at the same time," Madeline replied, ignoring Brett's comment. "In order to give you a chance to interact during the day."

"Good thinking," Allie said, her mind flipping briefly into detective mode. "But my problem with this is, how am I supposed to look like I know what I'm doing in calculus and physics?"

"With any luck, you won't be there long enough for anyone to notice," Madeline replied. "And, although none of the teachers know about this, they should understand a bit of the trauma of the situation — that you two children just lost your father."

"And why the hell am I in all these loser classes and then college prep English?"

"Some kids are brighter in some areas than they are in others," Leisa explained.

Brett said, "So our dad just died and we suddenly had to move?" Madeline nodded.

"You say none of the teachers know," Allie began. "Does that mean you have suspicions about some of them?"

"Well . . ." Leisa said thoughtfully. "You might say that. I know that a lot of schools don't screen their teachers properly — or even their maintenance crews or contract employees."

"I just read an article about that," Allie said. "Michigan is not one of the best states to know what their school employees' backgrounds are."

"Aw, c'mon," Brett said, "this is a small town — they've got to know these things. People know everything about each other in small towns."

"Not necessarily," Leisa said. "I read that same article," she said to Allie. "It was part of what made me start worrying about this, otherwise I might not have thought much about my feelings. But kids just don't get into trouble by themselves."

"Fuckin' great," Brett finally grumbled. "We can't trust anyone."

"We, Madeline and I, selected the classes for several reasons," Leisa began, pulling her mind off more worrisome thoughts. "First, to get a mixture of students and teachers. Second, to uphold your covers, which include the fact that Allie will be going to college next year, whereas Brett has failed a few years and just wants to graduate."

"I just want to graduate?" Brett asked, remembering how well she had done, at least with classes, during high school. At that time she *had* been going to college the next year.

"Yes," Madeline said. "Part of an uncle's inheritance to you hinges on the fact that you successfully complete your high-school curriculum."

"An uncle's inheritance?"

"We need a reason that will successfully motivate you to graduate from high school, even though you are older than most of the other students. It is not a lot of money, but enough for Brett Jameson to see as a good reason to do what he does not really wish to do."

"Wouldn't I just get a GED?"

Madeline shook her head. "Not possible. It is a part of the will. You must actually complete the curriculum and receive your diploma."

"Are we allowed to skip any classes?" Allie asked.

"You're supposed to be the good girl," Brett replied.

"Nobody's supposed to skip class," Leisa said. "But we did plan your fifth periods to be easier to skip than mostand like most seniors, you do have the sixth period off."

Brett and Allie stood near each other, examining the school layout and the positioning of their classes.

"Why do I have gym and she doesn't?" Allie asked, remembering the old horrors of gym. She had hated gym — partly because of the way other girls teased her about her body, even though she now knew it was great, and partly because of how she had wanted to look at other girls' bodies, but knew she shouldn't. She had even had a problem going to R-rated movies with her friends because she was worried somebody might notice how much she liked the naked women in them.

"Because Brett is such a jock he got that requirement out of the way back at his old school," Madeline explained.

"But I thought you had to take gym during your senior year?"

"He got those requirements waived by lettering in track and wrestling."

Brett began posing, as if she were some sort of a bodybuilder. "Why not football?" she suddenly asked.

"You're too small," Madeline replied tersely. Brett frowned at this.

"It's not fair," Allie pouted.

"Well, honey," Brett began, wrapping her arms around Allie's waist. "I can't quite imagine me trying to convincingly change in the locker room," she said, as visions of stuffing a jockstrap danced through her head.

"I can understand it," Allie whined. "But that doesn't mean I think it's fair."

"Look at it this way, baby, you get to hang around with a bunch of naked girlies," Brett said with a wicked grin.

"You chicken hawk you!" Allie exclaimed, pulling away.

"And damned proud of it!"

Madeline watched for a few moments as the two women tickled each other, then broke in. "Okay, you two, you have an early day tomorrow."

Leisa glanced at her watch. "Yes, I know. I need to get going too, not that I'll be getting much sleep. I haven't slept since this began, and I doubt I will until it ends."

Madeline walked over to Leisa and touched her cheek with her hand. "Poor dear, you really do look exhausted. Perhaps I might be able to make you something to help you sleep."

Leisa nodded slowly and smiled slightly. "I think I'd like that," she said, looking at the much shorter woman standing in front of her. Brett and Allie exchanged a glance.

"'Night Auntie," Allie said with a smile.

Brett turned to Allie with a teasing grin. "Would you happen to know the first derivative of $x$ squared?" she asked innocently. A look of pure terror creased Allie's face.

"I'm gonna fail!"


Leisa watched Brett and Allie and tried to pay attention, then she tried to not know. The not knowing was the hardest part of all to attempt to do. She knew Brett and Allie were women, were lesbians, and a couple. It was hard to see them as other than that.

But then she tried to shut off the knowing part of her mind and see them with fresh eyes, with eyes that had never seen them before. If she saw those two in the mall, what would she think?

She had to admit that she would think they were teenagers.

She had seen quite a few lesbians in her time, like when she was in college and a couple of her housemates were lesbians and talked her into going to the Michigan Womyn's Music Festival. She discovered there that lesbians came in all shapes, sizes, colors, and levels of butchness and femininity.

She knew there were women much more butch than Brett and women even more femme than Allie. But Brett's butchness was just right for this impersonation.

She hadn't thought it would work, but now she was convinced it would.

"What're you thinking?" Allie asked later that night, rolling over in bed.

"Back to school . . ." Brett said, letting her words trail off as she remembered her own difficult high school years. She couldn't quite shake the foreboding. She kept remembering her own first days of high school, the terror of walking in among hundreds of new faces. And even the faces she had known for years were different — they were now the faces of cheerleaders and jocks and nerds. Everyone had already formed cliques that she wasn't a part of.

"I know," Allie replied, cuddling up against Brett's shoulder. "It's funny to watch people fondly remember their high-school days."

"All the peer pressure . . . always feeling left out while you're trying your hardest to fit in and be one of the gang." She had never fit in, and now there were more people for her to not fit in with.

"And trying to balance work, school, studying, sleeping," Allie continued. Brett knew that although Allie's parents were pretty well off, they had still made sure that she had a job while in high school so that she would learn responsibility and the value of work.

The two women were silent for a few moments, each thinking of her own high-school days, with the accusations and the notes in and on lockers and books, notes calling them *carpet muncher, muff diver,* and *bulldagger.* This was especially painful for Allie, because her first girlfriend, her high-school girlfriend, the girl who apparently helped her through some of those things, was also the one who ended her old life, who killed her best friend and Brett's other lover at the time.

"At least this time I don't have to try not to be so fond of the girls," Brett murmured.

"Oh yes you do!" Allie exclaimed, sitting up slightly.

"I mean, at least I won't be called a *dyke*," Brett said with a smile as she pulled Allie back down.

"I know," Allie admitted. "I'm just not excited about having to be interested in boys."

"Just do a better job of it this time," Brett said lightly. She had started seeing Allie when Allie was a senior in high school.

"Easy for you to say. Big, smelly, hairy bodies — spitting and making rude remarks while trying to cop a feel."

"At least this time around you only have to do it out there," Brett said, rolling Allie on her back. "You get to come home and be yourself," she continued, running her lips along Allie's neck.

"Unless any of our 'little friends' are over."

"We'll have some time outside of it all," Brett assured her.

"Let's find the assholes real quick," Allie said with a little growl as she attacked Brett's neck.


The man lay in his bed, thinking about the videotape his young partner had made for him. It was better than his wildest imaginings. Some of his old friends would love to see that film. Granted, the girl was a little older than they preferred, but it wasn't so obvious because of her innocence.

He had to figure out how to talk his partner into making some more of them — and giving them to him. But who knew, maybe there were already more of them sitting out there, waiting to be viewed and sold. This could turn into something more lucrative than anything else he had ever done. Perhaps he could even be involved in further productions, be the director. He knew what his friends wanted, what they would pay top dollar for.

And of course, he would hardly consider being there, watching it all, maybe even participating himself, a tiresome task.

He got up, undressed, and went to watch the video again.

~ ~ ~ ~ ~

Brett was slinking down the hall of her old high school. The overhead fluorescent lights cast a grungy appearance across everything, and she hoped no one saw her as she looked about and dashed toward the next doorway. As she carefully peered around the corner, checking to make sure the coast was clear, she heard a deep voice behind her.

"Where's your hall pass?" the man asked, coming out of the classroom.

Brett bolted down the hall, her heart racing. She could hear his quick, heavy footsteps behind her. The adrenaline kicked in, and she turned right, then left, as the blood pumped through her veins and she heard the thumping of her heart in her ears. She turned into a room on her right. She thought she lost him when she slammed the door shut behind her.

Eyes were watching her, and she turned around to discover, slowly advancing on her with an evil gleam in their eyes, several leather-clad biker types. She ran back into the hall only to find the teacher waiting for her, his bulk and height looming over her like a god from ancient mythology. He grabbed her by the collar as the druggies came out of the room, surrounding her and the teacher. She turned, twisted, and pulled away, to take off running again.

She ran out of the school, slamming the door behind her, with all the minions of hell on her heels. She ran with all she had — right into the football team coming in from practice.

"Hey!" the fullback yelled as she ricocheted off him and into the arms of another, who grabbed her and threw her against the spray-painted outside wall of the school. It held the imprint of some gang, which one Brett couldn't tell because blood ran into the corner of her eye from the force of the blow.

"Get her!" the teacher yelled while another jersey-clad figure slammed his fist into her ribs. She fell to the ground and tried to curl into a ball, but their kicks kept coming. Rolling out of the way, she tried to cover her head against their blows.

But then she remembered she was no longer a high-school student: She was an adult. She wondered why she didn't have her gun, but it suddenly appeared in her hand. She wielded it with the force and power of Excalibur. Jumping to her feet, she faced her unknown accusers, their faces indiscernible in the sea of color and light and dark. They began to melt into ominous dark shadows.

"Stay away," she warned, "stay away or I'll shoot." She felt the weight of the gun in her hand, and it felt good. Its weight gave her power, force, and the ability to stand straight and tall.

The figures advanced on her and, without thinking, she lifted the gun and began shooting. One figure after another dropped to the ground. As they lay in pools of warm blood, her stomach churned at the spectacle. Steam slowly rose from the blood pools into the cool night air.

The figures, seeming to multiply like amoebas, kept advancing like the biblical swarm of locusts, each one breaking off into two. She ran out of bullets as they swarmed around her, enfolding her and blocking out her sight. The sounds were muffled as they enveloped her into their own being, trying to force her to become a part of them . . .

She awoke with a start, looking madly about as she jumped from the bed to stand with her back against the wall. When her eyes acclimated to the light, she realized the only other person in the room was Allie, who still slept in the bed.

# 4

The alarm went off.

"Fuck," Brett said, disentangling herself from Allie and reaching over to slam the button on the snooze alarm.

"C'mon baby," Allie said, crawling over Brett's body to get out of bed. "We've got a lot to do, and we don't want to be late."

"Mmm," Brett moaned, stopping Allie on top of her, running her hands over Allie's body. "This is gonna be a real fucked-up day, I can already tell. Any day that begins with waking up in the morning is going to be a problem."

~ ~ ~ ~ ~

When Allie got out of the shower, Brett was again fast asleep. "Brett, Brett, c'mon, get up."

Allie blow-dried her hair while Brett quickly showered. It drove her nuts that Brett could get away with taking so little time getting ready in the morning. All Brett had to do was shower, throw some gel in her hair, dress, and eat and she was ready. And now, of course, Brett didn't even have to shave her legs at all because they wanted her to be much hairier than she had been. She hadn't shaved since they first took the assignment.

Allie had to shower, blow-dry her long hair, put on makeup, get dressed (which took much longer than it took Brett), and eat. Then she was ready — usually at least a half-hour after Brett was, sometimes as much as an hour after Brett was ready to go. Her time depended on how confused she was about what she was going to wear. But it was going to take Brett a bit longer to get ready today; after all, she had to wrap herself down and do other things to properly disguise herself.

Brett got out of the shower and started dressing while Allie finished with her hair and applied her makeup.

"Honey, can you help me in here?" Brett called from the bedroom. When Allie entered, she found Brett dressed in a pair of fairly loose jeans, her new black Doc Martens boots, and a poorly wrapped Ace bandage over her breasts.

"Oh for crissake Brett," Allie said, walking up to her and undoing the long, wide Ace bandage. "What am I going to do with you?"

"Anything you'd like." Allie rewrapped the bandage, much more tightly and securely. "But, babe, I would like to be able to breathe some time today. Not a lot, just occasionally."

"You'll get used to it."

"I thought you two might enjoy some coffee this morning," Madeline said, entering the bedroom with two steaming mugs. "And breakfast is almost prepared."

"Thank god," Brett said, grabbing one of the mugs and taking a long swallow before grabbing a shirt out of the drawer, where she had decided to keep all her shirts so that they would not look as if they had been pressed, ever.

Allie reached into Brett's pants, took firm hold of her boxers and pulled them up so that they could be seen.

"Oh no you don't. You've got me looking like a scumbag already — unpressed clothing and baggy jeans, for bloody hell. I am not wearing my boxers over my shirt."

"But, Brett, that's what everybody does these days."

"And if everyone was jumping off bridges I suppose you'd expect me to do that too."

Allie giggled. "You sound just like my mother."

"Let's eat."

"I wouldn't mind mornings so much," Brett began, smoking a cigarette and drinking a cup of coffee while Allie drove, "if they didn't come so bloody early in the day."

"You'd better be careful with that go-go juice," Allie replied. "We still don't know how easy it'll be for you to use the john."

"Shit," Brett replied, dumping the rest of the coffee out the window and throwing the empty container into the backseat. "This is gonna be a real fuckin' fun day, I can already tell."

"You should just be glad you gave a good enough argument about smoking," Allie replied, glancing at the cigarette in Brett's hand.

"Well, it's true," Brett said, taking a puff. "If I'm who I say I am, I'd be a smoker." She and Allie had constant controversy about Brett quitting smoking.

"As soon as this is over, though . . ." Allie began, meeting Brett's eyes.

"I know, I know," Brett admitted, tossing the butt out the window. Allie pulled the Jimmy into the quickly filling parking lot and shut off the engine. She looked at Brett.

"It's showtime!" Allie said, feigning enthusiasm. Her excitement had dimmed as soon as she got in the car. It was an adventure before; now it was a nightmare as old anxieties began to roil her stomach. The building seemed to loom like a nightmare over them.

"We're supposed to go to the office to get our locker assignments and all that hot shit," Brett mumbled as they walked.

~ ~ ~ ~ ~

Although Madeline, posing as their aunt, had already filled out most of the paperwork, it still took several minutes for the office to finish with Brett and Allie and send them to their first classes armed with maps of the school and class schedules. Brett was glad to be out of the office — the air had smelled old and stuffy, and the drab furnishings had looked used and worn. It was not a pleasant place.

Brett walked into Algebra I and observed the layout of the class. It seemed like a normal enough class, with bored-looking students watching the energetic teacher who stood at the board explaining a problem. They all turned to stare at her.

Brett donned her most laid back stride and uninterested look to approach an empty seat.

"That's taken," a rather large fellow said as he tossed his books over on the empty desk. Brett glanced over his broad shoulders, taking note of the football jersey, thick neck, and close-cropped hair. Mr. Marin turned from his place at the board just as Brett was about to speak.

"Sorry I'm late, Mr. Marin," a peppy young brunette said as she bounced into the classroom and took the formerly disputed seat. Just before she sat, she glanced up at Brett with deep brown eyes.

"You are . . .?" Mr. Marin began as Brett found another seat across the room.

"Brett Jameson," Brett replied offhandedly and tossed her single notebook, with a pen in its spiral, on the desk and sat. She had forgotten how small and uncomfortable the seats were. She tried to push the chair back from the desk, to give her more room, and realized the two were connected. This was really going to be hell.

"Ah, yes," Mr. Marin said, looking at a piece of paper on his desk. "Brett Jameson. You're a new student."

"Yeah, that be me," Brett grunted, careful to keep her voice at a lower, more masculine pitch.

"Then perhaps you should come up here and get a book," Mr. Marin replied, studying Brett's face as if he were looking for something there.

"You mean I can't just wing it?" Brett said, not moving. She silently watched Mr. Marin pick up a text and proffer it to her, then

43

waited a full beat before slowly standing and taking it. She slouched back to her seat. Once seated, she met Mr. Marin's stare, and realized most of the class had their attention on her.

"Maybe you'd like to wing your way through problem twenty on page ninety-eight?" Mr. Marin said, still staring at her. Brett opened the text to the appropriate page. She glanced down at the problem:

$$4x - 16y = 24$$

Avoiding showing the elation she felt at such a simple problem, she returned Mr. Marin's stare and walked up to the board. She picked up a piece of chalk and scrawled across the board:

$$4x - 16y = 24$$
$$+16y \qquad +16y$$
$$4x = 24 + 16y$$
$$/4 \quad /4$$
$$x = 6 + 4y$$

She looked over at Mr. Marin and returned to her seat, amid the joyous snickers from the class at one of their own being victorious over a teacher. It gave her a certain cockiness to get her first problem right, even if it was something so simple. What had she been so afraid of?

Brett felt someone staring at her neck. She turned nonchalantly, met the deep brown eyes, and only then did she allow the beginning of one of her most charming smiles to play across her lips. She knew the football player was glaring at her as well, but Brett allowed herself to slowly undress the girl with her eyes nonetheless, knowing that this was how she could get it all started and moving. She was an investigator now. She had to do what was expected of her, and she had a role to play — one that required her to be bad, something she was very good at.

The brunette wore a simple blouse with a tight jean skirt, and her long legs were already tanned. Although she was slender, her breasts caused the front of the blouse to billow enticingly. The shirt was open just enough to show off the beginning swells of lusciously soft breasts.

Brett finished her evaluation, looked back into those deep brown eyes, and smiled again. A slight color touched the girl's cheeks, as if she knew what Brett had been thinking.

For the rest of the class, Brett tried to stay awake. She tried a variety of techniques to do this, including studying, as nonchalantly as possible, the faces of her classmates (even as they obviously studied her) as well as glancing through her textbook. But for Brett, who had studied calculus, beginning algebra was a joke.

At the beginning of second-hour chemistry class, Ms. McNeil informed Brett she was in luck, as they were just going to assign lab partners that day for the next round of experiments, and now Brett made the class even numbered. When Ms. McNeil announced this to the class, Brett glanced over at the brunette, who was in this class also, but sans boyfriend.

As the class started milling about, getting together with partners and lab stations, Brett continued to sit and watch the girl, who turned down other lab partner choices on her way across the room.

"Brett, right?" the girl asked, facing Brett. Brett met her gaze and nodded. "I'm Kathy Moran," the girl continued, "I think we've got the same math class."

"Yeah, we do," Brett admitted, allowing a teasing smile to play across her lips.

"Where do you come from?" Kathy asked, lightly sitting on a nearby desktop.

"Detroit," Brett said as she trailed her eyes down Kathy's body. Kathy shifted on the desktop. "Which station do you want?" Brett added, not looking at Kathy's face.

"What?" Kathy asked, a slight flush coming to her face.

"Which lab station — you did come over here to ask me to be your partner, didn't you?" Brett asked, ensuring that she kept her voice modulated to a monotone.

Kathy nodded slightly, then led the way to a station against the far wall, where they both put their books on the black countertop. Brett grabbed a stool, moved it near the wall, and sat on it, leaning it back on two legs so her back was against the wall. She watched as Kathy primly adjusted her seat and carefully laid her purse on the counter before opening a notebook to a clean page and pulling a pen from her purse.

Brett knew she had Kathy on edge with her assumptions and looks. But Brett also felt half-dead in trying to adequately portray a teen boy. The short sentences and total attitude were wearing thin already.

Kathy was too bouncy and flaky to really catch Brett's interest, but her boyfriend, on the other hand, definitely had Brett's interest, but not in a sexual way. Brett figured the only way for a druggie type like her to get through to a jock like him was via his girlfriend. But she had to admit she was surprised that a teen girl would make the leap to ask some new guy to be her lab partner. She thought there might be more to Kathy Moran than was first apparent.

Ms. McNeil cleared her throat to indicate that she was about ready to begin.

"Big guy — he's your boyfriend," Brett stated to Kathy's back.

"What?" Kathy said, turning to face Brett.

"The big guy you sat next to in math — he's your boyfriend."

"Yes, yes he is," Kathy slowly said to the floor. "His name is Brian."

Ms. McNeil cleared her throat again. "Ms. Moran and" — she looked at a piece of paper on her desk — "Mr. Jameson, is there a problem?"

"No, ma'am," Kathy replied quickly.

Ms. McNeil's eyes came up to meet Brett's. "Mr. Jameson?" she asked.

"Not yet," Brett slowly replied to Ms. McNeil, "but I'm sure you'll give us one real soon."

"You," Ms. McNeil replied, with steel in her voice, "are off to a very poor start at a new school, young man."

"You mean you will not be giving us a problem to solve?" Brett shot back with a raised eyebrow, again to the amusement of her classmates.

As soon as Ms. McNeil had started passing out test tubes of mixed chemicals for them to titrate and identify, Kathy glanced up from her book to look at Brett.

"You're gonna get me in trouble, aren't you?" she said.

Brett let her eyes slide slowly over Kathy's firm young body before she looked into Kathy's eyes. "I don't plan on getting you 'in trouble' but I wouldn't mind comin' close," she replied, leaning close and letting her insinuations land where they might.

Kathy's eyes widened as she realized exactly what Brett had said, and meant. "You're awful!"

"Oh, then my reputation has not preceded me." Brett began to think that her vocabulary and speeches were not quite suited to the character she was playing. Fortunately, however, it appeared Kathy was enjoying herself far too much to notice. Brett thought that perhaps teenagers were too busy thinking about sex to enjoy the finer nuances of flirtation, and that if Kathy had been seeing Brian for a significant length of time, she had not enjoyed such attentions in a while. Brett knew she needed to watch it.

"Ain't it weird to be getting new lab partners this late in the term?" Brett asked Kathy.

"There was an odd number of kids in this class, so Ms. McNeil wanted to make sure nobody was odd man out all year."

"As if," Brett replied, starting to set up the lab equipment. It was amazing how all this stuff was coming back to her. It was as if her hands knew better than her mind what she was doing. If she had tried to remember on her own, she never would have been able to do it. Brett finally winked at Kathy, took a beaker, and turned it upside down over a Bunsen burner before turning on the burner's gas.

"What are you doing?" Kathy asked.

"Just this," Brett replied, turning off the burner and pulling out her lighter, which she flicked just below the still inverted beaker. The gas in the beaker vanished in a puff of flame, which, unfortunately, Ms. McNeil noticed.


Allie knew she was in hell. She had to have done something very bad in a past life to have to be in high school again. It was just not fair.

Every bit of excitement she had ever had about going undercover again vanished in a puff as soon as she walked into the school — the griminess, the way kids looked at her in the hall, the small desks.

All the kids ... All the kids? God, she was already starting to think like one of them! They all looked at her when she walked into first-hour physics. They knew she was an outsider right from the get-go. Not one of them.

Some scrawny-looking guy sat next to Allie. A total nerd, she thought. He glanced nervously over at her. "You're new here, aren't you?" he asked, adjusting the glasses on his nose.

She heard a commotion behind her, turned, and saw that several other kids had entered the room. They didn't appear to be quite so geeky as the boy next to her.

"I'm Jim, Jim Taylor," he said, reaching a hand out to her. He nudged his books back on the table that they had instead of a desk.

"Allie . . . Jameson," she said, having to pause over her name. Her eyes wandered back to where people who actually spoke to one another were. Maybe that would be a more profitable venue for her to investigate.

Another geek walked up and sat net to Jim. "Oh my god, Jim, did you see —" his eyes flipped up to meet Allie's. "Um, did you see . . . that particularly interesting species of . . . um . . . it was outside just before school."

"Allie Jameson. I'm new here. And you are?" High school really wasn't so bad once one realized how young all the other kids were, how inexperienced and naive, Allie thought. She had nothing to be afraid of. She had the confidence of having been through this before, as well as the knowledge of her years. She just had to keep this in mind and not become one of them.

She looked up to see a girl with short brown hair giving her a hard look, as if she were jealous of the attention the boys were giving her. This was going to be more difficult than she imagined.


"Hey, Teach," Brett said as she strolled into third-hour English just after the final bell rang. She laid her pass on Leisa's desk and glanced over the classroom. Apparently either Kathy or Allie had saved her a seat, because there was a vacant one sitting between the two.

"Brett Jameson, your aunt asked me to watch over you. What were you doing in the office?" Leisa asked, forcing Brett to face her, which was a good thing, because otherwise the entire class may have noticed the slight flush that brushed Brett's face from the idea of sitting between her lover and the girl she had been flirting with all morning.

"Visitin' ol' lady Simons," Brett replied, turning back around to go to the seat.

"That is not the way you should refer to your principal, young man," Leisa replied.

"Whatever," Brett said with a shrug as she slouched into the seat, stealing glances at both Kathy and Allie.

"Remove that cap," Leisa said, staring at Brett. Brett shrugged and pulled off her baseball cap, then ran her fingers through her short hair. Allie smirked and slouched in her seat, but Kathy stole another glance at Brett.

"We will continue our study of *Beowulf*," Leisa said, leaning against her desk. She began a lecture on the historical perspective of the poem and how its time frame affected one's full understanding of it. While Leisa was writing on the board, Allie slipped a note to Brett.

*What's with the chick?*

Brett glanced at it and wrote underneath:

*She was in my first 2 classes. She's going with some guy from the football team.*

Allie took the note, read it, and glanced over. Kathy was staring at her.

*Then why's she giving me the evil eye?*

Brett looked at the two women and then held her head in her hands for a moment before she wrote:

*I've been flirting with her all morning, using her to get to her boyfriend.*

After she handed the note back to Allie, Brett became aware of yet another gaze locked on her. She looked up to see that Leisa was giving them an icy cold stare. The room was dead silent.

"Allison," Leisa began slowly, studying the two, "I expect such behavior from Brett, but you?"

Allie shrugged and glanced away from Leisa.

"Your aunt sure took on more than she bargained for when she took you two in," Leisa said before returning to her lecture. Kathy continued to try to assess Brett and Allie's relationship.

The class seemed especially well-behaved, and Brett thought Allie was doing an exceptional job of portraying the model student, conscientiously paying attention and taking notes on what Leisa was saying. Brett saw that Kathy paid attention in class too, but she kept looking at her and Allie. Finally, near the end of the hour as Leisa was winding up her lecture and the class was becoming somewhat restless, Kathy passed her a note:

*How do you know Ms. Kraft?*

Brett looked at her, then wrote:

*She's my aunt's best friend, and Blondie over there is my sister.*

Brett watched a slight smile touch Kathy's lips when she read the last part of the note.

Leisa finished her lecture, then requested that Brett and Allie see her in the conference room just off the classroom. She closed the door behind them and positioned herself so the class could not read her facial expressions.

"You are one pain in the ass," she told Brett.

"How'd you get sent to the principal's office already?" Allie asked.

"I filled a beaker with gas and lit it in chem class," Brett admitted, shrugging. Both Allie and Leisa smirked at this.

"If that doesn't get you in good with some of the students," Leisa said, "then hitting on Brian Ewing's girlfriend certainly will, which, by the way, may not be one of the smartest moves you've ever made."

"Why's that?" Allie asked.

"He's big and has a temper. He also enjoys picking on guys smaller than he is."

Brett smirked at this, thinking about other large men she'd taken on in the past, and just how she had dealt with them. Like a cat, she always landed on her feet. She cocked her head toward the room. "Is Kathy a cheerleader?" she asked.

"Captain of the squad," Leisa replied as Allie frowned at Brett. Brett wanted to reach over and take Allie in her arms, tell her she loved her. But she couldn't, because more than a few people in the class were glancing in through the windows of the room.

Instead, she put her thumb in her hip pocket and snarled, "Well, y'know, I'm already madly in love with this chick named Allie."

Allie smiled at her as the buzzer signaled the end of class.

~ ~ ~ ~ ~

Brett entered the men's room, noting that the stalls did indeed have doors. She was headed toward one, pulling out her pack of cigarettes, when a thin, grungy-looking fellow in black leather addressed her.

"Are you an idiot or what?" he said.

"What?" Brett said, putting on her best confrontational attitude.

"Kathy Moran belongs to Brian Ewing. She's got his brand on her ass," he said, as Brett identified him as being in both her math class and English class.

"Do I look like I give a shit?"

"Then you're one stupid motherfucker," the fellow mumbled. But as Brett took a step forward, as if to mess him up, the fellow lit a cigarette and added, "But I like that — name's Jerry."

Brett leaned back against a stall and lit one herself. "Brett," she said, not extending her hand.

"You sure took a shit in McNeil's Cheerios this morning," Jerry said with a grin.

"Hell, that broad's got a stick shoved so far up her ass it's comin' out her mouth," Brett replied.

"So where'd you transfer from?"

"Detroit."

"No shit?"

"No shit," Brett replied.

"Anything's got to be better than this little shit place," Jerry said, stomping on his cigarette as he prepared to leave.

"Hey," Brett began, "what can you tell me about Moran?"

Jerry shrugged. "Head of the titty shakers, been with Ewing since they were freshmen. Ewing's the captain of the football and soccer teams."

Brett shook her head a bit. "With all that energy, I bet she's one wicked ride in bed."

Jerry smirked and left, leaving Brett alone in the bathroom. She quickly used the facilities, making a mental note to try to use them during class when there would be less chance that she'd be caught, then headed for government, where the teacher, Caroline Thatcher, managed to be later to class than Brett was.

Class passed rather uneventfully, as did lunch, which Brett spent mostly in the smoking area with Jerry. She learned that many kids left the grounds for lunch, and she made another mental note to discuss this with Madeline, Leisa, and Allie.

In fifth-hour shop, she found herself transported to an entirely different world. The class was divided into smaller groups of students, mostly sitting and drinking soda. Brett noticed only one girl in the class, and it was toward her group that Jerry directed her.

"Steve, Jake, and Beth, this is Brett," Jerry said, introducing her around the circle. All of them looked grungy and unkempt, all wearing blue jeans and high tops, with Steve sporting a shadow across his chin.

"I've heard about you," Beth said, giving Brett the eye.

Brett heard a beeping as she assessed Beth's dark eyes, short dark hair, and the frown that seemed molded into her face. Dyke-city. No one could pay me enough to be in her shoes right now, Brett thought. She couldn't imagine really having to go through it all again.

"Bad news travels fast," Brett quipped.

"Your sister is one hot piece of meat," Jake said, pounding Brett's shoulder. "I wouldn't mind giving her the ride of her life."

"Then I'd have to fuck you up real bad," Brett said, glaring at Jake as white-hot rage spread through her limbs. She silently reminded herself that he was just an overeager adolescent male who didn't fully understand the implications of what he had said.

"Where's Scott?" Jerry asked, breaking the uncomfortable silence.

"Aw, he took off early," Beth said, still looking at Brett.

"Who's Scott?" Brett asked.

"Scott's the bossman," Steve replied, picking up a chisel.

"Or so he thinks," Jake added.

"So you comin' with us Saturday?" Beth asked Brett.

"I didn't ask him — figured we should check with Scott first," Jerry replied.

"What's Saturday?" Brett asked Beth, meeting the girl's eyes with her own. Beth quickly looked down toward the floor.

"Everybody goes to the Hot to Trot," Beth replied nervously. "But we get together first at Scott's to get warmed up."

"The Hot to Trot," Jerry explained, "is Lansing's teen spot." Lansing was about an hour's drive from Alma, and the nearest real city.

52

"I can't make it this week," Jake shot in. "My aunt's comin' to visit," he explained with a sneer.

"Shit, man," Steve interjected. "You'd better keep her the fuck away from Scott."

"Your aunt?" Brett questioned, curious.

"Yeah," Jake said mockingly. "My Auntie Randi from Detroit."

"Hey, man," Jerry said to Brett, slamming Brett's shoulder. "Maybe you know her!"

"Detroit's a real big place," Brett replied slowly, as a prickling sensation melted through her brain like water soaks into a sponge.

"Scott don't like her 'cause she's a cop," Beth added, watching Brett's reaction.

"Yeah, Officer Randi McMartin," Jake added, with a smile. "She don't care much for my friends," he added, but Brett wasn't paying attention. Ice-cold liquid fear slowly dribbled down her spine. She and Randi had a bit of a history.

# 5

The man walked into his bedroom and began hanging the photos he had gathered over the past few days. A few he had taken himself, when the girl was not looking, and others were gleaned from the pages of recent yearbooks. She was a senior now, so he had several years of books with her in them available to him. The ones he took himself gave him a special satisfaction, as she was not posing, not ready for a camera. They made him feel like a spy. They made him feel all tingly and excited. They gave him an intense feeling of anticipation.

When he was through arranging the photos, he lay back on his bed and stared at them. A slow grin spread across his face. He could imagine what she would be like with him.

A fleeting thought went through his mind about the new girl.

He'd like to see those two get to know each other. Get to know each other well.

He undressed and turned on the VCR.


Brett didn't say a word to Allie as they walked toward their car after school. As soon as they were locked inside its little cocoon, however, she turned to Allie.

"We've got to get the fuck outta Dodge," she said, with deep feeling.

"What do you mean? We're nowhere near finished yet."

Brett sighed and started the engine. She stared at the road and Allie looked at her in concern. In the same expressionless voice Brett said, "I met Jake McMartin today. His Aunt Randi's coming for a visit this weekend."

"No, no, it can't be," Allie said shaking her head. "Lots of people have the same name."

"She's a cop from Detroit," Brett said.

"Shit," Allie said, dropping her head into her hands. "Shit, shit, shit," she added while pounding her head against the dashboard. She looked up at Brett. "Listen, we really don't need to worry — your friends don't seem like the type to introduce their friends to their family."

"Allie!" Brett said, turning to face her. "I live by Murphy's Law: If something can go wrong, it will."

"But —"

"But nothing. If she sees us, we're going to have a huge mess on our hands!"

"Brett, we can't just back down now. They're counting on us!"

"You know I want to help them, but to have Randi back in my life again . . ." she trailed off and shook her head.

"Hear me out. There's something going on around here, and ever since we helped them nail Jack and his team we have nothing to worry about with Randi. And," she quickly continued before Brett could cut her off, "the chances of us running into Randi are slim to none. Plus, because of your disguise, and the fact that you're dead, she probably won't think twice about it if you do."

"But she'll recognize you! You're not even working under an alias, Allie."

"And we'll say that I'm working for the police. Which would make sense. You're just another narc. But she won't recognize me because I am now a teenaged girl. She'd never think twice about us like this. If she did, she'd convince herself that she's just delusional."

"I don't like Randi. That's it, point-blank."

"There's nothing she can do to us anymore, Brett. She can't touch us. We've got to do it, Brett," Allie said, turning to face her. "If we keep running every time something bad happens or something from the past pops up, we'll never have any peace. We know we're safe now. We have nothing to worry about."

Brett remembered Marie and nodded.

"You're right," she said to Allie. She was facing her fears one by one, and this was one she needed to face. She would eventually have to face Randi, and it might as well be now as later.

Maybe someday she might even face Dave and Alice Higgins. Her parents. Then it would be Matthew, Mark, Luke, John, Peter, and Paul. Her loving brothers. People sometimes wondered how her brothers had such biblical names whereas she was named Brett — without even a saint's name for a middle name (she didn't have any middle name at all). But Brett knew that her father, who had named the boys, couldn't be bothered with giving his daughter a name. So he had left it up to Alice, who must've randomly come up with a name, because she never could explain why she had finally chosen "Brett" when her daughter was five years old.

"I figured it was the only way to get through to Brian Ewing," Brett said over dinner that night. "I mean, a big jock like him would never have anything to do with Brett Jameson."

"You're right, there," Leisa replied, lifting a forkful of spaghetti. "But you just might end up starting a fight with him."

"But at least that would be interaction," Brett justified. "And there's no telling what Kathy might inadvertently say."

"I have a feeling that Brett might be more than willing to have direct interaction with Brian Ewing," Madeline said. Leisa, hanging on her every word, looked over at Madeline. Or at least that was how it appeared to Brett.

"Oh, I forgot to tell you," Allie said, putting more parmesan on her pasta and grinning at Brett, probably about the interaction between Madeline and Leisa. "Brian was in my government class, and Kathy was in both my government and my gym classes."

"It's interesting how you are both so interested in Brian," Madeline said. "It would seem to me that the athletes would be on the bottom of the list — he is an athlete, correct?" She paused briefly until she got nods of agreement. "They spend so much time practicing, working out, and trying to impress the girls, they do not really have time for much else."

"There's just something about Brian," Leisa admitted.

"Could you elaborate on that, perchance?" Madeline said, smiling at Leisa.

"He's the classic stereotypical jock who thinks he's the king — that he owns everybody and everything," Leisa said. "And I don't like the way he treats his girlfriend. He's so stereotypically male."

"But we're not just focusing on Brian," Brett explained, breaking Madeline and Leisa's eye contact, even as visions of her recent dream of having been attacked by football players ran through her head. "I also met some rather interesting types during shop class. And," she continued, before anyone could cut her off, "it seems rather stupid to just cut out whole sections of the school before further study. I for one have never believed in stereotyping."

"It's funny going back and seeing, kinda from the outside, just how the kids divide themselves up," Allie said. "I mean you've got the brains, goths, jocks, and the druggies, and of course the froufrou cheerleading types and all that."

"People always seem to want to differentiate themselves from those around them," Brett mused.

"That way," Madeline explained, "they are aware of the status quo. They know what they can and cannot get away with doing to whom."

"And they can always look down their noses at somebody in another group," Leisa added. "Kids have to feel special. They have to either claim that they're leader of a pack, that they belong to a pack, or that they don't need a pack to hang with. That they're individuals."

"Kids," Allie said. "They want to be different and the same all at once."

"Now you know why I didn't want to go back," Brett said.

"But didn't you wish somebody would help you when you were their age?" Allie asked.

"We've got to help them," Leisa said. "You can't give up."

"Well, then," Brett said, standing to clear the table. "We've got our start. We know how we can divide the kids up to keep track of who we're meeting and what we're finding. I'm just glad it's a small school."

With that, she went into the living room and began listing the teachers and the students, with each group taking a different page in her notebook. Allie, Madeline, and Leisa soon joined her, and they all began making lists and notes, comparing thoughts and knowledge.

Brett began by listing all the people she had met that day while Allie made her own list, and together they compiled the master, with blank lines between descriptions so they would have room to fill in information as more came in.

"About Lucy McNeil," Leisa began, "I think —"

"No," Madeline said. "I do not think that you should tell us your thoughts at this point. We do not wish for Brett and Allison to be partial to your thoughts quite yet. For you, as any human, will have opinions, and at this point I think their impartiality is a valuable asset to us."

"You're saying that it's too early in the game for me to say anything?" Leisa said, and Madeline agreed.

"Precisely. Untrained and unsubstantiated thoughts and opinions might be red herrings for Brett and Allison."

"What about your opinions?"

"I am an impartial player in this."

"Lover's quarrel," Brett said to Allie.

Allie laughed. "Now what about Kathy Moran?" she said with a raised eyebrow.

"You already know my thoughts on her and Brian Ewing," Brett replied. "You got anything on her?"

"She asked me to join the cheerleading squad. Apparently they are planning on doing a few more events this year, and one girl had to quit the squad recently because she was pregnant."

"Huh?" Brett said.

"One of the cheerleaders got pregnant recently, so she had to drop out of school," Leisa said. "I hate it because it's so close to graduation — I don't know why she couldn't just stick around a little longer, even though she is due at any time."

"Teen pregnancy, teen suicide — even though high school is supposed to be a time of fond remembrances, it is not until after it is all over that we can think of it fondly," Madeline said. "As has been said, it is what we learn after we know it all that counts."

"But every year more stuff gets thrown at kids," Leisa said.

"You are a teacher," Madeline said.

"And you're a professor," Leisa replied.

Even sitting across the table from them, Brett could feel the chemistry between the two women. She had always thought of Madeline as neither straight nor gay, as basically asexual. She really couldn't imagine her with this woman who was about twenty years younger, but sitting here, watching them flirt, she could feel the attraction.

Life was always full of such surprises.

"So . . . ?" Brett said to Allie. "What're you gonna do about this cheerleading gig?"

"I'm going to their practice tomorrow night and give it a whirl."

"That's strange," Brett mused. "For her to so quickly invite a newcomer into the clique."

"I figure it either means that she really likes me or that she's trying to get to you through me."

"Either could be a reasonable explanation of her actions," Madeline said. Normally she would have said something cryptic at this point. Brett had a feeling that Leisa was distracting her from her usual behavior.

"That's quite possible," Leisa said, still looking at Madeline.

Brett nodded as a thought occurred to her. "You said you had gym with her?" she asked.

Allie smirked and nodded. "Yup, I got to see Kathy in her full glory."

"And you call me a chicken hawk!" Brett retorted.

"Nya-nya-nya!" Allie teased, making a face at Brett.

"Why you little slut!" Brett said, standing.

"Children! Stop behaving like adolescents!" Madeline proclaimed, to which Brett responded by sticking her tongue out at Madeline. "Do your homework!" Madeline added, stomping out of the room. Brett rolled her eyes at Allie.

"I think she's taking this all a little too seriously," Brett said to Allie and Leisa. Allie was already pulling out her textbooks.

"Well, I don't know about you, Brett, but one sure way for me to blow my cover is to look like I haven't the foggiest notion what's going on in class." Allie pulled out her calculus book and looked at it morosely before adding, "which I haven't."

"Oh, c'mon. It's high school. We both have bachelor's degrees — we shouldn't have to study."

Allie looked up at her. "I don't know why we need imaginary numbers when we have real ones," she said, remarking on calculus.

"Imaginary numbers?" Brett asked, staring at her. "You're kidding me, right?" She winked at Allie. She knew all about imaginary numbers and hated them with a vengeance. She hated calculus, even though she had learned enough to get through the class.

Leisa looked at the two of them. Brett said, wanting to torment her about her flirtation with Madeline, "We're not keeping you here, you know." She winked at Leisa, who flushed a shade of pink before standing and leaving the room.

Allie paused for a moment, watching Leisa follow Madeline. "It feels like I just walked into a room and saw my folks going at it."

"Yeah, I know the feeling," Brett said, staring in the same direction. "So how did Kathy look?"

Allie stared deep into Brett's eyes. "Perky full breasts, toned legs, a nice flat stomach, a tight ass, and not an ounce of flab on her." Allie walked up behind Brett, pulling her back against her. "Her legs are nice and long, just like you like them. Her skin is nice and smooth. Not a single sign of age on her — not a single wrinkle, bag, or drooping bit about her." She caressed Brett's hair back, licking lightly along her earlobe and neck. Brett moaned. "Her nipples were erect and hard when she climbed out of the shower and started to dress. Her panties and bra were smooth, silky, and very tiny." She fondled Brett's thick, black leather belt. She always shivered whenever Brett pulled it off. "I bet you'd love to bury your head between her thighs. She's just your type — except she's not blond and her eyes aren't blue. Even the triangle of hair between her legs is dark."

Brett turned around and, in a single, quick movement, pulled Allie onto her lap. "Oh baby, you know you're the only one I want. Your legs are the ones I want to be between." She wanted to slip her hand between those legs because what really turned her on was to feel Allie's wetness against her skin. It was a moment Brett often put off, feeling Allie's wetness, because it always made her groan. Always got her wet.

It was her greatest enjoyment.


"You couldn't take your eyes off him, man!" Jerry said to Beth that night. She had come by his place for a beer after school.

"So what's the problem?" Beth said, going to the kitchen for another beer.

"Well, y'know, I ain't never seen you act like that before."

"Jake, get to the fuckin' point already," Beth said, sitting on the couch and throwing her feet up on the table. She lit a smoke and didn't look at Jerry.

"I mean, man, I always thought of you as one of the guys, so's it's weird seein' you act like that. I mean, it's like, your sister's a different story, she's not cool to just hang with like you."

"Yeah, you guys only keep her 'cause she puts out."

"Fuck yeah!"

Beth grabbed the remote and started surfing, looking for anything to stop this conversation. She was uncomfortable with it herself, 'cause no guy had ever made her feel like Brett did — there was just something so totally different about him that made her want to spend time with him.

For fuck's sake, she was seventeen years old and still a virgin, so she knew something was wrong with her, and she thought she knew what it was, but there was no way she was going there, ever. She couldn't let anybody know just how fucked up she really was.

"Yo, dudes," Scott said, coming into the house without knocking. Becky was behind him, her fingers locked into the belt loops of his jeans.

"You got anything for me, Jakey?" Becky asked, sitting on the arm of his chair.

"Hey, baby, I got something for you," Scott said, grabbing his crotch. "And I think you'd better do something about it if you know what's good for you."

Becky walked over to Scott and fell to her knees in front of him. She rubbed her face over his crotch, then reached up to unzip his pants. "Oh, Scottie, you taste so good," she said, pulling him out of his jeans.

Beth got up and went to the next room. She didn't like it when the boys ganged up on her sister. She didn't like seeing her sister like that, and she didn't like the sight of their dirty bodies.

She also didn't like seeing how far Becky would go to get her fix. The price she was willing to pay for the high she wanted. Her sister was an addict, and Beth hated it.


"I am unaccustomed to not saying precisely what I mean," Madeline said without looking up when Leisa joined her on the back porch.

Leisa sat down on the chair next to her. "Then why don't you?"

"Because I do not know exactly what it is I wish to say."

"I know how you feel."

"Then how do I feel, my dear?" Madeline asked.

Leisa laughed and looked away. "I love and respect you. I'd say you were a wise old crone, but . . ."

"But what?"

"You're wise, but you're no old crone."

"Remember, to be called a crone is a compliment. But, yes, my dear, a vast crevasse of years separates us."

"Then you have thought of it."

"You are young. I am not. You are beautiful and have your entire life in front of you. I do not."

"You didn't answer the question."

"But you are intelligent."

"Sometimes you can drive me batty, Maddy."

"Only sometimes?" Madeline said.

Leisa had only been with a few guys in her life and had never been with a woman, but something about seeing Brett and Allie together made her suddenly look at Madeline in a different light, see something different in their relationship than what she had previously seen. And then there was the way the two of them had been looking at her and Madeline all night, on top of the lover's quarrel joke.

It had made her see Maddy in a different way. Leisa suddenly realized how much she looked forward to spending time with this intense, intelligent, beautiful woman. How much she looked forward to each moment they spent together.

She had known Maddy for most of her life, albeit barely. Over the past few years, she had gotten to know her better, but over the past year or so they had actually developed a friendship. Maybe it was meant for more. Brett and Allie were making Leisa question it.

"Are you all right?" Madeline finally asked.

"Um, yeah. I think so," Leisa quickly said.

"I find that it is never good to act with direct relation to an incident. Anything that should be done will be done at such a point that it is proper."

"Maybe you're right," Leisa said. It was only on her drive home that she realized Maddy had been simply buying time, that she was as afraid as Leisa.

Leisa suddenly knew that Maddy was feeling exactly what she was, but that Leisa would have to be the one to make the first move. It was a strange feeling, to suddenly realize that somebody you love and admire so much is just as confused as you.


Randi clasped her gun between her two hands. Adrenaline, more potent than any drug, pulsed through her veins. Every nerve, every muscle in her body was at attention. She was ready for action. No woman could ever match this feeling. She was doing not only something she knew was right, but something she believed in. That combined with the fear, the knowledge that she could die, was the greatest rush in the world.

Fear when combined with bravery was almost better than orgasm . . . almost. Even now she knew there was something beyond this, and that was why she would live through tonight, for the something better that lay ahead.

She was focused, waiting for the sounds that would key her body into action. She listened for the right sounds to signal her move into action; she had to be ready to shoot the gun tensed between her slightly sweaty palms.

This night especially pissed her off, got her riled. They were going to catch a cop gone wrong.

Mitchell Symans was a sergeant, and he was in with the bad guys. That was all Randi needed to know — well, that and the proof that a cop had gone wrong. He was selling drugs, helping get them through Detroit Metro Airport, and was now even so cocky as to deliver them to these slimebags so they could infiltrate other territories with their poison.

A cop gone wrong was the worst criminal of all. Cops were supposed to be trusted, so when one went wrong it was bad. About the only thing worse than a cop gone bad was somebody who committed incest or abuse.

Before Randi could continue to wax eloquently within her own mind about all of this, she heard what she needed to hear. Symans had been confronted on the front porch and had opened fire on his fellow officers.

She flipped around the corner, yelling, but even in her hyperactive state, she waited and was prepared for the shot of gunfire before she pulled the trigger. Repeatedly.


Her one killing of the night would later prove to be justifiable. But to her and her fellows, killing the creep wasn't at all questionable. He had killed one of their own that night.

~ ~ ~ ~ ~

"Girl, what you whining about?" Her father's voice was slurred and his breath and body stank of the beer he had been drinking since he'd gotten up that morning. His face was in hers, his hand yanking her hair. He had come into her bedroom after she had gone to bed to sleep. When she had pulled away from him, he had grabbed her by her hair and tossed her to the ground.

She crawled into the corner. "No, please, no."

"Girl, what you whining about? I've had my fingers in you since before you could walk or open that smart-alecky mouth of yours. When you was still in the crib."

"Please, Daddy, don't."

"You gonna be a good girl now?"

"I want my mommy."

"That good-fer-nothing, two-bit whore don't give a shit about you. Ain't you figured that out yet?" He sat on her bed, unzipped his pants, and pulled himself out. "Now, you gonna make me happy, or are you gonna piss me off worse than you already have?"

Brett rubbed her healing ribs and crawled to her father, wincing on her recently broken arm.

She was six-years-old.


This time she didn't wake screaming. She bolted upright in bed. Allie murmured and crawled in closer to her. Brett smiled down at her and tucked the covers in about her. She kissed her forehead, murmuring calming words, then got up and went to the kitchen, where she poured herself two fingers of Glenfiddich single malt scotch.

No matter how hard she tried, she couldn't forget. She'd think she'd forgotten, but then something would take her back, would make her remember. Would wake her up in the middle of the night.

In a way it was good because it never let her forget that the only one she could really rely on, really depend on, was herself. But it was bad for those same reasons.

She wanted this deal done and over with, because she now knew she wouldn't get a good night's sleep until then. Something had set off her subconscious again, and she knew it had to be this deal. There had to be a reason for it, and this had to be it.

She took a sip of her scotch and then stared at the glass, remembering the stench of beer on her father's skin.

She poured the rest of the glass down the drain and went to curl up next to Allie, pulling her in tight.

# 6

"Out of my way, pindick," Brian Ewing said the next morning, coming up behind Brett in the hall and shoving her out of his way. Brett would've gone after him, except that Allie laid a calming hand on her arm.

"Easy, he's not worth it."

"I sure as hell hope he's involved, 'cause then you'll let me really take care of him," Brett replied, while Kathy, who was walking next to Brian, looked back apologetically.

In chem class Kathy walked right up to Brett, who was already at their lab station. "I'm sorry about Brian this morning," she said. "He can be such a jerk sometimes."

"An asshole is more like it," Brett replied, setting up the equipment while Ms. McNeil passed out the chemicals they were supposed to break down into their component parts and identify. They had had a simple mixture yesterday as a warmup, and now they were on to a more complex compound. They would have a week to complete this one.

"Allie says you asked her to become a cheerleader," Brett said, trying to open new roads of conversation.

"Oh yes," Kathy said, turning to face Brett. "Your sister's really sweet," she continued, as Brett poured the unknown chemical into a beaker and set it over the Bunsen burner. "But she told me you used to be quite a jock yourself," Kathy continued.

Brett faced her. "Only did it to get out of gym," she growled.

"Letters in track and wrestling?" Kathy said with a smile. "Too bad it's so late in the year. You could've gotten on our teams —" she broke off as Ms. McNeil walked up to watch what they were doing.

"I don't think Jameson would even be able to wrestle *you*," Ms. McNeil commented. Brett gave her a look that could freeze hell, but Ms. McNeil continued. "One nice thing about switching schools is that you can make your past anything you want it to be."

Brett stood up to confront Ms. McNeil, but Kathy broke in. "Ms. McNeil's the wrestling coach."

Brett burst out in laughter. "Oh really?"

"I'll look forward to seeing you at practice on Monday," Ms. McNeil said, smirking. "Then we can see what you're really made of." With that she walked away.

Brett fumed over what she had just gotten herself into while she connected tubes. "Hold on," she said to Kathy. "Why am I doin' all the work here?" Kathy had simply been watching her preparations.

Kathy grinned shyly. "Because I have no idea what to do."

"Okay," Brett said, pushing her own stool near the wall. "Then I'll tell you what to do," she added as she sat down and leaned against the wall.

"But —" Kathy began.

"No buts. You're not gonna fail this class 'cause of me," Brett replied. It had suddenly dawned on her that Kathy's apparent math and science deficiencies were probably due more to the fact that Kathy had been brainwashed into thinking that girls weren't supposed to do well in them than any real lack of ability on Kathy's part, because it didn't make sense that she was apparently taking some advanced classes in other areas but was taking lower-level classes in math and science.

"I'm not going to fail," Kathy said.

"Yeah, but if you're goin' to college, you're gonna need to know some of this shit."

"I don't see why. It's not like it'll be my major or anything."

"Gen ed," Brett said, then to Kathy's questioning look she elaborated, "general education requirements. There's certain shit they make you take no matter what."

Brett then instructed Kathy on the use of the equipment, and how, by gradually increasing the temperature, she could slowly boil off different parts of the mixture. The temperature that each chemical boiled at was their first clue to its identity. When they had two chemicals isolated, Brett had Kathy determining their density as she herself boiled out the rest.

"Isn't it kinda strange for you to ask a new girl to join the cheerleaders?" Brett asked Kathy.

"Yes, but we are short one, and I don't really want to do tryouts again with just a few more events to do. All the girls that would turn out for it I've already seen before, and they have no rhythm or ability."

"Ain't that gonna piss off some girls?"

Kathy shrugged. "I'm leaving soon, so I don't really have to worry about it. Are you upset about me making friends with your sister?"

"Nah, 'course not." It did make some sense to Brett, but she couldn't shake the feeling that Kathy had an ulterior motive.

"You're not quite what you appear," Kathy finally blurted out.

"Whaddya mean by that?" Brett asked, momentarily flustering Kathy, who looked down at the floor.

"I just meant, well, you really seem to know what you're doing . . . but you pretend that you don't."

Brett laughed. "Just don't let it get around." Their eyes met, and Brett felt as if Kathy were studying her.

"Are you and Allie twins?" Kathy asked. When Brett paused, she continued. "I mean, you're in the same grade and all."

"Well, um, actually I'm almost twenty. I failed a coupla times."

"But you're so smart."

"Aw, let's just not get into it, 'kay?"

Kathy put her hand on Brett's shoulder. "There's something you're not telling me, isn't there?"

"Nope," Brett said, handing Kathy another test tube with a separated chemical. "The boiling temp of this was one-oh-two."

Kathy took the test tube from Brett, their fingers lightly brushing. "Could you maybe help me in math?"

By the end of the hour, when they turned in their report, Kathy knew more about chemistry than she had planned on ever knowing. At the end of class, they were the only team able to identify all the chemicals in their compound mixture. Brett realized that Ms. McNeil had just wanted to show the class how much they didn't know.

"What are you doing in this class?" Ms. McNeil asked Brett.

"She did all the work," Brett said, indicating Kathy.

"Oh, so I should give her an *A* and you an *E*?"

Kathy began to object, but Brett cut her off. "Whatever turns you on, Ms. McNeil," Brett said sarcastically. "Because you can probably use all the turnons you can get."

When Brett finally got into Leisa's class, with another hall pass from the office, she discovered a slight variation from yesterday's seating: This time, Kathy was in the middle. Brett had to fight to keep from smirking at the idea of Kathy really being in the middle. Just the thought of doing both Kathy and Allie at the same time was enough to cause Brett to have to adjust herself.

"What did you do this time?" Leisa asked as she sat down.

Brett looked up at her and intentionally replied in an appropriate linguistical phrasing. "I remarked on Ms. McNeil's sexual life, or, more precisely, the probable lack thereof." With that, she calmly turned toward Kathy and Allie as the class burst out in laughter.

"Your father, rest his soul," Leisa said, "obviously did not raise you in the best manner possible."

This garnered a shocked look from Kathy, who at the end of class looked at Brett and Allie. "I'm so sorry. I didn't know."

"No big deal," Brett said with a shrug. Allie averted her eyes from Kathy, who then gave her a hug, a sight that sent a thrill through Brett.

~ ~ ~ ~ ~

Jerry Johnson went with Brett after class to have a smoke in the john.

"Did you really say that to McNeil?" he asked.

"Yup," Brett replied.

Jerry chuckled at the thought of Ms. McNeil's expression when Brett said that. "You know what though?"

"What?" Brett asked.

"You've really fucked me up about Beth."

"Whaddya mean by that?"

"I mean, I always thought she was some sort of a fuckin' dyke."

"So?"

"So? If I didn't know better, I'd think the bitch has got the hots for you, man."

Brett shrugged. "Guess she's not a dyke, then."

"I don't mind dykes," Jerry said. "It's the fags that get on my nerves."

Brett again shrugged. "I don't care what anybody does, so long as it doesn't fuck with my shit."

Jerry shrugged. "Oh, by the way, I talked with Scott this morning, and he says it's cool if you hang with us Saturday."

"Cool, just let me know when and where."

The warning buzzer sounded, and Jerry headed for the door.

"Catch you there, man," Brett said, heading into a stall. "I gotta take a shit."


After school, Brett waited for Allie by the football field where the cheerleaders were practicing. Allie watched for a bit, then Kathy took her by the hand and pulled her into the group, getting her to give it a try. All the girls had changed into shorts for practice, so Brett had quite a view of nice lean calves and thighs. So good a view, in fact, that she had to force herself to turn to the soccer field to assess her competition.

Brett had briefly wondered what a big jock like Brian was doing playing soccer, but then she had remembered that soccer had gotten

71

bigger since the World Cup. It made sense that a jock like him would want to do something throughout the year.

Still, she couldn't figure out the entire attraction.

Brian Ewing was obviously the center forward, although he was the largest fellow on the field. She quickly discovered that he was fast as well. Amazingly fast for his size. If he played his cards right, he could have a chance at pro football someday. She knew that he wanted to do football. He was the quarterback then, and boys like him liked being in control.

He would have to really work to get a spot on a Big Ten football team. He probably had delusions of grandeur, but his chances would be less because he was from such a small school.

Brett moved a bit higher on the bleachers so she could watch both the team and the cheerleaders without turning around. Kathy smiled and waved at her, and Brett thought that Kathy and Allie side by side was quite a lovely view. So lovely, in fact, that Brett was reminded of her earlier thoughts of Kathy being in the middle. Brett was almost amazed that she was getting so turned on at the thought of Allie being with another woman, but it would be Allie touching another woman with Brett being right there, watching and participating.

She suddenly felt a boot toe push into her ass. She looked up.

"You Jameson?" said a tall blond fellow wearing a leather jacket, torn jeans, and combat boots.

"You got a problem with it?" Brett said, standing to face the boy. She noticed Jerry and Steve standing on the ground just beyond the bleachers.

"Not yet," he replied. Brett gave him her best sneer. "But my boys tell me you're innerested in joinin' us."

"If it's worth my time," Brett growled.

"You got that wrong — you gotta be worth our time," he replied. Brett saw that Steve and Jerry were nervously pacing. Brett suddenly realized she was probably speaking with Scott Campbell, the infamous leader of the pack.

Brett looked at her watch. "Cut to the quick already, man, I got things to do."

Scott sneered at her. "I'm not sure if you're worth it," he said as he turned to leave.

"Scott Campbell," Brett mused aloud, stopping Scott. "You think you're all that with a cherry on top, and you really just ain't nothing."

"Buddy, you s'posed to be kissin' my ass right about now."

"I think," Brett continued, "that I'll have to go back to Detroit to do anything I ain't already done, or go anywhere I ain't already been."

"You just a boy playin' on man's turf."

Brett spit a big loogie. She had been working on this particular talent of late and was glad to finally have a chance to show it off. "I'm used to business, and you just talkin' play with me, man."

"You think we're just talkin' play here? We're chartin' new territory, and it's all my turf."

"You and I both know that I be way out of your fuckin' league. I can teach you shit you only dreamed of before." Brett was almost having fun with this pissing contest.

Scott spit out a big loogie. Brett imagined this was rather like both of them raising their legs to mark their territory. "Listen, man, if you're half of what you think you are, we might be able to do business," Scott said, sizing Brett up just before he turned and left.

Allie saw Brett sitting in the bleachers, watching. She smiled at her handsome lover and started to wave, but realized that might be inappropriate for a teenage girl to do to her brother, so she settled for the smile.

She knew Brett had come out today to watch the soccer team, but she was apparently watching both her and the soccer players. Allie wondered if Brett was remembering how old she had been when they first met. At that time, Allie really had been seventeen.

She glanced over at Kathy, wondering if perhaps Brett was remembering all that while looking at the wrong woman.

"That new student is a pain in the ass," Lucy McNeil said to Leisa after school.

Before Leisa could reply, Fred Marin said, "Yes, he is, and I'm not really sure his sister should be in my calculus class. She has supposedly taken advanced mathematics, yet she is having incredible difficulties with the idea of imaginary numbers."

"But she sure is one good looking broad," Carl Rogers grunted, looking up from the table where he sat with the swimsuit issue of *Sports Illustrated*.

"You're a pig, Carl," Lucy McNeil blurted out.

"Please," Leisa said, frowning down at Carl, "just give them time. They've been through a lot this past year. They're the niece and nephew of my best friend, and their father recently passed away."

"I don't care. That is still no excuse for the way that boy behaves," Caroline Thatcher interrupted.

"Talking about Brett Jameson?" Margie Simons said as she entered the lounge for a cup of coffee.

"Margie," Lucy McNeil said, leaning against a counter, "I think he's been seeing more of you than I have."

"I've noticed," Margie commented dryly as she poured her coffee. Leisa turned away so no one would notice the grin that was spreading across her face. Brett was definitely leaving her mark on this school. Leisa assumed it was because she knew she had nothing to lose since she would only be there a short time. She was excited that everyone believed that Brett really was an adolescent male.

"One thing I'll say for him, though," Lucy McNeil started as Kelly Green entered the room. "He's not as dumb as he looks."

"Who're we talking about now?" Kelly asked, walking over to Lucy McNeil and taking her cup of coffee. Lucy McNeil grimaced, but went to get another cup for herself.

"The new students," Fred Marin said. "There's something definitely different about them."

Lucy McNeil turned around, and Kelly caught her eye. "Yes, there certainly is," Kelly said, with a supposedly private wink to Lucy McNeil that a few other people noticed, like Leisa.

"He's way too good in chemistry to be in that class," Lucy McNeil said.

"I think he's taken it a few times," Leisa said, trying to cover for Brett's chemistry aptitude.

"Then he should've passed it by now, especially considering how much he knows. He walked Kathy Moran through class today, and they did a week's assignment in one day."

"Kathy Moran?" Carl asked. "Doesn't she belong to Brian Ewing?"

"Belong to?" Kelly asked. "Last time I checked, Carl, slavery was outlawed over a century ago."

Carl snarled at her. "I'm just saying he'll get what he's asking for if he messes with my boys."

"Carl, that sort of attitude only leads to problems," Margie said.

"There's always been a status quo, Margie. There've always been the winners and the losers, and Brett Jameson is just one of the losers my boys will trample on their way up."

Lucy McNeil turned from Carl in disgust. "I'm going home," she said and left.

"Carl, I need to see you in my office — now," Margie, the principal said, following Lucy McNeil out of the teacher's lounge.

# 7

Randi had gotten up early to get a start on the day. It was technically her vacation, but she didn't like anybody fucking with her nephew. She already didn't approve of the crowd he hung with and knew just how liable he was to really screw up his entire future.

She knew what he could so easily become — she had seen it happen to hundreds of teens all over the Detroit metro area as well as to her own brother, Daniel. He was dead now, and Randi now understood that at the end Daniel hadn't been the same boy who had given her piggy-back rides when she was younger. He had become involved with drugs and crime, sinking into them and away from Randi and their family. Randi didn't want the same thing to happen to her nephew. She didn't care if Jake's dad thought he might be imagining things. She knew that he had gone to Alma to get away from the crime and problems of the city and to have a safe place to raise his family. Randi didn't like him even being suspicious that Jake was involved in crime or drugs.

Randi dreamed of the day when she'd be living for the woman she made a life for, but for now, she could only dream of such things. For now, she had her job, her family, the drive to affect a great many lives around her. She enjoyed knowing that she had a positive effect on so many others — that's why she regularly volunteered her time at Affirmations, Detroit's LesBiGay community center.

She wished she could be a Big Sister, but knew that her job's strange hours would cause her to disappoint a little sister if Randi had to cancel whatever they planned.


"Okay, see you tonight!" Allie called out the front door as Kathy left.

Brett looked down at her watch. Three P.M. Allie had been with the cheerleaders since that morning. They had decided they wanted her on the squad, but they were making her wait a bit to ensure that she had the routines down before she could join them at a game.

Last night the soccer team had smeared a neighboring town's team all over the field during the scrimmage. All the sports enthusiasts in high spirits, especially all of Brian's fans, who were talking about him like he was the next Michael Jordan. Tonight was to be at Scott's house at five P.M., to warm up for the teen nightclub. She sighed and stood to get ready.

"Hey, baby," Allie said, grabbing her by the waist and kissing her. "Miss me?"

Adrenaline rushed through Brett's veins, overtaking the tired feeling she had been experiencing. She grinned and grabbed Allie by the ass, pulling her in tight. "Like you wouldn't believe." She couldn't let Allie flirt so blatantly and get away with it.

"Is Maddy around?" Allie whispered as Brett put her hands under Allie's shorts and lifted her off the ground. Allie wound her legs around Brett's waist.

"Nope," Brett said. "She's doing the psychic thing tonight — reading palms in Lansing." Allie's skin was like silk under her fingertips.

"Shame on her, leaving the children alone," Allie murmured as

Brett ran her hands up Allie's back underneath her thin T-shirt. What had begun as a teasing flirt had quickly become something much more.

"I love you, but I still want to fuck your brains out," Brett whispered, placing her on the edge of the living room table and removing Allie's shirt and bra. Allie quickly pulled her own shoes and socks off.

Brett feasted on her lover's mouth, her tongue dancing with Allie's in and out of each other's mouth.

There were very few women in Brett's life who had gone beyond a one-night, or even a one-month stand. Allie was one of those few. Allie could quickly raise Brett's temperature from cruising level to down and dirty — and she did so successfully, knowing what she wanted each step of the way.

Sometimes she wanted gentle lovemaking, with lots of extended eye contact, lots of praise and worship of every inch of her body, from the beautiful silky hair that Brett loved to bury her face in, to the long legs that Brett loved to caress with her hands and mouth and tongue. Those times it was slow and tender.

Then there were the times that Allie wanted something more, something not quite so gentle, tender, and loving. Those were the times that she liked things a bit more wild. Brett would still spend lengths of time gazing deep into her eyes, her soul, but she would also tie her up, become one with her, or wind Allie's legs around her neck and lift her up off the bed.

No matter what Allie's mood, what she wanted, she could tell Brett what it was without saying a single word. Brett knew her woman and could tell what she wanted from multitudinous clues she gave off. Brett had learned early that each woman she was with was different and that there was nothing so bad as making love to every woman the same. Brett lived for the pleasure she gave; that was what really did it to her, for her.

This time Allie wanted something else. Not sweet and tender lovemaking, not even the more ferocious and energetic lovemaking.

Allie was attacking her quite blatantly in the middle of the afternoon. She was moaning and grinding against Brett with her every thought, making it known that Brett could do anything she wanted to and that she would enjoy it.

Allie wanted Brett to take her. To fuck her and make her scream.

Brett was more than willing to comply.

Brett leaned down and grabbed a nipple in her mouth, tracing her tongue over its contours while Allie tried to push it deeper into her, arching her back against her. Brett teased the nipple, enjoying its full hardness and the fact that she was driving Allie crazy with her hesitancy. Allie knew what she wanted and needed, as did Brett, but Brett wanted her to know who was in charge.

Brett's hands moved up over the silken contours of Allie's body. Her left hand cupped Allie's right breast, her thumb and forefinger grasping the nipple securely, teasing it and squeezing it.

She moved her mouth to that nipple, biting it gently, tugging on it with her teeth. Her right hand tended to the left breast and nipple. She pushed her hardened stomach muscles against Allie and pulled her in close.

"You're driving me crazy!" Allie moaned.

Brett pulled away to grin at her, then nipped the nipple, pleasing one while her tongue whipped back and forth over the other. Allie pressed her crotch into Brett, pulling Brett against her as hard as she could with her legs. Her legs were spread wide, circling Brett's waist. She arched against Brett when Brett increased the pace of her tongue across her nipple, while Brett bit down harder on her already extended nipple.

Brett ran her hands down Allie's back, down under her shorts, grabbing her firm ass roughly to bring her in as tight as possible against her own grinding pelvis.

Brett loved Allie, and her greatest pleasure came from pleasing her, making her happy. She wanted what Allie wanted. But she knew that teasing could make that pleasure even greater, even better.

She loved the feeling of so much of Allie's skin against her. She loved the feeling of power that having Allie half-naked gave her, and she loved knowing how hot and wet this made Allie, being half-naked or naked, against Brett. It was Brett's greatest turn on.

She bit on Allie's nipple and whipped her tongue back and forth over the enlarged bud as Allie groaned her appreciation.

Allie pulled off her shorts as Brett roughly pushed the books and papers off the table carelessly to the floor. She wanted Allie. She knelt on the table and pushed Allie's naked body down under her. Stretched her out on the table underneath her. Brett lay down on top of her, pressing her body against Allie's. Allie arched her pelvis up into Brett's hard stomach, and Brett grabbed her wrists and took them up over her head, stretched her out even further, holding her down tightly.

"Are you trying to drive me crazy?" Allie whimpered, her body under Brett's control.

Brett chuckled her reply, looking down at Allie, before roughly attacking Allie's neck with her tongue and teeth. Allie pushed up against Brett as hard as she could, groaning and writhing under Brett, while Brett worked her way down to Allie's tits with small bites and nibbles. She liked working Allie over from head to toe.

Allie loved it when Brett was rough. She thrilled to every touch and bite. She loved it in the daylight, with the blinds not quite closed and the windows open, in the middle of Madeline's living room. She loved the cool table under her hot body. She loved Brett forcing her to comply to her every whim. It left her feeling open and exposed. It made her give away the control she so tightly held in all other aspects of her life. She felt free. She felt free within the unbreakable restraint of Brett's hands and body.

There was an open abandonment when it came like this, when Brett took her like this. She felt as if she didn't have a choice, even though she knew she did. She liked Brett pushing her so she felt no obligation to even try to return the favor, to make Brett feel as good as Brett was making her feel.

Brett knelt between Allie's legs, her own legs kicking Allie's even farther apart than they already were. She brought her thumbs down to open Allie's wet and swollen clit, and she knelt there studying it in the light of day before she moved her thumbs in to run up and down the sides of the no-longer-hidden flesh. She sunk both her thumbs into Allie to bring the wetness up and around her entire clit as Allie lay stretched out over the table, whimpering softly as the sensations spread throughout her body.

"God, baby, you look so good," Brett whispered.

Allie met Brett's gaze while she continued lying back, fully exposed. "Oh, Brett . . ."

Brett laid a tender hand against Allie's chest to keep her down. "Oh, honey, just let me enjoy you . . ." Her heart swelled in her chest, filling her with love.

Allie moaned and arched under Brett's fingers as she watched the still fully clothed Brett examining her. She lifted her pelvis up, offering herself to Brett. Brett began running her hands over Allie, roughly, from her neck, over her breasts, hardened nipples, flat stomach and down to her cunt.

"Oh god, Brett," Allie moaned.

"What do you want baby?" Brett asked, fully knowing what Allie wanted. She slipped her hand down between Allie's legs and moaned when she felt the wetness.

"Brett, you know."

"Tell me baby, tell me." Brett kissed Allie's stomach, drew her tongue up over the full breasts and nibbled on the full nipples, from one to the other, wanting neither to feel neglected.

"I want to feel your tongue, I want to feel you."

"I'm already tasting you, sweetie." Allie's skin was salty-sweet. Brett wasn't sure if she could ever taste enough of her. She traced her fingers up and down Allie's clit.

"Oh god, Brett, eat me."

Brett lowered her shoulders so she could slip her arms under Allie's gorgeous thighs and lift Allie's beautiful ass up off the table. Allie's legs entwined Brett's neck, and Brett kept her hands on Allie's tits, pinching the nipples, her fingers repeating the pattern that her tongue had started on Allie's clit. Brett's tongue eagerly lapped up Allie's thick, sweet juices before it went inside Allie.

Allie moaned softly at the warmth penetrating her. Brett brought her hands back down to Allie's hips before she returned her left hand to its original spot on Allie's nipple. As Brett burrowed her tongue in the tender flesh between Allie's thighs, she brought her right hand to tease Allie's vagina before she inserted first one, then two, then four fingers into her, up to her knuckles.

Allie bucked at the pressure and the feelings caused by Brett's fingers working their way inside of her while Brett's tongue beat back and forth across her clit. Allie felt Brett's entire fist slide into her, and she could feel every movement Brett made with her fist as she twisted it around and clenched and unclenched it. She was on the edge, the very edge, being driven toward it, climbing toward it, with Brett's fist inside of her, Brett between her legs . . .

She started to writhe on the table, her body an instrument under Brett's hands and tongue. Brett was inside of her. Allie was Brett's.

Suddenly her clit felt as if it were ready to explode. All her bodily fluids seemed to course through her body to converge between her legs . . .

Her tits and her pussy were connected . . . The heat was spreading . . .

And Brett was one with her as the edge loomed nearer . . .

"Oh my god, oh my god," Allie screamed as she jerked Brett over the table. Brett held on with every twist and turn, riding out the storm as her fingers tightened and her fist stayed its course and her tongue beat back and forth, back and forth . . .

Allie was so tight on Brett's fist that she could almost scream, and she tightened harder and harder so that Brett couldn't move her fist at all.

"Brett! Oh god, Brett!"

Then Allie stopped writhing and lay back on the table, exhausted and spent. Brett slowly lapped up her juices, tenderly running her tongue over her lover as the last tremors slid through Allie's body. Brett kissed the insides of her thighs, then her stomach. Only then, when she was half lying on top of Allie, did she slowly and gently pull her hand out of that incredible woman's body.

Brett and Allie lay holding each other for several minutes on the hard surface of the table, not noticing the face just beyond the blinds.



He had already given the man the money, so he finished inventorying the lot and loaded it into his duffel bag.

The man pocketed the money and looked at him. "That video you gave me the other day — are there any more like it?"

"Yes, there are."

"I want to see them."

"I'm not sure —"

The man slammed him against the car, anger flashing in his eyes. "I want to see them. And then I might have a proposition for you — something that will make all we've made so far seem like peanuts."

"What?"

"Just bring me the movies." The man turned away and then, "How's Scott doing?"

"I'll be takin' care of him."

"Getting too big for his britches, eh?"

"He's just pissing me off," he replied, as he climbed into his vehicle and left, silently cursing the older man who insisted they meet so far from town. It ruined his entire night.

Brett had to rush to shower and change and make it to Scott's house before she was more than fashionably late. Her tardiness was quickly excused, however, because of the case of beer she carried under one arm and the bottle of Jack she carried in her hand. She had chosen to wear an old, black leather biker's jacket, well worn slightly baggy jeans, black boots, and a white T-shirt with an untucked gray-and-white Structure flannel over it. What no one could see, however, were the gun strapped to one leg and the knife strapped to the other.

Steve, Jerry, and Beth were sprawled across the furniture in the front room. The air was cloudy with smoke, both tobacco and pot.

"Where's Scott?" Brett asked, entering the house.

"In the bedroom," Beth replied, indicating its location with a nod of her head. Her eyes slowly slipped over Brett. That was when Brett heard the moans and grunts coming from the rear of the house.

"I'll take those," Jerry said, jumping up and taking the alcohol from Brett. He returned a few moments later with beers for everyone.

Brett slouched into a chair. "His folks ain't home, I take it."

"Hell, Scott's folks ain't never home," Steve grunted.

"His mom ran away when he was like two," Beth added. "And his dad's always either at work or at the bar."

"He don't give a shit what we do anyway," Jerry clarified.

Brett's seat faced the hallway. A naked girl strolled past the living room going from the bedroom to the bathroom. She moved slowly enough so that Brett was able to enjoy her full breasts, lean legs, and flat stomach. She turned briefly toward Brett, obligingly giving her an even better look at her hardened nipples and the dark triangle of hair nestled between her thighs.

Beth caught Brett's eyes and followed them.

"That's Becky," Beth said. Brett wondered if there was a touch of disappointment to her voice.

"Beth's *twin* sister," Steve said with a laugh. Beth gave him a cold look as Scott entered, shirtless and zipping up his jeans.

"Beer, cool," he said, taking Jerry's. Jerry looked up, about to say something, but instead shrugged it off and went to the kitchen for another. Becky entered wearing only a man's large shirt and sat in Scott's lap.

"Dad's getting pissed at you wearing his shirts," Scott said, downing his beer and placing his hand high up on Becky's inner thigh. Brett noted that the shirt wasn't buttoned down the first half. Becky saw Brett's look and adjusted herself to give Brett a better view, letting it be known that Brett could do her.

Jerry was just passing out another round of beer when they heard a car door slam outside.


"Hey, Jake," Beth said, saluting him with a beer when he entered moments later. Brett turned to look at him as he entered, but then noticed he was being followed by someone else. Brett caught a quick glance of dark eyes, darker hair, and a slightly short, barely female frame before she turned away and looked down.

"Scott, Steve, Jerry, Beth, Becky," Randi McMartin said from the doorway. "I'm using Jake's car tonight so his Dad can work on mine. Can one of you give him a ride home?"

"Yeah, we'll get him home safe and sound, Auntie Randi," Steve said sarcastically from his seat. Brett tried to crawl into her seat.

"I'm in a fairly good mood tonight, Steve," Randi said. "So I wouldn't suggest fucking with me."

"But you wouldn't mind it if Becky were to fuck with you, huh?" Scott asked. Becky turned around in his lap to give Randi a better look at her goods.

Randi turned away from Becky in disgust. "I don't give a shit that I'm out of my jurisdiction, asshole. I can still take on any of you, and fuck with your realities while I'm at it."

Jake stood back. Brett wasn't sure if he was embarrassed or scared by Randi or his friends.

"We love you too, sweet cheeks," Jerry said into the silence.

"Your manners are shot to hell, as well," Randi replied. "You haven't introduced me to your new friend." She turned on her heel and faced Brett. Their eyes met for the briefest moment before Brett turned around and lowered her head.

"Well, excuse me!" Scott cried, standing and dumping Becky onto the floor. "Officer Randi McMartin, I would like to introduce you to Brett Jameson."

"Brett?" Randi repeated, turning white. She obviously had recognized Brett.

"Yeah, that's what I said," Scott repeated.

"You said Brett . . . Jameson, right?" Randi said, apparently trying to regain her composure.

"What the fuck, copper, how many times I gotta repeat myself?"

Brett felt her stare burn into the back of her neck. "Don't I know you from somewhere?" Randi finally said.

Brett lit a cigarette and took a swig of beer while she kicked her feet onto the arm of the chair so that she faced away from Randi. "I dunno, but I thought I recognized you," she said. "From a really bad nightmare."

"I am all of your worst nightmares. And I'm sure you'll all be glad to know that I'll be here for at least an entire week. That should give me ample time to fuck you all up big time." With that, Randi slammed out of the house.

"Keep her the fuck away from me," Brett said, turning to Jake.

"She is one fucked-up dyke," Scott said, storming back to the bedroom followed by Becky.

Jake shrugged at the rest of them. "I didn't think I could even get away from Randi and my folks tonight."

"You know her," Beth said quietly to Brett from across the room. It wasn't a question.

"I think we ran into each other a couple of times," Brett admitted.

"How?" Steve asked, leaning forward.

"Let's just say it was in connection to one of my employers," Brett said, standing. "I gotta take a piss."

When she left the room, Jake looked at Steve, Jerry, and Beth. He went over to them and knelt between them.

"Randi's been involved with trying to stop organized crime in Detroit for a coupla years," he whispered.

85

"That li'l shit in there?" Steve whispered back, pointing to the bathroom.

"Only thing that makes sense."

"He is from Detroit," Jerry reminded them.

"Scott'll want to know this," Steve decided. "Beth, keep him busy when he comes back out." Beth nodded her understanding while the three went back into the bedroom. Brett returned a few moments later.

"Where is everybody?" she said, looking about.

"In the bedroom," Beth replied, carefully watching Brett's every movement.

"Doing what?" Brett asked, sitting on a chair across from Beth.

"Havin' a gangbang, for all I know," Beth replied.

"Your sister's quite a slut, I take it."

Beth shrugged. Brett drank some more of her beer and watched Beth watching her. "Is there something you want to say to me?" she asked suddenly.

Beth was embarrassed. "Uh, no," she said, turning away.

Brett looked across the room at the young woman. She desperately wanted to say to Beth what she'd wished someone had said to her when she was that young. But she couldn't risk it. She couldn't tempt fate to show up her guise. She couldn't, she couldn't, she couldn't. There was too much at stake, too much to lose . . .

Brett stood up and walked over to where Beth was sitting and sat on the arm of the almost threadbare couch.

She looked down at Beth. "You're right," she said. "I am different from any guy you've ever met." She caught a quick glance into Beth's eyes before Beth turned away. She had hit the nail on the head. When Beth didn't speak, Brett continued. "Unfortunately, we wouldn't work well together." She lit a cigarette as she carefully weighed her next words. "But I want you to remember me as a friend you can talk to about anything in the next couple of years." She knew she was taking a chance, but she couldn't stand to think of this young girl having to live through what she herself had barely survived.

Beth turned and looked up at Brett. Brett could see the questions and fears running through her head. Brett wished there were some way she could make it all easier on Beth, but she also knew that she couldn't rush Beth, nor tell her what to do. The only thing she could do was thank the powers that be that she herself was no longer seventeen.

"Whaddya mean by that?" Beth finally asked.

"You'll know when the time comes," Brett said, running her hand quickly and gently over Beth's hair. She stood and walked back to her chair. She looked back at Beth. "My guess is that they're in there talkin' 'bout me," she said, nodding toward the bedroom. Beth looked away. "Beth," she continued, "I'd like to think there's someone here I can trust. I'd like to think that person was you. And I know you want it to be you, even if you don't know why quite yet."

Beth looked into her eyes. "Who are you?" she asked.

"Just a schmo from Motown," Brett said with a smile. She felt she could trust Beth, if only because Beth feared that Brett knew too much about her. But Brett feared that Beth might need some help, and Beth could help ingratiate her with the boys. "I was working for a guy back home," Brett said, contemplatively studying her cigarette. "We were into all sorts of shit. What's important is that Randi McMartin met me while she was undercover. I slipped out the back door when they raided the place, and probably the only reason they didn't come after me was that she thought I was just some asshole kid running the ticket booth. Let's just say between you and me that she was wrong."

"What all did you do?" Beth asked.

"A little of this and a lot of that," Brett replied with a shrug. "If you all are into anything, Randi and I should never see each other," Brett concluded, getting to the heart of the matter. Beth nodded, and Brett knew the girl would do anything possible to make sure that Randi and Brett never again met.


Beth was hooked. She had never thought about kissing some guy, and really couldn't understand how so many women went through hoops for guys. They let the guys control them. Beth couldn't even picture getting lost in some guy's big, hairy arms. But she could see herself losing herself in Brett's arms, burying her head in his chest.

Girls would lose themselves in order to get the boy they wanted. They'd give up themselves, their opinions, their brains, just to lie with their legs spread beneath some sweaty jerk.

But she loved the way Brett's eyes changed color — and she also loved the understanding and sympathy in those deep brown eyes. She liked the way he seemed to own any room he walked into, the way nothing ever scared him. The implications he had just laid about his past just got her all the more excited — he wasn't one that just pretended, he had lived it all.

But she had no idea how to go about picking up a guy. Well, she could do what her sister did, which was basically take off all her clothes and shit, but she couldn't see herself doing something like that — 'specially not with what he had just said to her.

She had to stop this. After all, he just told her that nothing would happen between them — but then he said he'd be her friend. Talk about mixed messages. Just what did he mean by that?

She suddenly wished she had a good female friend, somebody to show her how to put on makeup and tell her what to wear. She couldn't believe she was thinking about it, but she was. She just knew if she did something to get Brett's attention, she might have a chance.

# 8

Brett entered the dimly lit and fairly packed "bar." She had driven over alone, but the rest of the group would be arriving at any time. She was amazed at the size of the cover charge, but figured the proprietors needed to make their money somewhere since they couldn't make it on booze.

She assessed the layout. The Hot to Trot was larger than she imagined it would be, but it was also much more crowded — Beth and Jerry hadn't been kidding when they said everyone came here on Saturday nights. Although Brett already had a slight buzz going, she still walked into a corner to spike her drink from her hip flask after purchasing a soda at the bar. The guys would know something was up if she was drinking only straight soda.

The one thing missing now, she decided, was the cloud of smoke that always hung over bars. No smoking or drugs were allowed inside the building on Saturday nights. She could imagine what was going on in the bathrooms and in the parking lot.

She cruised the place, casually nodding to the few familiar faces she saw while looking for Allie. She wanted to fill Allie in on the discussion she had had with the gang. Brett had showed serious doubts about the possibility of finding any action in this little shitville, but Scott said they'd give Brett more action than he ever thought possible, if he proved himself. Scott had concluded by saying Brett would be filled in later.

Brett wasn't watching where she was going, and when she turned around she smacked into the girl in back of her. As Brett began to apologize, she looked into the girl's deep brown eyes. An easy smile slowly spread across the girl's face.

"Where's the other half?" Brett asked Kathy while trying to regain control of her own body.

"At some macho football player's thing," Kathy replied, yelling over the music.

Brett smiled. "Shame on him, leaving you all alone with the wolves tonight."

"Are you calling yourself a wolf?"

"You know we're all after only one thing."

"Yourself included?"

"What do you think?"

"We all know what the big bad wolf did to Little Red Riding Hood."

"Is that what you would like — for me to eat you?"

"I, uh . . ."

Brett lightly ran her fingers up Kathy's bare arm. "Why don't I save you the work of finding a reply and just take you to the dance floor?"

Kathy looked nervously about.

"I know I'll like the way your body moves."

"Brett, I, uh . . ." She was flushed.

Brett took Kathy's hands in hers. "Dance with me." She led Kathy to the dance floor.

"Well, okay, sure," Kathy replied, halfway to the dance floor.

Brett didn't think about what a mistake this was until they entered the dance floor. She had forgotten that straight guys don't like to dance, especially when they're teenagers. Although the bar

90

was fairly crowded, there weren't many people on the dance floor, and only one other guy. But Brett was feeling good as the beat invaded her soul and her body started moving of its own accord. The music took her along on its wings of harmony and melody. Her hips were swaying, and her feet were dancing.

Kathy seemed impressed with Brett's moves, even though in the gay bars, Brett hadn't been the best of dancers. Obviously the gay bars had much higher standards. As the two bopped to the beat, Brett reached forward and took the lead, holding Kathy's hands in her own as she stretched her arms across her body. Kathy did the same and they twirled about in circles before Brett let loose of one of Kathy's hands to twirl Kathy in a circle under her arm. She caught Kathy's hand and pulled the breathless woman in close.

Brett could feel the warmth of Kathy's breath against her neck, smell the sweet mixture of perfume and sweat on Kathy's body, and imagine the swell of Kathy's laugh under the din of the music. She turned Kathy around and pressed herself against Kathy's back, enjoying the feel of the woman in her arms, enjoying the way their bodies fit together. She was oblivious to all else. She remembered only how much she loved to dance and how long it'd been since she'd last had the chance. Every time their bodies were pressed together, Brett was surprised at the swell and firmness of Kathy's breasts against her. They felt so good that Brett just wanted to touch and see them. She wanted to take them in her mouth and make Kathy moan.

She lost herself in the moment.

The DJ announced a retro block and began to play a few songs from Brett's own high-school days. Brett and Kathy were about to exit the floor when a dirty dancing number began. Brett grinned at Kathy and pulled her close, positioning her leg between Kathy's and executing some of her best dirty dancing moves. She leaned Kathy back, then pulled her up into her arms. Brett dropped to her knees, running her hands unabashedly over the curves of Kathy's body. Maybe the Baptists were right, Brett thought — dancing could very well be vertical fucking. All Brett knew was that she wanted to take Kathy to bed right then.

A heavy hand grasped her shoulder.

Brett looked up. Three rather large fellows surrounded her.

"Outside, now," the first barked. Brett stood and saw the look of pure fear etched across Kathy's face as one guy half dragged, half carried her out the back door. Brett would've followed just to see that Kathy was safe, regardless of the two thugs following just behind Brett.

The back parking lot was full of cars but devoid of people, and the full moon washed over it ominously as the spring breeze sent trash scurrying across the blacktop. When Brett looked into the eyes of the guy holding Kathy, Brett saw only a blank. The boys — jocks, she now realized — were on something, and she could only hope that they weren't too far gone.

"What are you doin', Thompson?" Kathy yelled at one of the two who stood behind Brett. The one holding Kathy tightened his grip.

"Protecting Brian's property," Thompson replied.

Brett told herself that none of these jerks were as big, or as fast, as Brian. "Brian doesn't own her," Brett said evenly. "She isn't a piece of meat to brand."

"We can fix that," the other fellow said, pulling a switchblade and advancing on Kathy.

"Kyle, you can't . . ." Kathy began.

"Like hell, I can't," Kyle replied. Thompson stood watching both Brett and Kathy.

"Your problem is with me, guys," Brett said, diverting their attention. She backed up and turned, so that she could see all three of her opponents. She knew she had asked for something like this, but she hadn't expected them to threaten Kathy or to try a three-on-one against her. She reminded herself of the insurance she had strapped to her legs, but remembered that their use could blow her cover.

"I thought you were with Brian," Kathy said, making an obvious attempt to change the subject.

"So that's what he told you," the fellow holding her said. Kathy tried to struggle out of his grip, finally biting him on the hand till he tossed her to the ground. "Bitch!" he yelled as she rolled to her feet.

Kyle quickly grabbed her. "Hold this bitch, Doug," he snarled, tossing her back to Doug. "We want her to see what we do to guys who try to move in on Brian's property."

"Yeah," Thompson said, turning to shove Brett back against the car she was standing in front of. Brett's ass hit the hood as Thompson moved on her. Brett brought up both feet to kick him squarely in the chest, which sent him sprawling to the ground.

Kyle ran forward as Brett bounced off the ground and brought a foot up to kick him in the jaw. The hard sole of her boot made a satisfying thud as it hit its mark. Brett turned to whip her calf against Thompson's stomach as he tried to stand. He doubled over and fell back to the ground.

"Bastard!" Doug yelled, throwing Kathy to the ground and lunging at Brett. Brett dropped to all fours, threw her weight onto her hands and sent her legs flying to his, striking his shins and sending him tumbling.

Kyle had twisted around on the ground and was now standing with his knife as Thompson also gained his footing. Brett quickly glanced both ways, trying to decide what to do as both boys advanced on her, but Kathy jumped to her feet and brought a large rock down on Thompson's head. Brett flew toward Kyle in a flurry of karate kicks. Kyle's head hit a bumper, and he collapsed to the ground as Doug took off running in the opposite direction.

Still holding the rock, Kathy stood looking down at Thompson. Brett walked over, felt for a pulse, and examined the welt on Thompson's head.

"He'll have one helluva headache," she pronounced, "but he'll live."

Kathy sat on the ground and stared blankly in front of her. Brett took Kathy's chin in her hand and looked into her eyes.

"You okay?" Brett asked quietly. Kathy nodded. Brett looked around. "I think I'd better get out of here," she concluded.

"Can I come with you?" Kathy asked.

Brett turned to again look into her deep brown eyes. The young woman was scared. "Yeah," Brett said.

"Allie brought Susan and me . . ." Kathy began as Brett helped her stand.

"You go in and tell Susan you're leaving," Brett said. "Don't talk to Allie. But tell Susan to come back here in five minutes. We want her to make sure these guys come to okay." Kathy nodded her understanding. "I'll meet you out front."

When Kathy climbed into the waiting Jimmy, Brett took off. She had already thought of a nice, quiet place she had found in her explorations of the area. It was in Alma — part of a park. They drove in silence.

When Brett finally parked forty-five minutes later, Kathy wordlessly climbed out of the vehicle and walked over to sit on a rock looking down at the river. Brett wrapped her jacket around Kathy and tenderly laid a hand upon her shoulders. Kathy looked up at her.

"He would've done it, y'know," she said. A tear trickled down her cheek.

"I know," Brett said, thinking of Kyle approaching Kathy with the knife. She knew the boys were hopped up on something, but, fortunately, not so much so that they were immune to Brett's "powers of persuasion."

"Bri was such a nice guy when we met," Kathy tried to explain. "But he's changed. He's such a hotshot now and thinks he owns me. He thinks he can say who I can be friends with . . ." She trailed off as another tear escaped her eye.

"Has he been any different lately?" Brett probed, looking for any evidence of wrongdoing on Brian's part. As if being an asshole wasn't bad enough.

"I could tell before, but it really started getting bad last fall," Kathy replied, turning to face Brett. The moonlight trickled down from the sky, reflecting off the water, as the slightly chilly breeze whistled through the trees.

"Have you noticed anything in particular?" Brett said, trying to stay focused. She longed to soothe Kathy's troubled spirit; as she yearned to stop Kathy's tears.

"Sometimes, like tonight, he says he's doin' one thing and I find out he's not doin' it. He's been more secretive about what he's doin'. I don't know," she said as she bowed her head into her hands. Her shoulders began to shake.

"Have you thought about dumping him?" Brett asked, kneeling beside Kathy with her hand still on Kathy's shoulder.

"I don't think I can. You saw what happened tonight," Kathy sobbed, still holding her head as she crumpled into a fetal position. Brett gathered her in her arms and held her, gently running her hands up and down Kathy's back and cradling Kathy's head on her shoulder as Kathy cried. Both women were on their knees, their bodies pushed tight against each other. Brett felt strong and protective.

A minute or so later, Kathy pulled away and sat up. "I'm sorry," she mumbled, brushing at her tear-stained face with angry fists. "I don't know —"

"It's okay," Brett said, cutting her off and taking Kathy's face in her hands. Brett gently wiped away Kathy's tears with her thumbs.

"Thank you," Kathy whispered, looking deep into Brett's hazel eyes. Brett didn't have a chance to think as Kathy slowly leaned forward with closed eyes. She didn't want to think . . .

Brett closed her eyes and brushed her lips against Kathy's. Kathy put her arms around Brett's shoulders, and Brett slid her arms around Kathy's waist, pulling her in closer.

Kathy's breasts felt good even through the thick T-shirt and Ace bandage Brett was wrapped in. When Kathy parted her lips, Brett gently entered her with her tongue, lost in the moment, lost in the warmth and tenderness of Kathy's kiss.

When Brett ran her hands up underneath Kathy's jacket, Kathy moaned softly, bringing Brett back to reality. Brett's mind flooded with images of Allie laughing, Allie talking, Allie loving . . . She pulled away from the young woman.

"Wow," Kathy whispered, almost inaudibly. Brett could've kicked herself. She had forgotten that boys and girls do not kiss the same, and that teenage boys especially haven't a clue as to how to properly kiss someone. They stick their tongues out stiffly, roughly. They're awkward and clumsy. They're not really thinking about kissing by itself, they do it merely as a means to the end. They just want to get laid.

They kiss and then fumble like big awkward animals toward a girl's breasts and maybe her crotch.

Okay, fine. She was stereotyping, but she'd heard it from enough girls and women, and had experienced it a little with her coarse and abusive brothers and father.

Brett kissed every woman differently, and when magic really happened, as it did with Allie — or with Kathy — she melted into that woman. Became one with her from just the kiss.

She looked into Kathy's eyes and said, "Brian's friends don't scare me, so we have all the time in the world."

Kathy melted into her arms again. Brett's mind raged, but her body complied. After all, it was only a kiss. A magical kiss, but only a kiss.


Allie glanced at her watch for the third time in fifteen minutes. Where the hell had Brett disappeared to? She hadn't seen her for quite some time. Normally, given this situation, she'd start to get worried — and she *was* worried — but, *but* . . .

She hadn't seen Kathy for several hours either.

The last time she had seen either of them was a few hours before, when they had been dancing together. Oh no, hold on. Not just dancing together, but seductively dancing together. Even dirty dancing. Grinding together.

And now, conveniently enough, they were both missing.

It was funny how her mind could work at times like these. On the one hand, she was pissed that Brett obviously left without telling her, and especially pissed since she probably left with Kathy without telling her. But she didn't want to get too pissed in case something had actually happened to Brett.

Yeah, right. Like maybe she was getting lucky.

"Hey, Susan," Allie asked, grabbing another girl from the cheerleading squad when she walked by. "Have you seen Kathy?"

Susan looked around, "You know, I think I saw her leaving with your brother a couple of hours ago. Your brother does drive a Jimmy, right?"

"Yes, that's our car all right." Allie looked down at her watch. Twelve-thirty. She knew closing time at this place was one. "I think I'm going to get going now," she said. She had borrowed Madeline's Tercel for tonight.

"Hey, you can still give me a ride home, right?" Susan asked. "I mean, I came with you and Kathy . . ." She shrugged.

"Sure, c'mon," Allie said, hoping the company would keep her mind off what Kathy and Brett might possibly be doing together.

Allie wasn't normally a very big drinker — just an occasional glass of wine — but tonight she couldn't wait to get home and have a beer. They climbed into the car, and Allie glanced over at Susan. She really was a pretty girl. The only problem was that Allie liked handsome women. She sighed, turned on the engine, and headed toward Alma.

"Don't ask me what happened, because I don't know," Allie said, walking in on Madeline and Leisa talking quietly on the couch. She went into the kitchen, found Brett's bottle of scotch, and poured herself a glass. She took a gulp, almost spit it out, but downed it and poured another with ice.

"Allison, dearest," Madeline said, coming up behind her and taking the glass, "come in here and tell us about it."

Allie, lost in her thoughts, sat on the love seat across from Maddy and Leisa. "I know Brett's gone through a lot of shit. I know I don't even know the half of what she went through growing up in that neighborhood, with her family . . ." She fell off, thinking about all that she thought she knew, what she had always imagined about Brett's past.

Madeline and Leisa sat side by side, watching her, listening.

"I'm sorry" Allie said, "I've interrupted something. I'll just go . . ."

"Tell us," Leisa said. She was becoming more like Maddy every day.

"I know Brett's been through a lot," Allie said, grabbing the scotch from Maddy and taking a sip while she paced, "but it's not like nothing ever happened to me." She sat down with her drink. "I try to relate with her. I remember things, how things happen. And that's the problem, that I remember. I was Kathy's age when I first met Brett. I wanted her from the moment I saw her, but I didn't know what to do about it at the time."

"So she brought you out?" Leisa asked.

"No, I was already out." Allie looked down into her drink.

"Maddy, I think . . ." Leisa said.

"Yes. I know." Madeline got up and left the room.

"Can I have one of those?" Leisa said, looking greedily at Allie's scotch. Allie handed over her own drink and went to the kitchen to pour her own.

~ ~ ~ ~ ~

97

"What is it you want to discuss Leisa?" Allie asked, returning with her drink and the bottle so that she could refill Leisa's drink as well.

"How do you know I want to discuss anything?"

"Maddy's rubbing off on me."

"This isn't the time. You and Brett are involved in something I cooked up for you, and she left you at the bar —"

"It'll get my mind off of it. Off of everything."

"Allie, I just . . .I don't know . . . I . . ." She downed the rest of the scotch.

"The only thing I ask is that you spend the night if you drink any more," Allie said, refilling Leisa's drink.

Leisa suddenly felt more loved than she had in years. "Deal."

"Where exactly do you think I'd send you to sleep?" Allie asked with a raised eyebrow.

Leisa flushed a brilliant shade of red.

"You like Maddy, don't you, Leisa?"

"Yes, I do. I've never felt . . . I mean, nobody's ever . . . I've never . . ." Leisa couldn't find the words.

Allie scooched over on the couch to wrap an arm around her. "It's okay, baby, just tell me."

"When I'm around her, I feel like I've never felt before in my life."

"Tell me, are you in love with Maddy?"

Leisa was silent, thinking. "Yes, I am," she finally said.

Allie grinned at this. "I knew it," she said softly.

"What?" Leisa asked. Her pulse was pounding in her throat.

"It's just, well, Brett and I knew there was something going on."

"How . . . ?"

"It's a feeling," Allie said. "Something you just know. Especially when you've been out and around like I have."

"So you're telling me I'm . . . I'm . . . I'm a lesbian."

"Listen," Allie said, leaning forward and taking Leisa's hands in her own, "no matter what, nobody except you can know about you for sure. We had a feeling, but that's still just a feeling. You're the only one who can ever know what you truly think and feel. But no matter what, Brett and I will be here for you."

"Thank you," Leisa said, leaning her head against Allie's welcoming shoulder.

"No problem," Allie said, wrapping an arm around her friend. "The question is, what are you going to do about it?"

"Allie . . ." Leisa buried her head in Allie's shoulder. It felt strange to do so with this woman she thought of as a student. "I don't know what to do."

"I had to seduce Brett. I had to kiss her first. I had to do it all. I know how you feel. Madeline won't come on to you, you know."

"You . . ." God, Leisa was really starting to feel the effects of the alcohol. "You. You and Brett . . . something about seeing you two together . . ." She was breathless. "Something about seeing you together, as a couple, has made me question exactly what it is I feel for Maddy." She looked up into Allie's deep blue eyes.

"Only you can know that for sure," Allie said. "But you've already said you love her, and it seems that you're in love with her as well."

"I'm not sure how she feels."

Allie grinned. "Ah, the eternal questioning of love. Makes you feel like one of your students again, huh?" She took a sip of her scotch. "You think of me as a student, and you don't know what else. You're confused."

That was it, Leisa thought. She wasn't used to not knowing, or even questioning, her own feelings, or what somebody else felt about her. She suddenly felt like she should be trying to pass notes in study hall about Maddy.

"The amazing thing about love," Allie continued, "is the risks you take. You have to take a risk to let your feelings be known, and that's the greatest gamble of all. You're risking embarrassment, idiocy, making a fool of yourself. But the payoff can be the greatest of your life."

When Brett finally got home several hours later, Allie was waiting up for her.

"What the hell happened tonight?" she yelled as soon as Brett closed the door behind her.

"I almost got the shit kicked out of me," Brett replied, looking at Allie's rage in amazement. She knew Allie had every reason in the world to be upset, but she couldn't let Allie know that.

"All I know," Allie fumed as she paced the kitchen, "is that I waited for you all night until finally Susan told me you left with Kathy hours ago." She went to the fridge and grabbed another beer.

Brett got Allie to sit down so she could explain the events of the night, editing out her interlude with Kathy. She explained that now that Brian's friends had taken a personal interest in her, anything else that happened could be shown as a feud — like, if Brett were to be caught spying on them. She also explained about the significance of what Kathy had said about Brian really starting to change last fall, and that was about the time that Leisa started feeling that something was wrong in Alma.

"I'm sorry," Allie said, wrapping her arms around Brett. "But what took you so long?" she added, looking at her watch.

"I took her out to the river spot we found this past summer —"Allie cut her off with a sharp look. "Babe, I'm sorry," Brett said. "I know that's our place, but this poor girl was almost branded, and then she thought she had killed someone . . ."

"Okay, I guess," Allie said, again snuggling up to Brett. "But are you sure you just comforted her?"

Brett could feel the tension in Allie's body. "I'm sure," she replied, justifying to herself that nothing much beyond that happened, and what did could also be considered comforting. Comforting to Kathy, but not at all comforting to Brett who was still raging at how her body responded to the kisses of an high-school student. Of course, Allie had been only seventeen when she and Brett had first met, but that was when Brett was younger herself.

After Brett filled Allie in on what happened with Scott's gang and with meeting Randi and what she had said to Beth and why, they went to bed.

Brett didn't immediately fall asleep, though. Instead she lay holding Allie's sleeping form and thinking about the night's events. On her drive home, she had told herself she should be like a time traveler, merely observing events without making any changes in their course. The person she most worried about affecting was Kathy. There was no way around the fact that Brett would have to eventually dump her, but she worried about whether or not Kathy would need to know that Brett was really female. Something like that could change Kathy's life forever.

# 9

A car was honking outside. Brett looked at her watch. Six A.M. She hadn't gotten to sleep until four. She rolled over and snuggled up to Allie.

Madeline knocked on the door. "Brett?" she whispered. Brett got up and opened the door. "I think it's some of your friends," Madeline said quietly.

Brett quickly taped herself down and pulled on her clothes from last night, topping her look off with a baseball cap. She ran barefoot out to the waiting car.

"Where the fuck were you last night?" Scott said from behind the steering wheel.

"You assholes, my aunt's ready to kill me," Brett replied, glancing back at the house.

"I hope you stuck it to her real good," Steve leered across the seat. He was the only other person in the vehicle.

"My aunt?" Brett replied in disbelief.

"No, asshole, Kathy," Scott replied, lightly cuffing Brett across the head. "We pulled in just when you were leavin' with her."

"Where were you motherfuckers anyway?" Brett growled.

"None of your goddamned business," Scott said. "Get in."

"Where we goin'?" Brett said.

"Nowhere — we just need to talk."

Brett glanced around, then climbed into the beat-up Ford pickup.

"Okay, asshole." Scott drove out of the quiet subdivision. "We think maybe you might be all right."

"Might be?" Brett growled.

"You keep givin' me shit, though," Scott said, "and I'll hafta kick your ass."

"In your dreams, asswipe."

Scott glared back at him, then continued. "But you'll hafta do somethin' to prove we can trust you."

"Like?"

"Like goin' into the school tonight and scorin' a half dozen VCRs," Steve said.

"What for?"

"You're pretty stupid for somebody who's supposed to got experience," Scott replied.

"I mean, what's in it for me?" Brett asked.

"You name it, we got it," Scott gloated.

"Fine," Brett replied. "Weed."

"You want fuckin' marijuana?" Steve said, amazed.

"Yeah, I want fuckin' weed. Number one, it's the only drug I use except alcohol, nicotine, and caffeine. Number two, I know even people in this little shit place'll use it."

"People in this li'l shit place will use whatever you can supply," Scott clarified.

"So you do have an established market," Brett said, trying to sound like an adolescent version of a businessman.

"Hell yes, we do," Scott said with a grin. "But we figger, if what we've heard is true, you may make a good addition to our team."

"You name it, I've done it," Brett replied with assurance.

"You ever kill somebody?" Steve said, with an eager glow in his eye.

Brett stared him straight in the eye. "Yes," she replied truthfully. "I have."


Randi McMartin awoke from her deep sleep with a start. Those eyes, she thought, remembering Brett Jameson's eyes. Where do I know those eyes from?

She lay back down, wondering why she had awoken with that thought. She had been dreaming about the night the Paradise Theater burned. Dreaming about Adrienne Moore, Brett Higgins, and Allison Sullivan. She hated that she had been dreaming about Allie and that it hadn't been an erotic dream.

All of the vivid images and sounds of the night had come rushing back to her in a wild maelstrom of emotions: the gunshots, the lightning, the ring on the finger of the charred body they carried from the building. No longer as much of a body as the cremated remains of her arch enemy, Brett Higgins.

Brett Jameson, somehow, reminded her of Brett Higgins. Maybe it was his cocky attitude or his quick tongue. She was too much of a seasoned professional to let something so simple as his name get to her.

She was a patient woman, and was good at putting together all the parts of a puzzle and figuring it out — or figuring out some way she could take the pieces she already had and get everything else she needed. She liked to think of herself as *methodical* and *intense*, but some of her coworkers might call her *obsessive-compulsive* or *anal-retentive*. She was focused on her vocation, on her duty, with a single-minded devotion that drove her day and night.

That was the other reason that she had come to help out her brother and his family — that she was so driven. The two things that kept her going were her family and her job. She knew that the good guys could finish first, and she intended to do just that. She would someday find her own Miss Right and settle down into a nice life, but she also knew that she had to work to make this a world that she wanted to settle down in.

Then she thought of Brett Jameson's eyes again.

Randi realized that her anger was what had always kept her safe, what had kept her fear at bay and had kept her going. She would obsess over things, obsess over criminals and their crimes, blocking everything else from her mind and heart. But now she was beginning to wonder if her anger at and hatred of crime and criminals, which blocked all else from view, were worth it.

She used to say that her life would change once she fulfilled her pledge to avenge her brother's death, but nothing much had changed.

Several years ago, on the anniversary of Brett Higgins's death, Randi had visited the graves of Brett and her brother Dan. She stood first at Daniel's grave, suddenly realizing that the body that lay in that ground was somebody disguised as Dan, not her brother. Daniel had died long before, on the day he started taking drugs. The man who died was a cheap criminal without much in common with the brother who had given a young Randi piggyback rides. If she hadn't have been related to him, she probably would've been happy to see another criminal off the streets.

She had then walked over to Brett's grave. She'd stared at the headstone and WILL IT MATTER THAT I WAS? chiseled into the stone under the name and dates. Underneath that was IT'S NOT THE YEARS BUT THE LIFE THAT MATTERS. Randi knew Frankie had taken care of Brett's remains, from buying the lot to choosing what to put on the tombstone, but she had a feeling it had been Brett, and not Frankie, who had picked out those phrases, that Brett had always been prepared to die. She wondered what it was like to know you were going to die at such a young age.

She had expected to feel disdain and rightful vengeance when she stood there, but she felt neither. Instead, she had sat on the ground for over an hour, remembering . The last time she had been with anyone in bed was when she was dating Allie — something that came about only because of her obsession with Brett. The day Allie walked out of Randi's life was the day that Brett was buried, the same day Allie said that Brett hadn't killed Randi's brother. Randi still didn't know whether that was the truth, but now she accepted that Allie was never coming back to her. They would never again make love. She knew that as far as Allie was concerned, Randi had set up Brett's death.

The day of Brett's funeral Randi vowed to put the past behind her and begin anew.

So when Randi revisited the cemetery, she realized that it had been two years and she hadn't done a damn thing to fulfill that pledge to herself. She was still alone and, in all reality, wasn't fit for anybody. She hadn't had a date since Allie, but she hadn't really wanted to date anybody anyway. Nobody since Allie had caught her interest.

She went to work every day, got home, had a double whiskey, nuked a frozen dinner, had two or three beers, watched TV, and fell asleep on the couch with the TV still on, only to start it all again the next day. Sometimes she'd do some work while she watched TV, and sometimes she wouldn't. On her days off, she often didn't shower or even dress. And she had stopped working out.

The night she had visited Brett's and her brother's graves, she began cleaning her apartment — scrubbing, throwing away, organizing, scouring. It took her close to a month to go through years of accumulation, especially since her time had been limited since she had started working out again. Her TV went for months without being used, and she realized her oven and stove still worked. She saved a fortune on beer and whiskey.

She had dated a bit since then, spent time with her remaining family and been a damned good cop. All her coworkers knew that she was a good cop, but sometimes late at night she thought that something was missing from her life.

Then one of her other brothers called to say he thought her nephew Jake was getting messed up with drugs. Randi had driven home alone from the gym, walked into her empty apartment, cooked dinner, and flipped on the TV for the first time in months.

There was a rerun of the *Golden Girls* playing, and in it a reference was made to the Twinkie Defense used by San Francisco Supervisor Harvey Milk's assassin, whose name Randi couldn't remember, so she jumped up and went to her overflowing bookshelf and found her copy of *The Mayor of Castro Street*, which she pulled off the shelf. From the heap of books, bills, magazines, and newspaper clippings stacked on the shelves, several things fell while she glanced through the book to find the name of Dan White.

When she picked up the items that had fallen, she found two old pictures of Allison Sullivan that she had taken from the file on Brett Higgins after Brett had died and Allie had left town.

Now in Alma, she stared at the ceiling. What had gotten her started on remembering all this?

Those eyes. No, no, she told herself. That dream. The dream of Allie and the Paradise Theater. Well, enough of that.

She lay back down and tried to return to sleep. The past was past, and it was over.

In another part of Alma, someone else awoke with a start, remembering a death, but as he remembered more and more of what had happened, he grew hard.

He had killed before, merely cleaning up any evidence that might've been left behind, anybody who knew too much. He had killed from necessity. Actually, the first time he had killed by mistake, allowed somebody to take too much, so it was his fault, but he hadn't been the one to shove the needle in the girl's arm. Regardless, he had enjoyed watching her die.

This would be the first time he would plan the situation in which to kill somebody — to have sex with a girl before he killed her. He had never before been intimate with his intended victim before. That would bring a special closeness to them this time.

When Brett returned home, she filled Allie and Madeline in.

"I'd better call Leisa," Madeline said, reaching for the phone.

"No," Brett said, stopping her. "The fewer people who know things, the less chance of being found out." Madeline looked at Allie, who nodded in agreement.

"I think we can pull this off without being caught," Allie said.

"No," Brett interjected. "I'll pull it off. Allie Jameson would never do anything like this."

"Who says she's in on it?" Allie replied.

"You're the one who just said 'we' can pull this off."

"Brett *Higgins* and Allie *Sullivan* can pull this off. Brett

106

*Jameson* will pull this off without his beloved sister's knowledge, but with her help."

"Okay Allie, I think you've been sniffing around the chem lab a bit too much. You've lost your grip on reality."

"Reality is something to rise above," Madeline said with a knowing grin.

"Maddy, Allie here is obviously flipping out — she's forgotten that we're playing figments of our imagination. That we've created our characters."

"Brett, calm down," Allie said. "I mean that you and I will go out later to run some errands for Madeline. Brett will convince Allie that he has to pick up something he left in . . . in shop class on Friday."

"Okay, so I go in to get whatever it was I forgot."

"Yes," Allie said.

"But where do you play in to this all?"

"Brett knows he'll need to make a speedy escape, but he won't want to leave a vehicle where the cops might notice and investigate it, destroying his escape. But if goody-two-shoes Allie is waiting in the car, the cops won't care."

"So we stop by the school while running errands and I go in and nab the VCRs."

"Finally."

"Is it all settled now, children?" Madeline asked.

"I think so," Brett said, pulling Allie into her arms.

"And last night you didn't want me to know about the fight because I would've been upset that you were fighting again. I'm very protective of you, you know. And I hate it when you fight."

"So, my dear, where precisely do I fit into all of this?" Madeline asked.

"You have to send us out on errands later."

"How is Brett to gain entry to the school?" Madeline asked.

"Leave that to me," Brett said with a grin.

"What are you up to, honey?" Allie asked.

"About five-ten," Brett said. "Other than that . . ." She brought Allie against her.

"I do believe I should go bake something. Or read some cards. Or something," Madeline said.

"Go make yourself scarce," Brett said. She had been horny ever since last night. This entire mission was turning her into a regular little horndog, in fact.

Allie's body was soft and melting against her, her mouth soft and yielding. Brett entered her first with her tongue, melting into oneness with her. She led her to the bedroom.

"You are my everything," Brett whispered into her ear, laying her down on the bed beneath her.

"Nobody will ever be your everything," Allie murmured back.

Brett knew she loved Allie, Allie was her partner, her lover, her . . . Brett could lose herself with Allie, feel the stress and worries drain out of her when she was with this magic woman.

Allie was so unlike her, so soft, so yielding, so silky. Like Kathy. Maybe Kathy's likeness to Allie at that age was what attracted Brett. Brett was reacting like some middle-aged man.

Brett fell asleep with Allie's naked body in her arms.

"Children? Children?" Madeline's voice accompanied a gentle knocking.

"Huh?" Brett asked.

"I need you to run a few errands for me," Madeline said without opening the door.

"What's going on?" Allie asked.

"We've got to go to the store," Brett said, glancing at the clock.

"Now?" Allie asked, pulling Brett's naked body back down to her, fitting them against each other.

"Arrgh," Brett replied. "We really need to do this."

"You're right, but . . ." Allie took one of Brett's nipples in her mouth, nibbling it while whipping her tongue over it.

"Oh baby . . ."

"Children, um, behave." Madeline said, still through the door.

"Yes, Auntie," Allie said, pulling her mouth away from Brett's nipple. "Give you something to remember and wait for," she said with a teasing grin.

"Madeline, I hate you!"

~ ~ ~ ~ ~

Allie wore something Allison Jameson would have, a pair of jeans and a nice pink sweatshirt, while Brett wore a black shirt, black-and-gray camouflage pants, and black high tops, an outfit totally appropriate for Brett Jameson. She put her lock-picking tools in her pocket and strapped a knife to her right ankle.

They ran a few "errands" for Madeline before heading to the school. Allie drove. She turned off the lights as she entered the school's parking lot and pulled to the rear of the building.

Scott and Steve had told Brett that the only door they could guarantee would not be chained shut from the inside was the one in the back of the building by the janitor's office. No one would be in the school that late at night, they had said.

Brett jumped out of the vehicle and ran over to the door while Allie turned the Jimmy around for a quick getaway. Brett efficiently picked the lock and entered the school. As soon as she was inside, she slipped a ski mask over her face and pulled on a pair of light leather gloves, wiping off the door with a handkerchief to ensure that she had not left any prints. She raced down the halls toward the media center, where she quickly picked the lock and gained entry. She knew the VCRs were in the back room, which she figured might have additional security.

Her heart beat in her throat as she flicked the light from her small flashlight over the door and its surrounding areas. Next to the door was a keypad into which a security code could be entered. Underneath that was an override keyhole.

She drew a small black turning wrench and a rake from one of her pockets. She brought the flashlight down to the lock for a quick inspection. She needed to know what she was up against. The distinctive cut of the keyway in the doorknob looked to be Schlage, probably a six-pin. Tough but not impossible. The alarm bypass looked to be a simple wafer tumbler, generic brand — not a problem. Every chain has its weakest link.

Tucking the flashlight into a pocket, she set the wrench into the bottom of the keyway and barely touched it with the end of her left index finger. Inserting the rake into the hole, she gave it a little pull to gauge the feel of the tumblers. Six, right. Standard high security product. Brett began raking, gently at first, then a little quicker, a little firmer, as she gained an understanding of the lock.

Now, she closed her eyes. She entered the lock, feeling her mind expand within that narrow space. The first two tumblers surrendered to her smooth, rhythmic strokes, locking delicately into place. "C'mon three," she whispered. Something gave, and the cylinder rotated almost imperceptibly as the fourth tumbler released its hold. She gently probed the keyhole with the tip of her pick. So far, so good.

Brett put the rake between her lips and reached for her diamond pick. Maintaining a delicate tension on the wrench, she entered the hole with her diamond, touching and feeling each tumbler in turn. One and two free-floated in their pinholes; they were picked. So was four and yes, six. The live springs behind each of the others invited her delicate touch. Carefully, she lifted number five, a thousandth of an inch at a time, lest she upset the rest. The softest click betrayed its surrender, and she drew the diamond out to touch number three, the only tumbler still resisting her touch. She felt a tangible wave of anticipation as she ever so gently raised the last tumbler with the tip of her probe. It popped and the cylinder spun open. Relief.

Brett took a quick breath through her nose and placed the diamond in her mouth, once again grasping the rake, and stuck her tools into the alarm bypass in the frame of the door. A few quick riffles and the disc-wafers accepted and surrendered. The plug easily turned 45 degrees as the tension wrench rolled it over to the Off position.

Brett put the tools back into her pockets, opened the door, and pulled the heavy sack from one of the large cargo pockets on the side of her pants.

A light flashed between the library and the back room. "Hey!" the security guard called as he entered the library and flashed his light on Brett. "What are you doing?"

Brett slowly raised her hands and turned around, walking out of the back room toward him. As soon as she was sure the guard didn't have a gun, she dove behind a nearby shelf of books. She crouched as she ran behind the shelves. The guard played his flashlight around the room, searching for her. He had pulled his night stick.

Although Brett had only seen him for an instant, she knew that he was a fairly old fellow, the sort that cheap services use because the guard's only function is to phone the police.

She felt guilty as she came up behind him, clamped her hand

over his mouth, and neatly threw him to the ground by taking his neck in one hand and pushing back — by doing this she could use his center of gravity against him and take him nice and neat. She knelt on his chest.

"Are there any others?" she growled menacingly. Her past had taught her how to play this threatening role quite well. The old guard shook his head frantically.

"Take off your shoes and socks," she ordered, grabbing his night stick. He wordlessly complied. She shoved his socks into his mouth and used his own handcuffs to secure him to one of the columns in the library. She then went to the back room, filled her sack with VCRs and the school's one camcorder, emptied the money box for good measure, and left. She opened the school's back door just enough to verify that Allie was still there, alone, before she removed her mask and gloves and bounded out to the vehicle.


"I'll be a blind motherfucker," Scott whispered to Steve. "He did it in less than fifteen minutes."

"The guard was probably takin' a fuckin' nap," Steve argued, watching the Jimmy leave the parking lot. The two boys stood up and walked back up the hill to where their car was parked a few blocks away.

"I think we may be able to use him," Scott mused to himself, even as he patted himself on the back for watching tonight's show. He had wanted to make sure Brett knew how to follow instructions and didn't pull any fast ones just so he could join the gang.

"I wonder what he told Allie?" Steve said.

# 10

Monday morning, Brett was bleary eyed and slightly unfocused from lack of sleep as she entered the school, which was abuzz with whispers. Students gawked at Brett as she went to her locker and headed to first hour. She wondered what had been said to whom.

"Hey," Steve said, grabbing Brett's arm and pulling her into the nearest boys' room.

"What?" Brett said, facing Scott, who was waiting for her by a urinal.

"Didja get it?" Scott asked with a slight grin.

"Yeah, of course."

"How'd it go?"

"Okay, 'cept you didn't tell me there was a guard."

"Who helped you?"

"Whaddya mean, who helped me?" Brett growled. "I did it by myself."

"Well, the guard says he was overpowered by a gang of big guys."

"Hell, if I'da had a gang, I would've taken every fuckin' thing in the school," Brett said. Scott nodded with that same grin. "I got Allie to drive, though," Brett admitted.

"Why?" Scott asked.

"Couldn't leave the car alone. Didn't want to come back to find the cops," Brett explained. "But she's so fuckin' stupid, man, she thought I was gettin' my homework from shop."

Scott chuckled at this. "I'll be by to pick them up after school."

As Brett walked to first hour, she heard whispers about the robbery, but she also saw people looking at her with awe and respect. She couldn't believe the guys would be so stupid as to ID her for the theft. Outside of first hour, she finally began to understand.

"You're dead meat, man," Brian said, catching Brett off guard and pushing her to the floor. Brett jumped to her feet as Brian bore down on her.

"Mr. Ewing, the principal's office!" she heard Mr. Marin's voice boom from a few feet away. Brian lunged again, but Brett easily sidestepped him. Mr. Marin caught Brian by the collar and dragged him down the hall. It was a ridiculous sight because Brian was so much bigger than Mr. Marin, and could easily have knocked Marin off his feet. But Brian probably didn't want to blow his chance at any scholarships, Brett thought. She brushed herself off and headed into the classroom. Kathy ran up to her, laying her hands on Brett's shoulders.

"Oh my god, Brett, are you all right?" Kathy asked with a worried look on her face.

"Yeah," Brett said with a shrug. "Brian's lucky Marin was there," she said as she cracked her knuckles and headed for her seat.

"Sit over here," Kathy said, indicating Brian's seat. Brett grinned and followed the command.

A wide-eyed, scrawny fellow looked over at Brett. "Is it true you took on Doug, Kyle, and Thompson all at once?"

Brett turned to look at Kathy, her eyebrows knitting a question mark.

"A couple of people were in the car Thompson threw you against," she explained. "They saw it all."

Brett nodded her understanding, briefly wondering how they could've just sat and watched the unequal fight. Mr. Marin returned and began his lecture. Brett propped her head up on her hands and closed her eyes, hoping Mr. Marin wouldn't call on her today.

"You're in my seat."

Brett looked up, then farther up, into Brian Ewing's angry face. She briefly studied his broad shoulders, close-cropped brown hair, tree-stump neck, and angry frown.

"It doesn't have your name on it, Brian," Kathy replied evenly, looking up at him with a dare in her eyes. Brett tried to blink the sleep from her own eyes.

"Yes it does. Here, let me show you," Brian said, reaching down toward the seat. Brett saw it coming and jumped up and over, grabbing Kathy on her way. As Brett landed, cushioning Kathy's fall with her own body, Brian grabbed Brett's desk unit and hurled it toward Kathy's desk. It bounced and landed on top of Kathy and Brett as Brett held up her arm to block its thrust from hitting Kathy.

"You asshole!" Kathy yelled, jumping up and pummeling Brian with her fists. Mr. Marin came charging across the room to pull the two apart.

"You," he said, grabbing Brian. "Over there!" he continued, indicating another seat across the room.

"This ain't over, Jameson," Brian muttered as he walked. Brett let her hand fall from its protective stance on Kathy's back to right the disarray of desks, pick up her books, and sit back down.

Mr. Marin saw Brian to the seat, then went to the front of the room to return to his lecture.

Brett looked over at Kathy and said, "Does this mean you're single?" loudly, for the benefit of the entire room.

Kathy looked at Brett, her ashen face regaining some color. "Yes, it does."

"Not for very long," Brett replied with a grin.

Half the class broke out in applause.

"Jameson, Moran," Mr. Marin said. "Either you will behave yourselves, or you two will be visiting the principal."

~ ~ ~ ~ ~

114

In first-hour physics, Jim Taylor approached Allie.

"What did your brother do back in Detroit?" he asked. Several other geeks were close to his side.

"What do you mean?" Allie asked.

"Don't you know about the fight?"

"What fight?" Allie exclaimed, trying to feign confusion and alarm, although she had heard some murmurs and whispers in the hallway prior to class.

"Brett single-handedly took on three of the football team!" Leon said, obviously quite impressed.

"Brett was in a fight?" Allie replied, trying to convey the impression that not only did she not know but that she was upset. "He promised he wouldn't get into any more fights!" she continued, pounding her books down on her lab station.

"I think it's about time somebody showed those bullies what for," Moiré said, sitting next to Allie.

"They've been shoving me in my locker since the seventh grade," Leon admitted.

"I just hope he finishes the job he started," Moiré ominously stated.

"What do you mean by that?" Allie asked.

"Just that this school has hit the sewers faster'n a hungry rat," Moiré answered. Jim shot her and Leon a look.

"What?" Allie again queried.

Moiré met Jim's glance. "As Bill Clinton would say, 'Don't ask, don't tell.' " With that she turned around and the group dispersed.

Allie had been beginning to think that Brett was getting all the fun, that her "nice" group would not yield any information. But now . . . Maybe everybody at the school knew something. Whatever was going on, there was a strange silence around it.

Her mind churned as the teacher droned. Brett was getting involved, but Allie didn't like how close Brett was getting to Kathy in the process. But Kathy was just a high-schooler, so Allie had nothing to worry about. Right? Right.

At the end of algebra, Mr. Marin told Brett he wanted to talk to her, alone, after class.

"What'd I do now?" Brett asked with a sigh, approaching Mr. Marin's desk as the class emptied out. Mr. Marin got up and closed the door.

"By the activities of this morning, I assume what I've heard is true," he began, leaning on a desk so that he was eye-to-eye with Brett.

"Depends on what you've heard," Brett replied with a shrug.

"Let me be straight with you. I cannot condone violence in any way, shape, or form," Mr. Marin replied. "But I'm glad you kicked their asses," he continued with a grin.

"That's something you don't hear every day," Brett admitted. She was starting to like this fellow.

"The whole football team's become a bunch of asses ever since Carl Rogers took over as coach a year ago," Mr. Marin confided, relaxing a bit now that Brett had lost her attitude.

"You don't like Mr. Rogers much, I take it?" Brett asked. Carl Rogers had only been there a year?

"Let's just say he's got those boys thinking they're gods."

"Well," Brett said with what she hoped was a charming smile, "I ain't never been one to buy in to whatever shit they're selling."

Fred carefully studied her. "I think Ms. McNeil is right — there's more to you than meets the eye."

"Ms. McNeil said something nice about me?"


By third-hour English, Allie Jameson knew about Brett's escapades that morning, and knew that Brett had walked Kathy to their second hour, carrying her books for her.

Allie confronted Brett on the issue of the fight. Brett informed her that she had done her best that morning to avoid a direct confrontation, and that Saturday night she had been ambushed.

"You knew they wanted a fight when you went outside with them, Brett," Allie responded.

"It's not like I really had a choice," Brett said.

"And David knew there was a fight involved when he took on Goliath," Leon added, having eavesdropped on the conversation. Allie gave him a stern glance. He was in all her first three classes, and his nerdiness was getting on her nerves.

"Allison," Brett began, putting her arms on Allie's shoulders as she pulled her aside. "I am who I am, and I'm not gonna back down because some assholes tell me to." She made sure she spoke loudly enough for anyone who wanted to listen.

"That doesn't mean I have to like it," Allie said, stomping off to her seat.

After class, while they were walking to government, Allie asked Kathy if Brett was taking her to prom that weekend.

"I don't know," Kathy began. "He hasn't asked me."

"He probably hasn't thought of it yet," Allie replied. "But, of course, I'm assuming you're not going with Brian now."

"No, I'm not."

"Allie, I need to ask you something," Brian said as soon as they entered the classroom.

"Go ahead, Brian," Allie said, not sure what she should try to convey as she looked at him.

"I was wondering if you'd like to go to prom with me?" he asked Allie while looking at Kathy.

"I'm not sure . . ." Allie began.

"You don't have a date yet, do you?" he interjected.

"It's less than a week away, Brian," Kathy flatly stated.

"But she's new in town, *Kathy*," Brian retorted.

"Well, do you?" Kathy asked Allie.

"No, I don't."

"Then you should go with Brian. All the good guys already have dates."

"Well . . ."

"I'll pick you up at six," Brian replied, walking over to his seat.

"Are you sure you don't mind?" Allie asked Kathy.

Kathy laughed and shrugged. "I don't mind you going out with him," Kathy replied. "Just watch yourself."


Carl Rogers already had the class hard at work when Brett entered, so she didn't have a chance to talk with anyone until they were cleaning up near the end of the hour.

"Hey, stud," Jerry said, punching his shoulder. "Hear you kicked ass Saturday night."

117

"Yeah, man," Brett replied. "Where were you?"

"Giving us a hand," Scott said, walking up to the two. "We still on for tonight?" he asked Brett.

"Yeah, we're still on."

"You ask Kath to the prom yet?" Steve asked, approaching with Beth.

"Shit — that's this weekend, isn't it?" Brett replied.

"Yeah, it is," Scott said with a grin. "And I hear your sis already got a hot date, man."

"Whaddya mean?" Brett asked with a frown.

"She's goin' with Brian Ewing," Beth replied, her look telling Brett that she expected some sort of an outburst at this point. Brett quickly glanced over her comrades.

"The fucker's gonna pay for that," Brett growled as a cold chill ran through her.

"He had to do somethin' to you for stealin' his woman," Scott replied, smirking. "And you do seem rather *protective* of your sister."

"So you gonna ask Kathy or what?" Beth earnestly asked.

"Yeah, I guess I might do that," Brett allowed, watching a shadow cross Beth's face. Brett couldn't decide on whether Beth was disappointed to lose Brett to Kathy, or Kathy to Brett.


He knew he would eventually have to tidy up all the loose ends, and he would quite enjoy doing that, even though the girl wasn't as young as he usually liked them. He had quite a bit of money saved from his previous activities that he could live on fairly well for the rest of his life — and these last things would ensure that. They would make him a bundle.

He knew how others often thought they could go on forever and would get greedy, wanting more and more money. He wouldn't let that be his downfall as well. He knew when to call it quits. He was smart. And these last adventures would not only ensure him money, but also some very happy thoughts.

When he had first realized he would have to kill again, he was a little uneasy with the idea, although it did get him hot. But now he was definitely beginning to relish it. He was beginning to enjoy the thought of having somebody's life in his hands, of having that sort of power. A power almost sexual in its essence.

This would definitely be something he would enjoy.


After school, Brett hit the bathroom to have a smoke and quickly change into sweats for the wrestling tryout. Although she hadn't shaved in a week and a half, she knew her legs and arms didn't look convincingly male enough, so she covered as much of her body as possible.

She had studied several books on wrestling over the weekend and was grateful that because of her weight she could only oppose a few scrawny underclassmen.

"No wonder you lettered," Ms. McNeil said as Brett jumped off the scale. "There's nothin' to ya."

"Good," Brett said, making a move to leave. "I got places to go and women to do —"

"Hold it right there, Jameson. Do you want everybody to know you aren't man enough to stand up to those few in your weight class?"

Brett turned to look her in the eye. "I never chicken out of anything."

McNeil glanced at what Brett was wearing. "You can't wrestle in that get-up."

Brett pulled off her sweatshirt. Underneath she was wearing a white T-shirt. Ms. McNeil carefully studied her.

"What the . . ." McNeil began, staring at Brett.

Brett looked down. The Ace bandages could be seen through the thin material. "Cracked ribs."

"When'd that happen?"

"Just before I left Detroit — almost fixed now, though."

"You can't wrestle like that."

Brett walked onto the mat. "Bullshit. I can take on any of these asswipes."

"Watch that language, young man!"

"First you call me a chicken, now you tell me I can't fight?"

"Come back when you get them off."


119

"Fine," Brett said, pulling on her sweatshirt and stalking out. "Suits me just fine."

Outside, Brett went over to watch the cheerleaders and soccer team again. When the girls stopped to take a break, Kathy walked over to her.

"Hey, how'd the tryout go?" she asked Brett.

"McNeil kicked me out," Brett said as Allie approached.

"Why?" Kathy asked, concerned.

"I told you she wouldn't let you wrestle," Allie said, overhearing the conversation. She looked at Kathy. "Remnants of the last fight," she explained.

"I didn't know he was behind me," Brett justified.

"Oh," Allie said. "And that makes four cracked ribs okay?"

"What?" Kathy said, looking from one to the other, concerned.

"Some asshole jumped me from behind and knocked me across the chest with a blackjack a few times. McNeil saw the bandages and told me I couldn't fight."

"Are you okay?" Kathy asked, kneeling in front of Brett. Brett caught a glimmer of jealousy flash across Allie's face.

"Yeah, babe," Brett said, nonchalantly reaching over to chuck Kathy under the chin. "Takes a lot more than that to really hurt me."

"Why didn't you tell me about it?" Kathy queried, reaching over to run her hands where she assumed the bandages were — right around Brett's breasts. Allie's glimmer of jealousy grew.

"No big deal," Brett replied cavalierly. "Didn't want to worry you." She moved Kathy's hands from her breasts.

"Yeah," Allie said. "And he doesn't like admitting he's lost any fights."

Brett looked up at Allie, then noticed that Allie was now staring beyond her to the soccer field, where Brian stood, staring at them. As Brett watched, Brian approached, wearing shorts, a T-shirt, and gym shoes.

"Hey! Allie!" he yelled, jogging up. "You doin' anything tonight?"

"No, not that I can think of," Allie replied, shaking her head and shrugging. "Why?"

"Wanna go out to a movie?"

"Sure, why not?"

"Great. I'll pick ya up at seven," he said, then jogged back to the field when the coach began calling after him.

"Hope you don't mind," Allie said to Kathy.

"No, not at all," Kathy replied as a whistle called them back from break. "Oops. Gotta go," she said, turning to leave. When Kathy and Allie were a few steps away, Brett called to Kathy.

"Kat!" she cried. When Kathy turned, with Allie watching from a distance, Brett stood up and looked at her. "You got a date for prom?"

Kathy shook her head.

Brett looked at the ground, studying her shoes. "Wanna go with me?"

There was a pause. Brett looked up shyly into Kathy's warm, deep brown eyes.

"Yes," Kathy replied with a smile as she stepped forward to take Brett's hands in her own.

"How 'bout I go fer broke and ask about dinner tonight?" Brett asked. Kathy nodded her head. "Great, I'll call you after your practice." The whistle sounded again, and Brett looked over at the cheerleaders to make sure Allie had turned before she leaned forward and kissed Kathy lightly on the lips. "You gotta go."


Randi McMartin had spent the day going over files at the police station. She had heard about the Sunday-night burglary and had decided to see what the computer could cough up.

She started by running histories on most of Jake's friends, as well as on Jake himself. She figured the computer might announce things he had never bothered telling his parents. So far, the entire gang had come up surprisingly clean. At least as far as the newspaper and police were concerned.

She sat back at the desk, knowing that much police work is tedious and the rest is intuitive. She had learned to trust her intuition, and right now it was screaming that something wasn't right with Brett Jameson. She had several of the younger officers looking for records pertaining to him, looking for proof that he was who he said he was.

Her brother had told her that Jake was running with the wrong crowd and that he thought that maybe drugs were involved. But her brother didn't know how to help Jake out.

Randi smiled at the thought of Jake as a baby. He had been so cute and cuddly then, but now . . . . She thought with a grimace of his so-called friends. She had to do anything possible to get him away from these kids.

Jake was her first concern, but she was intrigued by the patterns of the recent robberies in Alma and the neighboring town. Piecing together the clues would be a challenge.


When Brett got home, Scott was sitting in the driveway.

"What took you so long?" Scott asked, jumping out of his pickup.

"Brian asked Allie out tonight, and she's goin' with the jerk," Brett responded, parking the Jimmy and leading Scott into the house.

"Izzat so," Scott said, glancing at Brett with a strange smirk on his face. He followed Brett to the garage without another word, but broke out into a large grin when Brett pulled the electronics out from under the bench where she had stashed them.

"I grabbed a few extra things, as long as I was there and all that horseshit," Brett said, standing over Scott as he knelt to examine the loot.

"And nobody saw you?" Scott said, standing to face her.

"Nobody 'cept the guard, and he's too busy tryin' to make himself look good to give the cops a clue."

Scott looked her in the eye and nodded. "I'm thinkin' that maybe between you and me, we can take this town over," he said.

"Whaddya mean by that?" Brett asked, hoping this was the crucial point she had been waiting for.

"I mean that Steve, Jake, and Jerry are a bunch of chumps," Scott replied. "They'll do whatever I tell them, but they're clueless when it comes to initiative and new ideas. Whereas you," he continued, putting an arm around Brett's shoulders, "may be just the man I been lookin' for — that is, if half what I've heard is true."

"What have you heard?"

"Just that you did a little more than go to school in Detroit."

"That's putting it lightly," Brett responded. "Just tell Jake to ask his aunt about Frankie Lorenzini and Brett Higgins, and you'll find out about the crowd I hung with." As soon as the words were past her lips, she realized her mistake. All she needed was to give Randi another clue as to her identity.

"Who're they?"

"My old employers."

"We can talk later," Scott said, looking at his watch. "I've got a meeting now." With that, he grabbed the bag and headed for the door.

"And that's all you're gonna say now?" Brett asked.

"That's all you need to know, now," Scott said, climbing into his vehicle. "Except that I'm really enjoying watching you and Bri go at it. Keep up the good work."

When Allie arrived home an hour later, Brett was sitting at the dining room table rereading *Beowulf*. She looked up when the door opened.

"I can't believe you're goin' out with that asshole," Brett said.

"You said you wanted to know more about him. What better way?" Allie said flatly.

"Make sure you take your pepper spray," Brett said, approaching Allie and leaning against the kitchen table.

"I should give you the same advice," Allie replied.

"It's not the same thing."

"The hell it isn't, Brett," Allie cried, tossing her books onto the table. "Why the hell are you going out with her tonight?"

"Allie!" Brett said, reaching for her. She pulled away. "I'm just gettin' under Brian's skin. He hates me so much he's liable to do something rash!"

"Y'know," Allie began, turning to face Brett, "at first I thought you were just barking up the wrong tree, but —"

"But what?"

"But too many people seem too happy about what you're doing."

They quickly filled each other in on all the details of their days, and Allie agreed to make another go at getting more information from the school's "good" kids. Allie was eager to discover that Scott was looking at Brett as lieutenant material, but she wished he would hurry up about it.

"What're you wearing tonight?" Allie asked Brett finally.

"Oh crap, I dunno."

Allie walked to the bedroom. "Well, you'd better decide soon," she said, picking out an outfit for herself.

"Hold on," Brett said, "you ain't gonna wear that, are you?" She didn't like the short length of the skirt Allie had selected.

"Brett, I know you don't like it, but I've got to look my part."

"Well, then, at least wear a long-sleeved shirt." Allie had selected a sleeveless top so that overall the outfit would be showing a great deal of flesh.

"Brett, I'm letting you do all this stuff with Kathy, I'd think the least you'd be able to do is trust me as well — especially since *my* hot date is with a boy."

Brett grunted and pulled her dark blue suit from the closet. She also grabbed the deep red-and-blue tie, light blue shirt, and deep red suspenders that she always wore with it.

"Hold on," Allie said, standing in the middle of the room in just her bikini briefs and lacy bra, "you can't wear that."

"Allie, I've been intimating that I worked with organized crime in Detroit, so if I'm trying to impress this chick, I'd dress fairly well. You never see mob bosses on TV wearing jeans."

"Then at least don't wear that suit. It's my favorite, and you look too damned hot in it."

"Yeah? So I want to look handsome."

"Brett, it's my favorite."

Brett acquiesced to this argument. No matter how pissed she was that Allie was going out with Brian, she couldn't distress her like that. She pulled Allie into her arms, slipping her hands down inside her panties to feel the damp, warm skin beneath.

Brett dropped to her knees and rubbed her head against Allie's belly and then down farther.

"Oh god, Brett, we don't have time."

"We always have time," Brett said, slipping the panties down to her ankles. Allie gingerly stepped out of them, and Brett rubbed her cheek against the short, blond hairs, inhaling the scent of her woman.

"Oh, Brett."

Brett pushed Allie against the wall. They were parts of a whole.

"Brett . . ."

Brett reached up and deftly undid Allie's nice, lacy bra, then allowed her hands to freely roam over Allie's naked body — down her soft, muscular arms, across her plush breasts with their hardened nipples, down to her tight tummy, down to where she could push Allie's legs a little wider apart.

She loved that Allie gave herself up so freely.

"Oh god, Brett, I can't stand."

Brett ignored her plea, leaving her standing naked, with her back against the wall. She put her hands between Allie's legs and spread open Allie's lips so that she could freely run her fingers up and down Allie's swollen and now exposed clit.

Allie's scent filled Brett, intoxicating her. All Brett ever needed to become reenergized was to know that Allie was that turned on by look or touch or smell. No matter how tired she was Brett always wanted Allie.

She felt a shudder run through Allie's body as soon as she put her tongue to her. "You're mine and you know it," Brett growled. She buried her tongue in Allie, knowing there was no time to tease her, but making her remember who was naked and who wasn't, who was exposed and who wasn't. She loved letting Allie know who was in control.

Brett took Allie wholly and completely, and Allie had no choice but to give herself to Brett, wholly and completely.

And Brett knew Allie loved it.


Thirty minutes later they helped each other finish get dressed for their dates, Brett wearing her loose fitting, double-breasted, dark purple suit with matching tie, black suspenders, and black shirt. When she thought about it, it seemed particularly apropos because she had always referred to it as her gangsta outfit.

# 11

The man put the new pictures up next to the other ones. These photos were of the new girl, plus a few shots of the two girls standing next to each other at cheerleading practice. He ran his fingers lightly over their outlines, carefully noting their athletic legs and short shorts. His eyes wandered up the curves of their inner thighs, and he imagined what lay beyond. He especially liked the photos where they were holding hands or touching in other ways, as cheerleaders often do.

He had been inconspicuous enough taking those photos, because he had also taken several shots of the soccer team while he was at it. Perfectly natural for someone in his position to do.

Seeing the girls together like that excited him. It made him hard. He lay back on the bed and let his mind run free while he masturbated. He imagined them hot and sweaty after practice having an ice-cold soda together, then one would lean over and kiss the other, licking the sweat from her face. Slowly their hands would begin to wander over each other's body as their clothes slipped to the floor.

He imagined himself joining them, but it wasn't until he visualized their faces when he strangled them, and felt the warm blood running over his hands, that he was able to get off.


Kathy was wearing a miniskirt and light summer top when Brett picked her up that night. Brett allowed herself a few seconds to admire Kathy's nicely tanned legs before she realized Kathy was speaking.

"I didn't know we were going anywhere fancy!" Kathy cried, apparently distressed by Brett's suit.

Brett allowed a leisurely grin to sprawl across her face. "You look fine, babe, I just wanted to make a good impression for your folks." Well, that and she wanted looser clothing so her figure wouldn't be so easy to identify.

"I should've told you. They're out of town."


Brett took Kathy to Clara's in Lansing. There really weren't any good restaurants in Alma. Besides, Brett thought there might be too good of a chance for someone to recognize her there because she had been, albeit briefly, an adult resident of Alma.

"What do your folks do for a living?" Brett asked after they had ordered their dinners and sodas.

"They're in advertising, a freelance creative team. Dad's a graphic designer, and Mom's a writer. Because they do freelance and are pretty good at it, they're out of town quite a bit, traveling to meet with agencies and prospective clients."

"I guess that means you have a lot of parties at your place?"

Kathy laughed. "No, not at all. I learned real quick that if people knew they were out of town, they'd want to come over and rip the place apart, so I don't tell anybody anymore."

"You told me."

"You're different."

"You don't seem to be the normal high-school girl either."

"Well, like I didn't have a normal childhood, so . . ." The waiter brought their sodas and appetizer.

"What do you mean by that?"

"When I was born my parents were in the Peace Corps and then after that in Africare. They stayed for quite a few years after I was born until they finally got out and moved back here. They had both been born in Alma, and now say that there really is no place like home."

"Where all did you live?"

"Mostly they were stationed in Africa, but we lived all over there. A coupla times we had to move in the middle of the night because a coup went down."

"Wow? Really?"

"Yeah." Kathy looked down and began tracing figures in the sweat on her water glass.

"Kathy?" Brett reached over and put her hand under Kathy's chin, tilting her head up so that their eyes met. "What's going on?"

"I just haven't told a lot of kids about it. I mean, it put me a year behind in school. I don't want everybody thinkin' I'm slow or something."

"So you're eighteen?" Brett asked. Oh god, if she was, that would mean she was legal. Brett had been telling herself that she couldn't do anything with a woman who was underage. Although knowing her age was a relief, it also took away one of Brett's main reasons for leaving Kathy alone.

Kathy nodded, still looking down.

"I'd never think you were slow." Brett smiled as she reached over to take Kathy's hand into her own.

"I'm . . . I haven't gone out with anybody but Brian for some time now. And whenever we went out, he just wanted to talk about himself."

"So you're not used to talking about yourself that much, eh?"

"Are you and Allie really close?" Kathy asked with a quick shrug.

"Nice change of subject." Brett looked deeply into her eyes.

Kathy focused on the artichoke. "You two look nothing alike, but there is something . . ."

"Like what? Al and I are as different as Arthur and Morgana."

"Well, it's more of a feeling. You two feel the same," Kathy replied as Brett stared at her. "You know what I mean," Kathy concluded. Brett shrugged and looked down at her food when the waiter brought their meals. Brett had ordered a steak, Kathy the chicken Kiev. "I think it's cute the way she worries about you."

"It can be a pain in the ass."

"Brian asked her out just to get even with you. You two really seem quite close for brother and sister."

"Whaddya mean by that?"

"Nothing. I think it's cute the way you watch out for each other."

"I don't like Brian. I don't like the way he treated you, so I know sure as hell I ain't gonna like the way he'll treat Allie."

A cloud passed over Kathy's face. "Please, can we not talk about him. I . . . I still can't believe the way he attacked us in class today."

"I know his friends were hopped up on something the other night, but I don't know what it was."

"Brett, please . . ."

Brett waited a moment, then said, "Did you want to go to a movie or somethin' after dinner?"

Kathy looked up and into Brett's eyes. "Um, well," she began nervously. "I was thinkin', since my parents are out of town and all, maybe we could just rent a movie and go back to my place."

Uh-oh. Back to her place. What a concept. The two of them alone and in private. Brett wanted it and was scared because of it. "You ready for some dessert?"

"Um, I really shouldn't."

"You have a hot body, Kathy. Don't go gettin' all worried about it on me. Don't want you becomin' an anorexic or anything like that."

It had been quite a while since Kathy had been out on a date with anybody other than Brian. She had almost forgotten what it was like. She wasn't used to being so abashed — she couldn't believe she was acting like this, always looking down and being unable to meet Brett's eyes.

But there was something so different about Brett. One minute he acted like somebody soon to drop out, and the next he was the most intelligent guy Kathy had ever met. The smartest and most feeling guy she had ever met. He wasn't afraid to discuss anything, so the two spent a half-hour over dessert and then the entire drive home talking about movies and books and the fact that Brett could cook a better chicken Kiev than Clara's, which Kathy was surprised to hear. She wasn't used to guys admitting to being able to cook anything — or to sampling their date's dinner either.

She had only ever had sex with Brian, but she had done it because it seemed the thing to do after they had been dating awhile. It didn't do anything for her, but he seemed to enjoy it, so she figured she could put up with it to make him happy. But that made it all the more surprising when she found herself studying Brett's hands and wondering what they would feel like on her bare skin. On her inner thighs and nipples.

He was funny, sweet, charming, and smart. Kathy thought maybe it was because he was slightly older that he had such an effect on her, but sometimes when she looked into his eyes — which intrigued her all the more as she came to realize how they could change colors from green to brown, visiting all the shades in between — she would've sworn he was far older than the nineteen years he claimed. But still his face was young, and his body had not yet gained the bulk that so many men acquired, sometimes even in their late teen years. Brian was like that.

Kathy knew Brett would have a hairless chest, and she thought that was so sexy. Brian was proud of the hair on his body, but Kathy didn't care too much for it. She loved the idea of a nice, clean chest. And she really wanted to kiss Brett again. His lips were so soft and tender, they cut right into Kathy, slicing through her. The touch of his tongue was like being struck by lightning. The way he entered her was invasive, penetrating, but nice. She wanted that feeling again.

The other night when he had held Kathy and kissed her, Kathy was glad for the strong arms around her because she knew if she had tried to stand, she would not be able to. Brett Jameson was strong and brave and bold, but unafraid to show his softer, smarter side with her. She thought it was cute the way that he so looked after his younger sister, and she really liked Allie as well. Not many boys would show their caring side like that.

She felt guilty that she hadn't really warned Allie about Brian — she had only cautioned her to watch out — but Allie seemed so happy to be asked out. After all, she was the new girl in school, and he was supposedly the best catch around.

It didn't make sense to Kathy that she was throwing herself at Brett. She had never wanted or thought about anybody like this before, but she knew that if Brett asked, she'd sleep with him tonight. She probably would've slept with him the other night.

She flushed at this thought, at the thought of them together, at the thought of Brett inside her, and just then Brett looked over from the driver's seat. "What're you thinking about?" he asked with a grin.

"Nothing," Kathy said, quickly looking down and hoping Brett hadn't figured out what she was thinking.

"'Nothing?' No one who looks like that is thinking about nothing."

Kathy took a deep breath, reached over, took Brett's hand in her own, and laid them on her own bare thigh. Brett looked over at her and took a deep breath of his own, then squeezed her hand lightly. Kathy knew Brett had to be feeling the same thing she was, she just knew it. But what if he wasn't? What if all the attraction was on her side? What then? What if he just wanted to get laid?

"The first time I drove into this town, I saw all the signs that said PICK YOUR OWN . . . this and that. I was expecting to see a sign that said, PICK YOUR OWN SNOWBALLS."

Kathy laughed, "So you've been to Alma before?"

"Yeah — visiting my aunt. I was just thankful the entire town didn't smell like it does right when you get off the highway."

"The refinery. Yes, it does stink up the town quite a bit. There's a video place just around the corner here."

Brett had originally written Kathy off as a fluff-brain. And then she'd look up and catch Kathy secretly looking at her, and she'd smile back. The girl was interesting and funny and had a naive openness that appealed to Brett.

After they rented the movies, they returned to the Moran residence, where Brett set up the VCR and turned to see Kathy sitting primly on the couch. Brett was transported back to her first nervous date with Allie all those years before. Allie had been a year younger than Kathy was now.

Brett glanced around the room, which was furnished with rich textures, subtle colors, and wood. Obviously, the Morans had money but didn't see a need to flaunt it, preferring a comfortable residence to a showplace.

"Nice place."

Kathy shrugged. "It's okay."

Brett stared at Kathy, who met her eyes. Brett felt as nervous as a teenager on a first date. She wasn't sure what she was supposed to do, or where this was supposed to go. And Kathy seemed just as nervous as she was.

It was a relief to know that Kathy was eighteen, but still, there was Allie. And Brett was madly in love with Allie, but yet she was attracted to Kathy. She wanted to sleep with Kathy, make tender love with Kathy.

Years before, Brett would've done whatever she wanted to, whatever felt right at the moment, but now it wasn't right. She shouldn't lead Kathy on; she shouldn't do this to Allie, even if it was only a kiss. That was as far as this really could go, because Kathy thought Brett was a guy . . .

"Oh fuck it," Brett murmured, advancing on Kathy.

"What?" Kathy asked as Brett leaned down to bring their lips together.

Brett could almost feel the tension drain out of Kathy as their lips met. Kathy's lips opened warmly, inviting Brett's tongue to enter her. Brett did so, entering her and caressing Kathy's hair with her hands, the soft skin of Kathy's face under her fingertips, as Kathy drew her down to her. She heard a low moan escape Kathy's lips as she pulled gently away.

She sat next to Kathy, facing her with one arm encircling her shoulders, the other wrapped around her waist.

Kathy grabbed Brett's hand and kissed it. "Why do I feel as if I've known you for a very long time?" she asked Brett without looking at her.

"Some people say that we go through the world looking for a

person who will fill in our missing parts — and that when we find that person, we find the rest of ourselves. Other people feel that we are reincarnated alongside those we've spent eternity with."

Kathy looked at Brett for a long time, then gently kissed her before bringing her head to rest on Brett's shoulder. She sighed heavily as Brett's arms wrapped around her.

"You're only the fourth guy I've ever kissed," she admitted.

They watched the movie, a romantic comedy, with Kathy leaning against Brett. By the end of the movie, they were lying on the couch, with Brett spooning Kathy from behind — one of Brett's arms around her waist and the other beneath her head. At the end of the movie, as the cassette rewound, Brett rolled Kathy to her back. Kathy looked up at Brett and began to tremble slightly.

"What's the matter, babe?" Brett asked as she lightly played her fingers through Kathy's hair and down to her waist, carefully avoiding any of Kathy's more interesting locations.

Kathy looked down toward the end of the couch. "I guess I'm a little scared."

Brett chuckled lightly. "Honey, as far as I'm concerned, we have all the time in the world. We won't do anything you don't want to."

Kathy looked up at her. "Why do I believe you?"

Brett shrugged. "Because I'm telling the truth?"

They continued to kiss until the movie had rewound.

Brett looked up. "I guess I should change the movie," she said, not getting up. "Have you ever been with a guy?" Brett suddenly asked, not quite sure why she had asked.

Kathy slowly nodded.

"Just Brian?"

Kathy looked away and slowly nodded. "Yeah," she said.

Brett gently pulled her back to face her. "Did he ever make you do anything you didn't want to?" she asked gently. Kathy looked away, and Brett felt a rush of anger pulse through her veins. "I'm not Brian," she said finally.

"I know," Kathy said, turning back to face her. "You're not like anybody I've ever met before."

"What did he make you do?"

"I, I'm not really sure," Kathy began, stuttering. "I, I . . ."

"You what?"

"There's been a few parties where, where I only drank soda and

133

I don't remember half the night and, well, I . . ." A tear slid down her cheek. Brett tenderly kissed it off with her lips.

"Did you feel drunk at all?"

"For a while."

"So you woke up and couldn't remember what happened?"

"Yes, that's it," Kathy said, burrowing her head in Brett's shoulder.

"Did you experience any hallucinations?"

"No, no I didn't," Kathy said, confused. She turned away. "I also . . ." she put her head down in her hands.

"What is it, baby?"

"I can't tell you."

"Honey, you have to." Brett turned Kathy so that she could look into her eyes. "You have to if you want me to help at all."

"I was really sore, and there was dried blood . . . down there."

Brett pulled Kathy into her arms, gently stroking her hair and back. "It's okay, baby, it's over now. I'll never let that happen to you again." She silently vowed to get even with Brian for Kathy.

"It's okay, baby," Brett said, kissing Kathy's forehead. She couldn't voice her suspicions to Kathy.

"All I know right now is that I want to be with you," Kathy suddenly blurted out. She looked shocked at her own words. Nonetheless, she moved Brett's free arm beneath her shirt to her bare stomach.

Brett felt a jolt of electricity at the smooth, soft skin of Kathy's stomach. She felt herself flush as she explored the softness of Kathy's ribs, up to just below her bra. Brett traced her way back down to the waist of Kathy's skirt, allowing her fingers to feel the upper part of Kathy's stomach. She knew Kathy would let her do whatever she wanted, but she knew she had to stop. She thought of Allie and took a deep breath.

Kathy was studying her face, then pulled Brett down for a kiss, a tender, loving kiss. Brett brought her lips over Kathy's ears and down her throat, tracing her collar bone lightly with the tip of her tongue. Kathy moaned.

"I should go," Brett said, looking down at Kathy.

"No, you shouldn't," Kathy contradicted, moving Brett's hand up to rest on her clothed breast. She was trembling slightly, and her eyes were closed.

Brett moved her hand. "Then maybe we should watch the other movie . . ." It was incredibly thrilling to Brett for Kathy to place her hand in such an intimate location.

"No."

"But . . ."

Kathy looked up at her. "Are you attracted to me?" she asked with a gulp of air.

"Oh god yes," Brett breathed heavily and quickly, unable to believe she was saying such a thing out loud. She wanted to be with Kathy.

"Brett, I'm scared, but I need you to touch me."

"If you're scared, then maybe we shouldn't —"

Kathy placed a finger against Brett's lips. "I've never felt like this before," she whispered. "I liked Brian when we first met, but . . ." Brett looked at her with concern. "I think I'm in love with you," she finally blurted. Their eyes met and locked. Brett looked away. "Will you make love to me?" Kathy barely whispered.

Brett's eyes were glued to Kathy's as she unbuttoned Kathy's blouse and undid her front-clasp bra, exposing Kathy's breasts to the flickering light from the television screen. Kathy closed her eyes, and Brett looked down at the beautiful, creamy mounds of flesh topped with hardened cherries that poked up at the ceiling.

"Oh god," Brett moaned as she placed her hand on a breast. Kathy moaned her reply. Brett rolled on top of her, and was all too aware of the softness beneath her, of the gently curving flesh, of the legs she lay between. She kissed Kathy deeply, even as she told herself she needed to find an excuse and leave. She moved down to tease her tongue over Kathy's nipples. Kathy groaned and arched herself up, offering herself to Brett.

There could be no question any longer — Kathy wanted Brett, and Brett wanted Kathy.

That was when the gunshot, accompanied by the squeal of tires and breaking glass, rang out in the night air.

"What the fuck?" Brett yelled, jumping to a crouch on the floor, automatically reaching to her shoulder, where for years she had carried a gun. Tonight, however, she had come unarmed. "Wait here!" she ordered Kathy, who was sitting on the couch, covering herself up.

Brett hurried toward the front door, running in a near-crouch position so as to stay below any windows. At the front door, she loosened her tie before gingerly easing the door open and crawling out into the night. Once outside, she listened for any strange noises, and, hearing none, she stood.

On the Jimmy's dark blue panels someone had spray-painted, in fluorescent orange, the word *deadman*. The single gunshot had taken out two of the Jimmy's windows. A high-school impression of a "subtle" threat.

"Is everything okay?" Kathy asked when Brett reentered the house.

Brett looked at her and shook her head. "I don't think somebody likes me much," she said. Kathy walked forward, then turned to look out the window.

"Oh, Brett," she said, seeing the Jimmy. "I'm so sorry."

"Shh . . ." Brett said as she reached forward and took Kathy in her arms. "It's not your fault."

Kathy stood back and leaned against the wall, looking at Brett. Brett grinned and ran a finger down the buttons of Kathy's blouse.

"You're done up wrong," Brett said.

Kathy looked down and almost began rebuttoning her blouse in front of Brett when she thought twice about it.

She looked up at Brett. "What is it you do to me?" she asked, her arms hanging limply at her sides. Brett shrugged, and she continued. "I'm not usually like this, or —" indicating the couch for clarification — "that."

"I'm sorry. I didn't mean to take advantage of you —"

"I wanted it," Kathy replied, cutting Brett off. "And I still do and I'm not like that and I don't know what it is about you or what you're doing to me," she spit out in confusion. "I wish you could tell Ms. Jameson that you were spending the night at Scott's or Steve's . . . and really spend the night here, with me."

Kathy was offering herself to Brett, totally and completely. Brett took Kathy into her arms, murmuring that she had to do something about the Jimmy and silently wondering what Kathy saw in this bad boy from the wrong side of the tracks. Except, maybe, the woman underneath.

~ ~ ~ ~ ~

Brian arrived ten minutes late to pick up Allie for their date. Allie was not impressed in the least. Why did Brett get to go out with somebody like Kathy and Allie get stuck with Brian? It wasn't as if Allie could make Brett jealous with Brian, or even with any of the other cheerleaders. Allie was simply not in a position to make Brett jealous at all.

Allie could almost hear Brett laughing, "What would two femmes do in bed together, anyway? Paint each other's toenails?"

The doorbell rang. "Madeline? Could you get that?" Allie called from the bedroom where she double-checked herself in the mirror and spritzed on some perfume before heading to the front room.

Brian was sitting on the couch across from Madeline, chatting. Allie and he exchanged quick once-overs while Madeline looked on with a bemused smile.

Allie supposed he would be considered good looking. He was tall and broad-shouldered and had nicely trimmed jet black hair and a good tan. He obviously took good care of himself, but he also probably knew how good he looked dressed in a pair of neatly pressed khakis, a white polo shirt, and nicely polished brown oxfords.

When Brian and Allie headed to the door, Madeline took Allie's arm and pulled her aside briefly.

"Does Brett have any idea what you are wearing?" she asked.

"Don't wait up, Auntie," Allie said with a quick peck on the shorter woman's forehead.


Brian took Allie all the way into East Lansing, to El Aztaco, a Mexican restaurant that a lot of the college crowd from Michigan State University went to.

"They know me here," Brian whispered when they sat down.

"Bri, what can I get you?" the waiter asked, coming up to the table almost immediately. The place wasn't very full. It was a Monday and the regular college year was over and summer term had not yet begun.

"How about two margaritas?" Brian said, looking over at Allie and raising an eyebrow. She nodded.

"Coming right up."

"They serve you here?" Allie asked. She really could use a drink.

"Yeah, I've got my connections. This place usually cards everybody because of the college and all, but if you've got it, you've got it."

"And you have it?"

"That's right. I know you're new in school and all that, but I'm pretty important around there and I have a lot of friends all over."

He was obviously full of himself. Maybe she could use that against him? "So then tell me about yourself," she suggested.

"Well," he said, leaning back in his chair and taking the drink the waiter brought. "I'll be going to U of M on a full-ride football scholarship in the fall."

"What're you going to major in?" God, she was almost disgusting herself with the way she apparently was hanging on his every word, leaning forward on the table and everything.

"Business. My dad wants me to go to work for him after graduation, but I think when I get done there I'll move to New York. That's where all the action is."

"Really?"



Madeline heard a car door slam. She glanced at the clock on the wall and realized it was merely eight-thirty — far too early for either of her girls to be home, unless something had gone terribly awry. She jumped to her feet, then realized that nothing was wrong, at least not with Brett or Allie.

By the time Madeline answered the front door, just after the chime rang, though, she was nervous. She was unaccustomed to feeling nervous. When she put her hand on the doorknob, she realized her palms were just a tad damp.

"Hi," Leisa said when Madeline opened the door.

"Hello, my dear," Madeline said, trying to look away from the deep green of Leisa's eyes. She turned and led Leisa into the house. "May I get you something to drink?"

"What do you have?"

"Since the children moved in, I seem to have a wide variety of beverages available."

"How about a beer?"

"Very well," Madeline said, reaching into the refrigerator for a Labatt's Blue. The bottle felt so cool in her hand and it was such a warm night, a night that had suddenly gotten quite a bit warmer, that Madeline decided to take another out for herself. She handed one bottle to Leisa, but Leisa paused while taking it so that their fingers momentarily touched. "I believe I might partake myself," Madeline said.

She kept her distance from Leisa, sitting in the easy chair instead of nearer to Leisa on the couch. The night seemed so much warmer when she was near the bold blonde.

"Are they any closer to finding out what's going on?" Leisa said, leaning forward toward Madeline.

"I believe Brett had a run-in with some associates of Brian Ewing. She was also approached about other matters by somebody else."

"What?"

"Beyond that I cannot say."

"The break-in at the school."

"So tonight Allie is on a date with Brian while Brett is taking Kathy out."

"Brett seems to really like Kathy, doesn't she?" Leisa said, standing to look out the front window.

"Brett plays many roles, for that is what her life until now has been — roles to play," Madeline said, feeling like she should gulp air now that she could. She was glad for this brief respite to safer ground.

"What's going on, Madeline?" Leisa said, turning suddenly to face her. Her deep green eyes bored into Madeline.

"Brett is doing what she needs to do, such as she always has. She is doing whatever it is that she needs to do." Leisa walked toward her. "I'm assured that she is merely playing her role." Leisa knelt at Madeline's feet. "My only concern is that she will fall into the trap of thinking she is actually that which she portrays."

"We both know that's not what I meant."

"Leisa, I do not then know what you mean." What was going on with her? She was unaccustomed to feeling this way. She had never felt this way before. She knew that life was a series of challenges and that the uniqueness of each incident made life interesting. But still, she was used to knowing something of that which was to come.

Madeline could not pull away from Leisa's entrancing gaze. "Maddy, I spoke with Allie recently."

Madeline knew that she was not understanding something, though she had a queer feeling that somehow she did. "And did she have any interesting facts to share about the matter at hand, beyond which I would not know?"

"Yes, yes she did. But not about the school or drugs or Brett or Kathy or Brian."

"Then I do not know what you are referring to, my dear."

"Yes, you do." Leisa reached forward to take Madeline's hands into her own, warm, soft ones. "You're tripping all over your words, Maddy. You know what's happening."

Madeline suddenly became aware of the undertone of fear in Leisa's voice, just as she realized that Leisa could be understanding that there could be two reasons for Madeline's agitation.

"We can't keep doing this, Maddy. I have to know." When Madeline didn't reply, when instead she sat frozen in her seat, Leisa leaned forward and kissed her lightly and gently on her lips.

Years before, when she was young, Madeline had believed in romance and love, and she still did, just not with regard to her own life. And now, here, at her age, she suddenly had a very beautiful, very much younger woman kneeling at her feet kissing her. Kissing her, of all things!

And, even stranger, she found herself responding.

She gave up thinking and gave in to feeling.

Allie couldn't believe it and couldn't say no when Brian asked her to a movie after dinner. So far the evening had been a total bust, with Brian saying nothing out of the ordinary, or even interesting in any measure. She was so bored she could have fallen asleep.

Of course, she now had to endure his arm around her shoulders for an entire hour and a half. Allie usually found such short movies annoying because they never got far into character development or even adequate plotting and carry-through, but tonight it felt as if those ninety minutes lasted a millennium or two.

Then he insisted on holding her hand in his big, callused one the entire journey to the car and the whole car ride home. As a topper to the evening, he jumped out of the car to try to open her car door for her, but she beat him to that. But he walked her to the house, still droning on about himself.

They paused on the porch where Madeline had thankfully left the light on. Allie turned toward Brian, offering her hand, when he grabbed her and forced his tongue into her mouth. She briefly thought she'd have to knee him in the crotch, but fortunately Madeline opened the door right then.

Brian quickly pulled away from Allie, then bashfully said his good-night and backed down the steps to his car. Madeline did have a way with looks. She could probably stone Medusa from thirty feet if she felt so inclined.

Allie waved good-bye to Brian and rushed inside.

"Yuck! Gross!" she screamed as she ran to the bathroom to brush her teeth and gargle.

"Oh fuck, man," Jerry breathed heavily as he went outside to look at Brett's Jimmy.

"Listen," Brett said, "I wouldn'a come here, except all the shops are closed and Steve and Scott are out."

"There's no way you can keep this from Ms. Jameson."

"Well, no, duh, man, but I want it as fixed as possible."

Jerry slowly nodded, thinking. "Jake's dad, he's our best bet. He has total access to the shop he works at in town."

Brett looked at her watch. Nine P.M. "We'd better get a move on."

As it turned out, the paint used to vandalize the vehicle was a fairly cheap one. Mr. McMartin had Jake, Brett, and Jerry scrubbing at it when Randi pulled up behind them.

"Just the boy I wanted to see," Randi said, approaching Brett. "Where were you Sunday night?"

Brett looked up at her, glad that she had stripped down to her T-shirt and trousers. Randi might have recognized the suit. "Out runnin' some errands for my aunt with my sister," she replied brusquely as Randi surveyed the vehicle.

"You weren't anywhere near the school?" Randi asked.

"Nope," Brett replied, returning to her careful car cleansing. Mr. McMartin was already at the shop, preparing the equipment to put

141

the new windows in and making sure that the proper sizes were in stock. He had told the boys how to work at the paint so as to not mar the vehicle. He wanted it done here, while it was still as fresh as possible. They were to take the vehicle to the shop as soon as they were done, to put the windows in and polish and wax it.

"Did you report this to the police?" Randi asked, studying the damage.

"Nope," Brett replied as she put the finishing touches on her side of the vehicle. As it turned out, both sides had been emblazoned with that same catchy phrase.

"Why not?" Randi queried.

Brett turned to face her. "Because I don't like the fuckin' pigs, and the less I see of them, the better."

Jake ran around the car when he heard Brett's outburst. "Aunt Randi, Brett's just having a really bad night."

Randi stared at Brett. "I don't like you. What's more, I know there's a reason for it. And as soon as I figure out what it is . . ."

"I'm done over here," Jerry announced from the far side.

"You're going to the shop?" Randi suddenly asked Jake.

"Yes."

"Good, I'll see you there," she replied, walking back to her car.

"You're outta your jurisdiction, copper!" Brett yelled after her.


Allie was furious when Brett didn't get home until after midnight. She calmed down somewhat when Brett explained about the damage to the vehicle and the repairs thereof. Brett also told her about running into Randi, again, and how Randi had acted when Brett paid Mr. McMartin in cash.

"Listen, Allie, I'm just about positive that Brian dosed Kathy with a date rape drug, but I don't know which one."

"What happened?"

"Blackout or amnesia. She felt drunk but hadn't had anything to drink. She felt as if she was watching herself and got very tired. Then she doesn't remember."

"No hallucinations?"

"No, none. So I don't think it could be Special K," Brett said, referring to ketamine hydrochloride, a veterinary tranquilizer that was often used for date rape. It was also known as Vitamin K and just plain old K. One of its effects was that it caused hallucinations.

"So that leaves G or Roofies," Allie replied, referring to gamma-hydroxybutyrate, a.k.a. Liquid G and Liquid E, and Rohypnol, otherwise known as Roofies. All three, Special K, Liquid G, or Roofies could cause the effects that Kathy had described.

"I'm guessing Roofies," Brett said. "Roofies are the most common date-rape drug, and they have the least side effects that would be a real downer to a rape scene."

When they went to bed that night, they had agreed that Allie would ride to school with Madeline so that Brett could pick Kathy up, both in order to silence her from saying anything about the paint and the shots of the night before, and to burn Brian's ass when Brett showed up for school in an undamaged vehicle with Kathy.

Brett fell asleep, not being able to believe that some people took date rape drugs for recreational purposes, for fun.

# 12

Brett got up early the next morning to pick up Kathy for school. She hadn't set this up with Kathy, so she wanted to make sure that she caught her before she left.

As soon as Kathy opened the door, though, Brett knew the plan had been a mistake. Kathy was still damp from the shower, and she wore only a short, silky, red bathrobe.

"Oh my gosh!" Kathy squealed, seeing the car. "You got it fixed!" she threw her arms around Brett. Brett could feel every inch of Kathy's body pressed against her own. The silk did not so much cover Kathy's body as accentuate it. Brett pushed Kathy back into the house and pressed her against the closet door.

"Oh no," Kathy said, bringing her hands up to cover her face. "I don't have any makeup on! You didn't tell me you were coming!"

Brett pulled the hands down. "Make no mistake about it," she murmured, looking into Kathy's eyes. "You are beautiful in the morning." When Brett pulled back from the lengthy kiss, she noticed Kathy's nipples standing out through the clingy material. Brett's lips traced the line of Kathy's collarbone, and she gently pulled open Kathy's robe. She wasn't wearing anything under it.

"Oh god, Brett," Kathy moaned. "Don't do this to me before school." She pushed her bare breast into Brett's mouth. Her hands were in Brett's hair, pulling her head into her. She was tight against Brett's leg, which was between her own.

"I'm sorry, you're right," Brett replied, stepping back to admire Kathy's creamy breasts with their fully-aroused nipples. Her gaze lowered to the triangle of dark hair nestled between Kathy's thighs. She wanted to part those lips and feel how wet she was. Kathy flushed hot then demurely pulled the robe closed and went to change.

A few minutes later, Kathy realized Brett was standing in her bedroom doorway watching her. She boldly leaned back against the wall, looking at Brett over the bed. She had on her underwear and a half-buttoned shirt.

"I would've killed Brian if he ever did anything like that," she said to Brett.

"How many times do I have to tell you that I'm not Brian?" Brett asked from the doorway. "I'll never do the things to you that he did." She paused a moment, watching the expression on Kathy's face. "You need to show me your prom dress."

Kathy nodded and dug through her closet. Brett walked up behind her, inhaling her intoxicating scent. She was as close to the girl as she could be without actually touching her. Kathy seemed to sense her presence, stiffening slightly as she pulled the dress from her closet. Brett reached out to run her fingers over the fabric.

"Very nice," Brett said. "I can't wait to see it on you." She paused for effect. "And off you." She turned to go back to the kitchen. "You'd better hurry or we'll be late."

In the kitchen, Brett took a deep breath. They had to figure this case out soon because she was losing all control with Kathy. Hell, she had already lost it.

She couldn't believe she was doing the things she was doing; she couldn't believe the way she was acting. No matter how many ways she tried to justify it, she still knew it was wrong. She was acting like the Brett Higgins who had lost Allie those several years ago. She didn't want to lose Allie again.

Kathy stood back from the bathroom mirror, where she was applying her makeup, and looked at herself. She couldn't believe all that she was allowing Brett to get away with. She had only known him a few days, and already she was willing to sleep with him. In fact, she wanted to have sex with him. Make love with him.

She remembered how long Brian had begged and coerced her before she consented to sleep with him. Maybe that was the difference. She was the one pursuing Brett. Moreover, and again unlike Brian, Brett seemed to really listen to her when she talked. How often had she sat listening to Brian go on about his plans, and yet Brett asked her questions about herself and her life. He always looked at her, into her eyes, when she spoke, as if he really cared. She felt as if she could tell him anything, and she hadn't felt like that about anyone since her friendship with Beth had ended.

She briefly stopped and wondered, as she occasionally did, what had happened to Beth and her. They had been such close friends for so very long, and then high school came and they just sort of went their own ways. What had happened that made her pull away from her old friends? She had gotten involved with cheerleading. She had made new friends and forgotten the old ones. She had felt like a caterpillar that had just left its cocoon as a beautiful butterfly.

She had been overwhelmed by the attention from both boys and girls, all of whom gave her admiring glances. When the best looking boy in her class asked her out and then gave her his ring, she forgot everyone else. But now she was beginning to regret that she had ignored her old friends.

She knew she was at a turning point. High school was ending and college was looming in the not-too-far future. It was strange that Brett Jameson and his sister, Allison, had entered her life at this point. It wasn't just Brett, but Allie as well, who had the open honesty that she so craved. Both of them looked at her, really at her, when she spoke. They both listened, and she knew that already they cared.


Allie approached Jim just before class in the hallway.

"Jim," she began, "yesterday you seemed to imply some things . . ."

"I didn't mean to," Jim said quickly.

"Well, I've got a favor to ask. You see, Brett's birthday is coming up and —"

"I thought you two were twins?"

"Oh no. He's a bit older than I am, but see, I know what he'd really like, but I don't know how to get it."

"What is it?" Jim asked suspiciously.

"I hate to say it, but . . . he's been behaving really well, for him, and . . . I know he'd really like some speed or marijuana."

"Then you should ask Scott Campbell," Jim said, turning away.

"Either that or ask your boyfriend," Leon said as he approached, having overheard some of the conversation.

"What do you mean by that?" Allie asked, confronting him. Jim shot Leon a hard look.

"Uh, nothing," Leon said, quickly leaving for the classroom.


"Hey there!" Beth said cheerily to Brett as she passed Brett and Kathy in the hall.

Brett turned to face Beth. "Hey yourself. Whazzup?" She noticed that Beth was not looking at her, but at Kathy.

"Not much. Hey," she said, addressing Kathy.

A smile lit Kathy's face. "Hey you," she half murmured, her voice silky.

"You two put any more football players in their place?" Beth asked, still looking at Kathy.

"Not lately," Brett replied as the warning buzzer sounded.

"Oh shit!" Beth exclaimed. "My ass is grass if I'm late one more time!" She turned to dart down the hall.

Brett looked at Kathy. "Hey, you okay?" she asked, noticing a somewhat faraway look in Kathy's eyes.

"Oh yeah. I'm fine," Kathy replied, shaking her head as a faint blush touched her cheeks.


"Brett, Allie, I need to speak with you in my office for a moment," Leisa said at the beginning of third hour.

"Whatever it was, I didn't do it," Brett said.

"You really are making your mark on this school, young man," Leisa said, shaking her head. "Anyway, Madeline wanted me to let you know that she's having dinner with friends in Lansing and won't be home until about midnight." She turned to go back to the classroom, but Brett stopped her.

"Leisa, I got a quick question — is it true that Carl Rogers just started teaching here a year ago?"

"Actually, I think it was closer to a year and a half ago. Why do you ask?"

"Leisa, any teacher that started only recently is a very good place for us to start in our investigations," Allie said.

"Madeline didn't want me to say anything earlier; she didn't want me to bias you."

"Yes, I remember," Brett said.

"Why do you ask?"

"Mr. Marin said something about it, and I just found it curious is all."

"Fred Marin? He's only been here two years himself."

"Is that the usual turnover for a school this size?" Allie asked.

"Rogers took over for the old coach who had retired. And the school has been growing, so we've needed more teachers — thus Fred Marin, Caroline Thatcher, and Burt Jones. They all came from bigger schools, looking for something a little quieter now that they're a bit older. I started here about a decade ago, and I've seen several faculty and staff come and go during that time. More coming than going, of course."

"Great, just great," Brett said. "I was thinking I was on to something. If Carl started here when the trouble started —"

"Leisa," Allie said, "Who started when the trouble did?"

Leisa paused a moment, thinking. "I think the last one was Carl. And we don't contract any of our service employees — bus drivers, janitors, and lunchroom workers."

"So Carl Rogers was the last one hired in," Brett mused. She turned to Allie. "Hey, sexy, ya think you can squeeze me into your schedule tonight?" She slid her eyes over Allie, knowing that she couldn't touch her with the kids right outside. "So we could have a little quality time together?"

That night Brett and Allie went into Lansing to accessorize Brett's tux for prom. When they were finished at the store, Brett took Allie to a very nice, romantic restaurant for a candlelit dinner.

"I love you," Brett said as they held hands and sipped wine.

"And I love you. I'm sorry I've been so jealous about Kathy," Allie replied. "I really like her a lot. I guess I'm just afraid because . . ."

"Because?" Brett asked.

"Because I look at her and I see Storm and all the other young girls you weren't able to save."

Brett realized Allie may have hit the nail on the head. "I'll just be glad when it's over."

"Which should be any time now."

"Hey, if it's soon enough, I won't need that tux!" Brett cried gleefully.

"You're gonna stand Kathy up for prom?"

"Isn't that what you want? For me not to go with her?"

Allie shook her head. "You butches can be so thoughtless," she said. "Kathy will probably be prom queen, and she would be quite embarrassed if she didn't have a suitable date for the occasion."

They were laughing together by the time they got home and made their way to the bedroom.

"You're in for it now," Brett said, pushing Allie onto the bed and climbing on top of her. She had wanted Allie all night long and wasn't about to be gentle. Kathy had been driving her nuts, and at least with Allie she didn't have to feel guilty.

"Ooh!" Allie teased. "The big, bad letterman's got me scared."

Brett ripped open Allie's shirt and bra and buried her face in the softness of Allie's breasts. Allie moaned as Brett teased her nipples back and forth, then pulled her own shirt off as Brett ripped off her jeans so she lay naked on the bed.

"Oh god," Brett moaned as she knelt between Allie's legs and roughly pushed Allie's thighs apart. She could smell and see Allie's readiness, Allie's excitement, as she parted the lips and licked at the damp flesh within.

Allie leaned back on her arms as Brett's tongue tasted her, filled her, teased her. The warm summer breeze blew in the window as Brett's hands caressed every inch of her naked body.

"Oh god, Brett," Allie moaned, "I need you so bad."

"Then try this on for size," Brett growled. She pulled open her zipper to expose the cock she'd been packing all night.

"Fuck me, baby, fuck me!" Allie said loudly as Brett entered her.

Brett wrapped Allie's legs around her waist and rode her. Allie lay on her back on the bed in total abandon as Brett ruthlessly pulled in and out, all the way, over and over again, fucking her hard.

As Allie cried out Brett's name, the drapes blew open slightly in the breeze, but neither Allie nor Brett noticed the face peering in at them.


"Tell me about Randi McMartin," the man said first thing over the phone.

"She's Jake McMartin's aunt, a Detroit detective."

"I know that. What I mean is, do you know why the hell she's here?"

"She claims to be on vacation."

"Let me give you a hint: That is an incorrect assumption. I found out from Maggie's secretary that she's had several meetings with Principal Margaret Simons."

"Shit. Okay, we'll watch it."

"You'd better watch more than that. I think Brett Jameson's moves are a little too cool for some shithead teenager."

He let that remark slide. "You're right. He's a pain in the ass, and his ass is mine, but he checks out."

"How do you know that?"

"Newspapers, magazines, and a few phone calls. Let's just say I don't think a powerful man like Frankie Lorenzini would cover for no narc. *And* Randi almost busted Jameson a coupla times in Detroit. So even she has been giving him shit. She doesn't know who he is, at least not yet."

The older man briefly considered this. "I also don't like the way Madeline never grieved for her brother, so watch it. As for Scott's pretensions to the throne —"

"Scott's ass is mine."

"You say that a lot, but I haven't seen any results lately."

"That's because I keep letting fuckers like Thompson try to do a man's work."

"This isn't a child's game. No more scare tactics like spray-painting. I want results," the man said.

"Don't worry."

The man had a nagging feeling, but he didn't care about his employees, who would be the ones to take the fall, so he continued. "Okay, fine. Now, about those tapes you showed me of Kathy — I need them again." He had made copies that were adequate for his own viewing, but the copies were not good enough to duplicate for distribution.

"Why?"

"Let's just say we can make some real money off them," the man replied, before adding "of course, since it appears you've been seeing a lot of Allie Jameson lately, it wouldn't hurt to add a few of her to the collection."

A little grin began to pass over Brian's face as he hung up the phone. He had just been given permission to have his way with Allie, a thought that did not disturb him one bit, especially as he had already been planning it. That he would make money on it was only the salt on the Margarita glass.


"I cannot believe you talked me into . . . into playing hooky like this," Madeline said to Leisa over the dinner table.

"Yes, you can," Leisa said, then boldly reached forward and took Maddy's hands in her own over the table. "It can't be easy trying to play mother to those two for very long." The simple feeling of taking Maddy's hands into her own was enough to give her weak knees. No guy she had ever dated, kissed, or had sex with ever gave her weak knees like this.

"But what if Brett and Allie need me?"

"They'll be fine on their own for one night."

"How is it that you seem confident about this unusual turn of events?"

"Because I've been waiting for it my entire lifetime."

"Are you sure I'm not too much of a disappointment? After all, I am a great deal older than you and —"

"Shh. I've never felt like this before, about anybody."

"But you are so young and beautiful —"

"I said *shh*. And when I say that, I mean it. But I'll let you in on a little secret. I'm scared to death because I've never felt anything like this before. And don't ask me to think about the future, because I can't think beyond this moment. I am just so happy to be able to touch you like this."

"Leisa Kraft, you also do to me what no one else has ever done before."

Leisa wanted to jump up and down with joy, she wanted to run out of her skin, she wanted to scream at the top of her lungs. But she knew Maddy would find this inappropriate and embarrassing, so she settled for smiling across the table at the woman she loved.

# 13

"I like your style," Scott said to Brett Wednesday over lunch, which he insisted Brett join him, alone.

"Whaddya mean?" Brett asked as she grabbed another slice of pizza.

"You're ruthless, only lookin' out for one guy — and that's you."

"You gotta problem with that?"

"No, I said I liked it."

"Speakin' of likes and dislikes," Brett said, realizing she had to be direct with Scott or else he'd play his little games with her forever. "What about my stuff?"

"It's in the car," Scott said with a shrug. "Had to get you some crack with it, though."

"Why?" Brett asked suspiciously.

"He didn't have enough weed, but don't worry. It'll sell," Scott replied, nodding his head. "You done?" he asked, indicating the remains of the pizza.

"Yeah," Brett said, standing.

"I got some Jack in the car. We can have a drink while we discuss things in private."

Out in the pickup, Scott started the engine and reached behind the seat. He pulled out a bottle in a bag and drank directly from it, handing it over to Brett when he was done. They passed the bottle silently between them for several minutes as Scott drove through town.

"You seem to like Kathy a lot," Scott began.

"What of it?" Brett asked.

"I'm just enjoyin' seein' you put the screw to both Brian and her." Scott smirked. "Ewing's been a pain in the ass for quite a while."

"Puttin' the screw to *both* of them?" Brett asked in astonishment.

"I don't think Kath would be very happy if she knew what I knew," Scott said. "Not happy at all."

"What do you know?" Brett scowled. Had he figured out her secret?

"I don't let anybody hang with me unless I know them," Scott said. "So I always do some checkin' around. Well, I didn't believe it when I first heard it, but . . ."

"Cut to the chase, Campbell," Brett growled, impatient for the bomb to drop.

"I heard 'bout you being overly protective of your sis, then Jake told me, so last night I did some investigatin' of my own —"

"Investigating? What the fuck did you investigate, bastard?"

"I know you're fuckin' your li'l sis," he said, turning to look at Brett with an evil grin. "I was outside her window last night when you got back from your little date."

"You fuckin' bastard."

"And you really gave it to her, man. I always knew those sweet types had to be fuckin' hell on wheels in bed. Man, she was wild, lovin' every minute of it, and what a fuckin' body that broad has on her. I'll tell you, man, I wouldn' mind spending some time with those tits and that sweet li'l pussy of hers myself —"

That was it. "Listen, you slimy fucking piece of shit, you keep

154

your hands off my goddamned sister or I will rip your body into shreds and put the parts in trash Dumpsters across the state so they'll have to piece you together coated with moldy Big Macs and rotten French fries. You got that?" Brett barely controlled the urge to carry through on her threat right then.

"Hey, man, don't worry. Nobody's gonna know a thing, and I'll leave your little sister alone," Scott assured Brett, nervously pulling away from her. "Not unless you piss me off. And I can't say as I blame you. She is one hot number. And one fuckin' hot lay," he added with a smirk.

"What is it you want me to do?" Brett replied curtly. He could tell from the look in Scott's eyes that Scott knew Brett was serious but didn't want to blow his tough guy act.

"I'm thinkin' I may need a little help. You see, my supplier's always insisted he be the fence as well, and I think he's screwin' us —"

"So you want to go around him," Brett interrupted bluntly.

"You got it. And I don't think he'll be happy 'bout it."

"So you need me to make it as peaceful as possible," Brett surmised, "and to help set up a new distribution chain."

"Basically, that's it. I want to cut out as many middlemen as possible."

"And you'll tell Kathy and the whole world 'bout me and Allie if I don't comply."

Scott looked over at him and nodded, with the same smirk still on his face. "Got you by the balls, ain't I?"

"I take it, then, that Officer Randi McMartin verified my story?"

"We couldn't exactly point out why we was innerested, but Jake 'remembered' the names, and asked her a few questions. It looks like you might be who you say you are." He didn't add that Beth had done some digging at the university's library and had discovered several interesting articles about the two people Brett had referenced, and that Scott had himself phoned Frankie at the theater and talked with him. Frankie said merely that Brett Jameson had been a fine employee, trustworthy and competent, and he was sorry that he had had to move, because Frankie hadn't wanted to see him leave.

~ ~ ~ ~ ~

Randi stared at the computer screen. She kicked her feet up on the desk and leaned back with a cup of coffee in her hands. So far, she had been able to come up with nothing on Brett and Allison Jameson. She had called Pershing High School, which did have records backing up Brett's and Allie's story. But the address the school had for the Jameson family did not exist, and the phone number was for a local McDonald's. Beyond that, when she checked school records on Madeline Jameson, she discovered that the next of kin listed was a brother living in Alaska.

She noted that Madeline was born in Alma, and so she went to the office of the *Alma Sun* and researched her in their microfiche files. She discovered that her parents had died several years ago within a few months of each other and were survived only by their two children, Madeline and Timothy. When she called the number she found on the Internet for Timothy Jameson in Nome, Alaska, she got a machine, but it told her all she needed to know. A rather effeminate male voice said, "Hello, Timothy and Dwayne can't come to the phone right now."

She put down her coffee and lit a cigarette, studying the swirls of smoke as they rose toward the ceiling. Jake had asked several strange questions the other night. He usually wasn't interested in her work, and she tried to tell herself he was just curious. After all, the DeSilva/Higgins/Lorenzini case had been a major turning point in her career: The time she had taken the initiative to jump over her boss and implement a major strike against her opponent. Of course, it could just be that his friends were becoming a gang and needed some role models. But where would he have found the names?

Jake had asked about Frankie Lorenzini and Brett Higgins. He seemed particularly interested to discover that Higgins had been a woman, and, when he first began the conversation, he didn't seem to know that Randi had even worked on that particular case.

Although a fire destroyed most of the evidence they had against Frankie and Brett, Brett had been killed all the same, and Frankie alone would not be able to sustain the momentum of the DeSilva enterprises, which he and Brett inherited when Rick DeSilva died. Randi knew Brett had been the brains and that without her it was only a matter of time before Frankie crashed, thus ending one part of Detroit's organized crime history.

Randi pulled out her wallet and stared at the picture of Allie she had kept since Allie had dumped her. Dumped her because of Brett, even though Brett was dead. Randi knew she was dead because she had seen her burnt corpse, had gone to her funeral, had visited her grave. Brett Higgins was dead, she insisted to herself.

She reached over to pick up the telephone.

"Yeah," she began when it was answered. "I need a couple of phone numbers . . ."


Scott and Brett pulled into the school's parking lot a few minutes later. Brett immediately tracked down Allie and pulled her to a quiet corner of the school, which happened to be in the library.

"Scott saw us last night," she whispered to her.

"When?" Allie asked, concern crossing her face.

"I think he followed us for half the night. The long and short of it is, he still thinks we're brother and sister, but he thinks . . ."

"What, Brett?"

"He knows we're lovers, and he's using that to make sure I do what he wants me to."

"That may not be an entirely bad thing. He's figuring he can trust you now that he's got the dirt."

"But it concerns me that Brian asked you to the prom as soon as Kathy dumped him," Brett mused out loud. "Like he knew just how to get my goat."

"I don't understand. Scott just found out about us last night."

"But he said that Jake had mentioned something to him . . ."

"Is everyone watching us fuck?" Allie whispered fervently.

"And all along Scott's been acting weird when you've been mentioned in my presence."

"You're suggesting that Brian and Scott may communicate a lot more then they let on? Like Scott found out from somebody else and told Brian about it?"

"By the time Brian asked you out, Scott would've known that I was protective of you, and would've had some indication that we may be lovers — probably an eyewitness who saw us go at it when we thought we were alone."

"You're making an awful lot of assumptions," Allie pointed out. "But Brian did know where we lived."

"What do you mean?"

"He didn't need to ask directions. He —" Allie stopped when Principal Margaret Simons entered the library with Randi McMartin. "Oh fuck."

Brett turned to see what had grabbed Allie's attention. Before they could determine a route of escape from the library, Randi spotted them. Brett and Allie tried to make it to the exit, but Margie called out to them.

"Brett, Allie," Margie began. "Come over here, there's someone I want you to meet."

Allie pointed at her watch. "Gotta run, Ms. Simons," she said as she scurried out the door. Brett shrugged and tried to follow.

"Did you get your car fixed?" Randi asked. Brett turned to study her.

"Yeah, I did. Thanks for asking," she replied, not stepping any closer.

"I don't know what got into her, Randi," Margie began. "Allie's usually attentive and well-behaved."

"Not at all like her brother?" Randi replied.

"I should get to class —" Brett began.

"I understand you went to Pershing," Randi said, making sure Brett could not escape.

"You're finally right about something, Randi."

"That *is* in my jurisdiction, after all," Randi said with a smirk, indicating that she would soon remember where she knew Brett from.

"I know," Brett said, exiting. Outside, she quickly located Allie near her locker.

"That was a close call," Allie said, spying Brett.

"Too close for comfort," Brett replied before she detailed the rest of her lunchtime conversation with Scott. Allie stared in horror. When Brett neared the end of the story, Kathy came around a bend in the hallway, saw them, and walked over.

"Hi, there," she said. She gave Brett a peck on the cheek. She sniffed. "You've been drinking," she said.

"Yeah," Brett admitted nonchalantly. "I went out with Scott for lunch."

Kathy sighed, closed her eyes, looked down, and began to walk away. Brett reached out to grab her arm.

"Hey, what's the matter?" Brett asked. Kathy turned to look at her, hurt clearly etched across her features.

"I thought you were different," she said. Brett wanted to reach out and reassure Kathy, but she was quite aware of Allie standing next to her.

"Hey, it was just a little Jack," Brett justified. Kathy stood frozen.

"I thought you were different," she said again, coldly, before she broke out of Brett's grasp and went running. Brett and Allie exchanged glances, and then Allie ran after Kathy.


When Kathy got home from school that day, Brett was sitting on her front porch with a dozen red roses. Kathy ignored her.

"Kathy, I'm so sorry."

Kathy unlocked the door. "I trusted you!" Kathy cried. "Do you think I've ever acted like that with anybody else?"

"You *can* trust me," Brett insisted. Kathy pulled away and slammed the door in Brett's face. To no avail, Brett spent half an hour trying to get Kathy's attention. When Brett tried to look pleadingly in, Kathy pulled all the drapes shut. When Brett tried knocking on the windows and ringing the doorbell, she turned up the radio. Brett finally went behind the house and, after making sure no one was around, pulled out her lock picks.

Within moments she gained entry. She searched the house stealthily and found Kathy lying on her bed, holding her teddy bear, and crying.

"What do you want?" Kathy cried, sitting up, when Brett knocked lightly on the doorjamb.

"I want to talk," Brett said, holding out her hands.

"How did you get in here?"

"I've never hidden the fact that I'm from the wrong side of the tracks —"

"You didn't break a window, did you?" Kathy said, rushing out to inspect the house.

"No." Brett grabbed Kathy at the doorway. "I picked the lock."

"You bastard!" Kathy cried, pummeling Brett's chest with weak punches. Before Brett could grab the hands, as her intentions were, Kathy sank to the floor, crying.

"Not again. I'm not gonna let it happen again," Kathy cried. Brett knelt next to her.

"What, baby?" she asked gently.

"All my friends said you were no different, but I told them you were." Kathy stood up to pace. "They told me that you were stupid and crude and" — she looked up at Brett — "and I told them that they were wrong, that you were the only guy who could get me away from Brian." Her mascara was running, her eyes were puffy, and her face and lips were wet from the tears. Brett thought she was beautiful.

"You just wanted me to get you away from Brian."

"No. Not at all. But I was happy you didn't let him scare you."

"What aren't you gonna let happen again?" Brett asked.

"I know Brian was on something, and I know he was gettin' mixed up with things he shouldn't —"

"Like what?"

"I don't know! I just know he changed this past fall. We were starting to fall apart before then, but he was never so brutal, so possessive!" Kathy cried out, pounding Brett's chest. Brett pulled her in tight. "And I know Scott's gotta be involved somehow . . ."

"There's no reason to be scared, Kat," Brett said, running her fingertips down Kathy's back and then down her cheek.

"Yes, there is," Kathy said, taking Brett's hand and kissing it lightly. "I'm scared of you being friends with Scott, and of Brian dating Allie while hating you so much."

"Don't worry," Brett said, "I can handle it — and them."

Kathy pulled away and stared at Brett. "Yeah, right," she spat out vehemently. "And how many other guys these days have said those same things? How many other guys who are now six feet under with a bullet in their brains?"

"Kathy," Brett said, taking Kathy's hands in her own. "You just have to believe me. I'm not here to sell drugs or start a gang or anything like that . . ."

"Then what are you doin' with Scott?" Kathy replied, accusingly.

Brett ran her lips over Kathy's hands as she wondered if Scott was selling to Brian. "You've just got to trust me," she said, cupping Kathy's chin in her hand. "I know you want to, so just follow your heart and do what you know is right."

"How can you be so sure?" Kathy asked with a questioning glance.

"You need to trust me," Brett said with a reassuring smile. "Besides, you can't dump me now — Allie just helped me pick out my tux for the prom." A little white lie couldn't hurt at this point.

# 14

Thursday morning, Allie dropped Madeline off at the college so that Brett could use Madeline's car to do some investigative work.

Brett waited across the street until a bare-chested Scott rushed out of his house, carrying one notebook, his shirt, and a leather jacket. She crouched down as Scott drove by, then looked slowly up and down the street and over the entire landscape before she headed for the house. She walked to the back and checked for any lurkers, but saw none. A quick peek in the windows confirmed that the house was empty. After picking the lock, she entered the house and walked directly to Scott's room.

She searched the room, beginning with the desk and then the bureau, the bed, the mattress and pillows. The posters on the wall concealed nothing, as did the stereo. But among Scott's four hundred or so cassette tapes, Brett discovered more than two dozen boxes filled with cocaine, weed, and amphetamine pills. Scott's musical taste seemed to be focused on hard rock, but the containers that hid the various substances had soft-rock and pop labels. Based on this insight, she selected several CDs from his rack and discovered logs of exchanges made during the past year, as well as coded records of deliveries.

As Brett laid the records on the floor, she began to see the pattern. The boy really was an amateur. Scott arranged for stolen items to be delivered to his source, who would take them in exchange for drugs, which Scott, or his associates, would then sell, thus making their profit. She also realized that he was right: He paid too much for the drugs and received too little for the goods. But she knew that Sunday night's take should've been worth at least twice what he recorded as being received from it. Brett meticulously replaced everything before continuing her search.

At the top of his closet, Brett discovered four boxes that at first seemed to contain only old clothes. But as she lifted one to search around it, she realized it was too light to be filled with clothing. She pulled it down and dumped the contents on the floor. There, at her feet, was about one or two thousand dollars in cash. Each of two other boxes contained the same. The last box, however, contained something additional: four videotapes marked KATHY. Brett put the tapes to the side and replaced the boxes. She went out to the family room to view the tapes, but saw a car pull up in the driveway. She stepped to the side of the windows and peeked through a curtain to see Brian Ewing and Thompson climb out of Brian's car, look around, and approach the front door.

They knocked and rang the bell several times before going to the back of the house. When she heard the crash of glass breaking, Brett hid in the staircase leading downstairs.

"I don't see why you gave them to him anyway," Thompson was saying as they entered the house. Brett was paying close attention to the sound of their voices to assess their position, so she'd know to move if they got too close.

"It's none of your fucking business," Brian growled back. Their voices were coming from Scott's bedroom. Brett heard the two boys cursing at each other while they ripped apart Scott's room. "Like you've got room to complain, anyway," Brian continued. "Letting that pussy Jameson kick your butt."

"Leave it alone, Bri," Thompson replied. "At least I don't go givin' away thousand-dollar videos . . ." Brett looked at the tapes in her hands.

"All we gotta do," Brian said, "is grab both the bitches tomorrow night." Their voices moved to the living room.

"I don't know, I mean, makin' these tapes is one thing —"

"Listen, he's told me this shit will sell for a fuckin' fortune on the black market. Think about it, man. One of these old pervs will pay a coupla hundred for just one of these babies."

"But what if we get caught, man?" Thompson argued.

"How're we gonna get caught?" Brian asked. "Kathy don't remember a thing about any of the times we did it before." Brett felt a cold chill creep through her body. She knew what was on the videotapes.

"What could he have done with them?" Thompson said in exasperation.

"I don't give a shit," Brian said. "He's gettin' too big for his britches anyway, him and Jameson."

"You don't give a shit cause you want to stick it to his sister."

"*And,*" Brian clarified, "I want to teach Kathy that nobody dumps Brian Ewing."


Instead of going directly to school, as she had planned, Brett went back to Madeline's. She turned on the TV and popped the first tape into the VCR. Although the tape was poorly shot, every detail was crystal clear. They must have used a very good camcorder. Brett watched, outraged, disgusted, and ready to cry. She wanted to throw up. Instead, she got up, poured herself a stiff belt of scotch, downed it, and returned to her viewing.

She scanned the tape, stopping only occasionally to make sure the background voices were the same. She wanted to nail every single son of a bitch who had anything at all to do with this — who, so far as she knew right now, were the same as the guys on the tape. Brian and Thompson. She also wanted to nail whoever wanted these tapes to sell to other fucking perverts, even though that info wouldn't be as easy to discover.

She had to resist the impulse to throw a table through the TV.

When she was done with the first tape, she pressed the rewind button. After preparing another drink, she reluctantly inserted the second tape into the VCR.

When she finished scanning the second tape, realizing it was more of the same but on a different night, she finished her drink, rewound the tape, hid the tapes in her room, and went to school. She couldn't bring herself to watch any more.

Even when she had been involved in porn, she hadn't touched anything to do with anyone underage, or anything to do with nonconsensual sex. Both Rick and Frankie knew quite clearly where she stood on those issues, and they knew the one way for them to be forever condemned by her would be to become involved in such things themselves.

Brett knew the tapes were important evidence, but she wanted more. She wanted to get everyone who was involved, including the mysterious male whom Brian and Thompson had mentioned while they were at Scott's.

All their asses would be hers.


Brett gave Ms. McNeil her note from the office, which said she was late due to car trouble, and reluctantly headed to her lab station.

Kathy looked up at Brett and smiled. "I was worried when you weren't in first hour," she began, stopping when she saw the look on Brett's face. "What's the matter?"

Brett reached over to run her hand along Kathy's cheek, to look into Kathy's eyes. "Oh god, Kathy, there's something we need to talk about —" She wanted to pull the girl into her arms and protect her from anything bad that might ever happen again.

"Excuse me, Mr. Jameson," Ms. McNeil said, walking up behind him. "You may have an excuse to be late to class, but there's no excuse to not do your work while you're here."

Brett felt too drained for a witty repartee, so she merely shrugged and opened her textbook, telling Kathy they would talk that night.

Kathy spent much of that hour trying to get Brett to tell her what he wanted to talk about, but Brett said nothing. She just couldn't.

"You're comin' with me tonight," Scott told Brett as soon as she entered shop class.

"Where?" Brett asked, as the rest of the group crowded close.

Scott looked at Jerry, Jake, Steve, and Beth with open disdain. "To a meetin'."

"The meeting!" Jake cried, gathering the attention of most of the classroom. "You never let us go!"

"And why the hell do you think that is?" Scott shouted, grabbing Jake by the throat and pressing him against the wall.

"Scott," Carl Rogers said, collaring Scott and pulling him away from Jake. "Today's assignment is to work on your lamps, not to practice your taxidermy methods on other students."

Brett studied her teacher's short, stocky build, and nearly shaved head. She recalled having been told that he had briefly played professional football before receiving a knee injury that had relegated him to being a high-school football coach and teacher. She suddenly realized he had probably been a bully himself in school, and was probably a role model for Brian Ewing. She wondered if he knew anything about what was going on.

Rogers turned and looked at Brett. "Have you got a problem?" he asked.

"No," Brett replied, turning to her lamp. "No problem."

"Good," Rogers said, returning to his desk and the magazine he had been reading.

Scott pulled Brett aside. "It's at midnight," he said. "I'll call to let you know where."

"I might be at Kath's," Brett replied.

"You do have a gun, don't you?" Scott asked. Brett nodded. "Good. Bring it."

Brett looked at Scott, then turned to see Carl Rogers staring at them.

# 15

Brett stopped to watch the cheerleaders as she left school. They were going to have a late practice because of the prom and wouldn't be practicing for the rest of the weekend. She and Allie had been unable to break away to talk, so Allie still did not know about the meeting or the videotapes or Brian and Thompson's plans for her and Kathy.

"You used to hang with some pretty impressive people," Beth said, walking up to Brett.

"It all depends" — Brett turned to face Beth — "on what you consider impressive."

"Several million dollars is impressive."

"What do you mean by that?"

"Scott asked me to check out some of the names you mentioned to him."

"So you're his research department," Brett stated, wondering what else Beth knew.

"He just sticks me with what he considers to be the boring stuff. He called Lorenzini himself."

"He talked with Frankie?"

"You call him Frankie?" Beth asked, amazed. When Brett nodded, she continued. "What was it like, working for an organization that big and powerful?"

"Taught me a lot," Brett replied simply.

Beth waited for her to continue. When she didn't, Beth, looking down to the ground and tracing patterns in the dirt with her toe, asked, "What was Brett Higgins like?"

"Why do you ask?"

"Well, you just don't hear much of women making it big in shit like that."

"Women make it all the time. You just don't hear about them so much because it's the guys blowin' each other's brains out."

"I bet she was pissed to die before she had a chance to spend all that money."

Brett stood looking at Beth, with her simple evaluations of the entire complex landscape that had led Brett Higgins to across the country and back again. "It wasn't so much about money for Brett," Brett admitted. "Although she came from a family so poor they made you look wealthy. It was about power and respect and making her own way in a world she didn't think really wanted her."

"You really knew her," Beth commented in amazement.

Brett nodded. "I was one of the few who did." She looked up at the sky and continued. "The worst part of when she died wasn't that she lost all that money, it was that when she died she thought she was pretty much alone. There were only two women she ever loved, and one had been killed a few years earlier and the other, so far as she knew, no longer loved her."

"Women?"

"Yes, women. Brett Higgins was a dyke. Didn't your research turn up that bit of info?"

"No," Beth said in open-mouthed amazement. "It didn't. And that was all right with you?"

"Why not?" Brett said with a shrug. "Nothin' hotter than two women goin' at it."

"Y'know, you're talkin' real weird for somebody wantin' to join us," Beth said.

"Beth, we all make choices in life, and sometimes it ain't until it's all over that you realize you made all the wrong choices. Ya gotta know what is important is the big thing."

"What are you sayin'?"

"I'm saying you shouldn't glamorize crime — it's a dangerous living. You also shouldn't idolize the life Brett Higgins led, because she never fought the good fight. She chickened out. She never wanted to be a role model." Brett walked away, thinking of all the good fights she had walked away from in her life, fights like trying to make it in the legitimate world of business, or like letting her family get away with giving her crap.

"Brett!" Beth called from behind her.

Brett turned. "Can I give you a ride home?"

When they got into the Jimmy, Brett asked Beth, "This meetin' tonight — do you know who it's with?"

"I dunno. Scott won't tell us shit. I wouldn't be surprised . . ."

"What?"

"Well, see, Scott talks real big and all that, but . . ."

"Beth, tell me."

"All I'm pretty sure of is that it's with the guys above him. I don't know who they are, but I know I've heard some shit about Brian Ewing, which seems stupid, but I'd believe the crap I've heard about Mr. Rogers."

"Mr. Rogers? What have you heard about him?"

"Well, he obviously doesn't like us much, but he really likes his football players."

"Yeah, he does, doesn't he?" Brett lit a cigarette and offered one to Beth, who accepted. "Beth, I want you to know that I meant what I said before about us being friends."

Beth looked down. "I know. Do you have any idea what you're getting into tonight? I know it must all seem like kiddie stuff with what you're used to, but I know Scott's serious, and . . ."

"What?" Pulling the story out of Beth word by word was getting on Brett's nerves.

"I know Brian's serious as well. You're gonna be meeting with Brian tonight — he's the middle man. I don't think even Scott knows who gets the shit to Brian, or anything really."

"You know a lot about all of this, don't you?"

"I just keep my eyes open, is all. I prolly know more than Steve, Jake, and Jerry combined, but still, Scott won't give me a chance to show what I can really do 'cause I'm a woman."

"Don't go always thinkin' that the grass on the other side is greener, babe."

"It just pisses me off. I mean, I know that Brian is the middle man and that's why Scott needs you. If he gets rid of Brian, he ain't got a clue how to do what he does, but he does want to figger out who supplies Brian."

"So he needs me for that, huh?"

"Yeah, he needs you, man."

"And why are you tellin' me all this?"

"Well, it's 'cause, well . . . ."

Brett didn't need to hear the rest — Beth told her all that because she trusted and liked Brett.

After dropping Beth off, Brett looked at her watch and realized she had some time before she had to get ready for the night. She was to meet Kathy at eight at the Moran residence, and it was only four now. She needed a nice quiet place to think and prepare her plans for that night so she drove out to the river. Later she'd have to go home, grab her gun, and try to wire herself with the tape recorder before going to Kathy's. Kathy had given her the key, so that, if she was delayed, Brett would not have to wait outside. Brett figured that between eight and midnight she could stop at Madeline's to pick up Allie and bring her along for the meeting, as well as to inform her about all that had occurred that day. She'd keep Allie hidden so no one would know she was there. Brett wanted her for backup.

It was as Brett was thinking that, perhaps, she should let Allie wire her, as wiring herself was such a pain in the ass, that she realized she was being followed. She had been aware of the dark blue Chevy for some time, but until now it hadn't clicked that it was deliberately following her. She silently cursed at herself for not having a gun handy, but then told herself that she was no easily scared teenager. Not only could she easily outrun that vehicle, but she also knew how to lose a tail. First, though, she needed to know who was following her.

Brett was parked by the river for a full five minutes before she saw the figure watching her from the bushes. She climbed out of the Jimmy, sat on the same rock Kathy had sat on so recently, and pretended to stare at the lake. In reality, however, she had positioned herself to watch the lurking figure with her peripheral vision.

After a while, Brett stood, stretched, and pretended to go into the bushes to pee, but instead, she went through them to approach the hidden figure from behind. Even from a distance, Brett recognized the build, the stance, and the short brown hair.

"Randi McMartin," Brett said, without thinking, relieved that it wasn't someone looking for a fight. She knew that, at this moment, Randi had not identified her as Brett Higgins, nor did she have anything on her. So Randi was a lot less harmful than, say, Brian Ewing or Thompson. Of course, neither of them would have the patience or the know-how for the careful surveillance Randi was conducting.

"Brett Jameson," Randi said, turning to face Brett. "If that is your name." She didn't seem particularly surprised by Brett's sudden appearance behind her.

"And what would make you think it wasn't?" Brett asked, leveling her gaze on Randi.

"Maybe that you have no police record." Randi advanced on Brett.

"All that means is that I ain't the troublemaker you take me for," Brett explained with a grin.

"Well, then," Randi continued, looking Brett up and down. "Maybe the fact that Madeline Jameson's only brother is alive and well and gay —"

"Because my father is dead," Brett commented, circling Randi.

"I may not be able to say who you are," Randi replied, "but I know that I know you and that I intend to figure it out."

"Before I vanish in a puff of smoke, eh?"

Randi stepped right into her face. "Just know that your ass is mine," she said starkly.

"Sorry, hon," Brett said facetiously with a snap of her fingers. "You're not my type." With that she stalked back to her vehicle and left in a cloud of dirt.

Although it took her almost two hours, Brett finally lost Randi in Lansing and East Lansing after making several stops, including two Chinese restaurants, one adult bookstore, one general bookstore, and an art institute, as well as driving through all of the traffic circles on campus. She figured she would totally confuse Randi while she was at it.

Randi swore to herself as she glared around in all directions. The bastard was nowhere to be seen. She cruised the streets hoping to catch sight of him again, although she didn't think she would. He knew more than most teens, having been able to lose her without a high speed chase or any accidents. Most kids would've just run like hell. Not Brett Jameson, though. He methodically tried to confuse her by stopping at a wide array of establishments, without any rhyme or reason, doubling back, going below the speed limit, and taking a few quick turns.

Randi headed back to Alma, figuring that was where he had probably gone. She would drive by the hangouts and the homes of his friends to see if she could spot his vehicle, although she expected it to be a fruitless search.

This kid had gotten under her skin. The only real clue she had was that Frankie Lorenzini knew him and had said Brett Jameson had worked for him. Beyond that, she found nothing. She was beginning to think that Brett, Allie, and Madeline Jameson were all in this together, even though she couldn't find the connection.

Allie. That was one inconspicuous figure she wanted to look at more closely. Up until now, she really hadn't had a chance to do so. It seemed that the matters to do with Brett were of far greater importance. But Allison Jameson . . . Randi considered the quick glimpse she had had of the girl, the flash of blond hair, the aristocratic features. If she didn't know better, she'd say that was really Allie Sullivan. If she didn't know her Allie was twenty-seven, if she didn't know her Allie would never get involved with something like this. She knew Brett Jameson was part of the drug problem at Alma High, and she knew Allie Sullivan would never become involved with the drug trade.

Was she forever to be haunted by Allie and Brett? Was that to be her lot in life? Because she would swear that these two were really Allie Sullivan and Brett Higgins.

She pulled over to the side of the road, leaned back in her seat, and stared out the windshield.

This was it, she decided, she had really lost it. She was looking at an adolescent boy and seeing Brett Higgins. An adolescent boy. Not only was Brett Higgins female, Randi had never even known her when she was younger, and by now she'd be in her thirties and, for crissake, she was dead! Randi had seen them remove her toasted corpse from the building. She had gone to her funeral!

As for Allie . . . Okay, fine. This girl had the same name, but Randi had really only seen her from a distance, and lots of people looked like other people. It was a simple fact. Randi had had people walk up to her in elevators and say something that made it clear they were positive she was somebody else.

Her boss had said she was obsessed with Brett and Allie, but she had always claimed she had her reasons. But this was it. She had to accept the fact that she was obsessed, even after all these years.

She might as well pack up her bags and go home, because she couldn't function properly, do her job well, if she could not get over this. But she couldn't let Jake down. She had sworn to herself that she would help him, and she would.

She just had to come to terms with the fact that Brett was dead and Allie was never again going to be in her life.

She started the car and headed back toward Alma, where she could continue her investigation. But she would not attempt to locate Brett Jameson. She would force herself to realize there were other leads and ideas to follow up on. It was only a coincidence that Brett's and Allie's names were Brett and Allie.


As Brett drove back to Alma, she looked at her watch and cursed. She didn't have time to stop home before meeting Kathy, especially since she would have to switch cars so she could hide the Jimmy in Kathy's parents' garage, just in case Randi decided to drive by.

Just as she was finished switching the cars, Kathy pulled up and parked in the driveway.

"What's up?" Kathy asked suspiciously, seeing that her mother's car was parked in the driveway.

Brett nervously looked around. "I had to hide my car," she explained, trying to get Kathy into the house. The night was drawing near, and she was afraid she wouldn't notice Randi driving by in time, and she didn't have the time to lose her again.

"But my folks didn't leave their keys," Kathy complained as Brett dragged her toward the house.

Brett shrugged. "I hot-wired it."

"You can't hide from us, Jameson," Thompson said as he came around the corner to yank the door from Kathy's hands and enter the house.

Brett turned around in surprise and felt Thompson's fist hit her stomach as she saw Brian enter behind him. Kathy cried out as Brian pushed her against a wall and closed the door behind him.

Although winded, Brett pulled herself up and jumped to kick Brian in the chest, but Brian moved too fast. Kathy tried to hit him, but he threw her across the room as Thompson slugged Brett in the face. Brian grabbed Brett around the neck and slammed her headfirst into a wall before bringing his knee up into her chin. Kathy flew at Brian, but he tossed her over his shoulder and carried her into the living room, where he dumped her onto the floor and closed the drapes.

Thompson grabbed Brett in a headlock and dragged her into the living room where he pushed her forward into the carpeting. Brett darted to her feet, to kick Thompson in the groin, but Brian grabbed a table and brought it down on Brett's head.

When she came to a few minutes later, Brett saw that Kathy had a sock in her mouth and was handcuffed to the couch. She tried to jump to her feet, but her legs weren't working quite right. Thompson grabbed her from behind and pinned her arms behind her. She couldn't get the footing to toss him off.

"So this is what you left me for?" Brian said to Kathy, slapping Brett across the face. "You wanna see what I think of him?" he asked, slamming Brett in the stomach with his fist. Brett cried out as her knees started to buckle.

Kathy looked on in horror as Brian repeatedly pounded his fists into Brett's stomach and chest and face.

# 16

"Oh God, Brett?"

The world felt dark. "Hruaoooaaahhh?" Brett said, barely able to open her eyes. When she did, she saw Kathy's face, looking into her own with deep concern.

"Brett?" Kathy asked. "Are you okay?"

"Did you get the license number?" Brett murmured, trying to grin even though it hurt like hell.

"Oh god," Kathy moaned. "I'll get an ambulance," she said, standing.

"No!" Brett cried, trying to sit up. She threw an arm out to grab Kathy's leg. "Fuck," she said as pain coursed through her body.

"You need an ambulance," Kathy said, crouching by her. She was disheveled, her shirt was torn, her mouth was swollen, and one eye was bruised.

"No," Brett said. "I'm fine. No ambulances. No police."

"You need help."

"Did they do anything to you?" Brett asked, remembering the words of this afternoon.

"No, they didn't, but you . . ."

"I'll be fine," Brett said, trying to sit up.

"But —" Kathy argued.

"Listen, you can't just call an ambulance. They'll bring the cops." Her mind wandered. She was vaguely aware of Kathy's soft hands on her, Kathy's concerned eyes. "No cops," she said. The next time she woke, she felt a warmth and softness surrounding her.

She tried to lift herself, then realized she was in bed with Kathy, her head pillowed on Kathy's breast, her body cradled in Kathy's arms.

"What time is it?" Brett mumbled, feeling a pounding headache beating at her temple as she tried to lift her head.

"Two A.M.," Kathy replied, guiding Brett's head down again.

"Fuck," Brett said, giving in to Kathy and lying back on the softness. "I need a phone," she said.

Kathy told Brett she had called Jerry and that he had contacted Madeline to tell her that Brett was spending the night at his house.

"Did you tell him what happened?" Brett murmured. Her stomach flopped and her head pounded.

"No. He probably thinks we're celebrating your birthday."

Brett knew what it meant to Kathy to tell someone else they were sleeping together. Teenage girls never liked to admit such things for fear of what that would label them. But the thought barely had time to register with Brett before she had to run to the bathroom to puke. Kathy held her as she disgorged, then helped her stand, wash her face, brush her teeth, and take some aspirin.

"You need to rest," Kathy said, guiding her toward the bed.

"I need to call Scott," Brett murmured, reaching for the phone. It rang several before Scott's dad drunkenly answered. No, Scott was not home.

"What did you do that you didn't want me to call the police?" Kathy asked as she helped Brett into bed.

"I just don't like cops," Brett mumbled before she passed out again.

~ ~ ~ ~ ~

It seemed like mere minutes later when Brett heard a noise and woke up. She felt much better. Sitting up, she heard the shower running and pulled on her shoes and socks, the only pieces of her clothing she wasn't wearing. Thankfully, Kathy had not undressed her. She walked over to the dresser and used one of Kathy's brushes to comb her hair, wincing when it touched the bruises and bumps. As she was inspecting her cuts and bruises in the mirror, Kathy entered the room wearing only a towel. Brett's heart skipped a beat, but she wanted to cry when she noticed the bruises on Kathy's arms, legs, and face.

"Oh," Kathy said. "You're awake."

Brett looked directly at her. "Yes, I am."

"How're you feeling?" Kathy asked, walking over to her.

"Much better, thank you," Brett replied, letting her eyes slide over Kathy's body. "I still have a bit of a headache, though," she admitted, reaching out to touch Kathy's face lightly.

"There's some more aspirin in the bathroom."

"You're nuts if you think I'm leaving you right now." Brett picked Kathy gently up off the floor and lay her on the bed, lying on top of her, feasting on her mouth.

"You recover fast," Kathy said. Brett's leg was between hers, Brett's thigh pressed into her crotch. Brett looked down at her and grinned.

"We're gonna look like the terrible two tonight at the prom," she said, running her hand over Kathy's scratched and bruised face.

"Are you still up to it?" Kathy asked.

"Can't let them know they slowed me down at all," Brett said, thinking she had to talk with Allie as the day before came rushing back to her. She looked down at Kathy and realized this was probably the last time alone together that they would have. She ran her hand over Kathy's face as she moved to lie by her side.

"Brett," Kathy began, pulling away.

"What?" Brett said softly, concerned.

"I need to tell you something," Kathy breathed, turning on her side to study Brett's face. "Last night, when Brian and Thompson were beating you, when you wouldn't let me call an ambulance, but

178

let me hold you, and I was scared, and you wouldn't even let me put my dad's pajamas on you . . ."

"What, Kathy?"

"I realized that . . . I do love you, Brett."

Kathy said it so innocently, so completely. Brett had always had trouble saying that phrase herself, so it always took her unawares when someone else said it to her, even though Kathy was the third person in her life who had said it. Her parents had never said it, nor had her brothers. She had never told Storm that she loved her, nor had she told Allie until it was almost too late. Brett thought of Allie, then thought of Storm. She looked into Kathy's eyes. Brett leaned over and kissed Kathy, letting her hands wander down Kathy's naked shoulders, enjoying the warmth of her skin.

Brett knew it was wrong, she knew she shouldn't . . .

"I love you, Kathy," she whispered, barely audible, saying it as much to herself as to Kathy. It was an admission as much as it was a statement.

She reached down and undid the towel tied just above Kathy's breasts, keeping eye contact as she opened the towel completely. She realized Kathy was looking at her in stunned amazement, barely breathing. She wondered if Kathy had ever been totally revealed, in full light, to anyone before.

"You are so beautiful," she whispered.

Kathy moaned slightly as Brett ran her fingertips over her body, circling the enlarged nipples, tracing her inner thighs.

"I want you," Brett whispered into Kathy's ear. Brett brought her mouth to Kathy's chest. Kathy arched her body upward.

Brett knelt between Kathy's legs, looking down at the wonder spread in front of her. Kathy leaned forward slightly to tug at Brett's belt and zipper.

"No," Brett said, moving Kathy's hands. "I want this to be different from anything else . . . I want to be different." Brett brought her head down between Kathy's legs.

"Oh my god!" Kathy cried, pulling herself away after Brett barely touched her clit with her tongue.

Brett rested her hands on Kathy's hips, keeping Kathy from moving further away. "Relax," Brett said with a gentle grin. "Just relax."

"What are you doing?" Kathy asked, trembling and embarrassed as she tried to close her legs.

Brett lay down on top of her and whispered in her ear "I want to taste you, to feel you with my tongue."

"Oh god," Kathy groaned, as Brett again knelt between her legs and laid her tongue on Kathy's clit.

The warm sensation from Brett's tongue shot up through Kathy's stomach and down through her thighs. Kathy tried to relax, but Brett's warm breath kept her nerves on edge. She looked down and saw Brett's dark head between her legs. Kathy's body involuntarily arched up as she moaned aloud.

"Oh god, Brett, what're you doin' to me?" She moaned, gasping for breath. She spread her legs even farther. "Please . . ." Kathy moaned, "please, Brett . . ."

Brett brought her tongue up Kathy's clit, then sucked the swollen flesh into her mouth, beating across it with a swift, hard pattern. Kathy flung her body across the bed; Brett hung on, her mouth glued to Kathy. Kathy fell screaming over the brink of orgasm.

Brett ran into Madeline's house, jumped into the shower, and cleaned herself up, trying to be as gentle with her battered flesh as she could. She climbed out of the shower, ran a handful of gel through her hair, dressed, and looked at her watch. Second hour had just ended.

When Brett returned to Kathy's house thirty minutes later, she noticed a strange car parked out front. She circled the block, then parked in front of a neighbor's house before approaching the Moran residence.

She peeked in through the front windows but couldn't make out much. She walked around the house, peering in where she could. Everyone appeared to be in the kitchen. She finally walked up to the front door, braced herself, and opened it. She didn't want to knock because she wanted the element of surprise if it was Brian and Thompson again.

Kathy was sitting at the kitchen table; a middle-aged man and woman stood in the center of the room.

"Uh, hi," Brett said. She had been prepared for physical combat, not the combat of meeting Kathy's parents.

"Kathy, who is this?" the man said without moving.

"Mom, Dad," Kathy said, moving to stand next to Brett. "This is Brett Jameson — Ms. Jameson's nephew that I was telling you about."

"I am so very pleased to meet you, sir," Brett said, reaching out to shake Mr. Moran's hand. Brett then turned, took Mrs. Moran's hand, bowed lightly, and kissed it as she said, "I can see where Kathy gets her astonishing good looks from, ma'am."

"He is good," Mrs. Moran remarked to her daughter with a slight smile.

"Is my presentation that transparent?" Brett queried, taking a step back and flashing an impish grin.

"We're in advertising, son," Mr. Moran remarked. "We're accustomed to being the ones feeding people the lines."

"I'm Sally, and this is my husband, Rob," Kathy's mom said, introducing themselves. "He'll give you a bit of trouble because he liked his daughter dating the captain of the football team," she continued, referring to Rob, "but I always thought Brian Ewing was . . . less than what Kathy deserves."

"Their plane came in a bit early," Kathy explained.

"She was telling us all about you," Rob said, "and about last night, and about giving Brian his walking papers."

"I wasn't happy with him, Daddy," Kathy said. Brett slipped a protective arm about her waist. Both Rob and Sally watched the movement, but Brett didn't give.

"You're different," Rob said, eyeing Brett. "If I looked only at your apparel, I would give *you* your walking papers . . ."

"Rob!" Sally said.

"Looks can be deceiving, Rob," Brett said, using his given name with deliberation. "But I clean up quite well."

"But why wouldn't you go to the hospital last night?" Sally asked, her eyes full of concern as she assessed Brett's black eye and bruised cheeks.

"It's a long story, Sally, but basically, if we went to the cops right now it'd be fruitless. Just our word against theirs. They'd try to make it look like Kat and I got into a fight ourselves and were just trying to blame it on them."

"You've obviously been watching a lot of TV," Rob said.

"But he is right," Sally argued. "We have no proof it was Alma's pride and joy that did this."

"I don't want to pull Kathy out of Alma High," Rob said.

"You don't have to," Brett said, stepping up to him. "Give me until Monday."

"Big words from such a little man."

"I come from Detroit, which is an ocean to Alma's pond. I'm gonna fuck with these boys so badly they'll think they got it up the ass from King Kong himself. It's not just what they did to us last night. They've also brought a lot of drugs and crime to Alma."

"Why should we trust you?" Sally asked while exchanging questioning looks with her husband.

"Who else are you gonna trust?" Brett countered, knowing that time was running out. She still didn't even have a plan, and they were already pushing on fourth period.

"Nobody hurts my little girl," Rob said.

"I'm not going to hurt her, Mr. Moran. My goal is to help her, and everyone else who deserves a chance. I've seen the signs, man, I know where these things go."

"And how do you know this?"

"I've been there, I've done that. Mom was hoping to get me straightened out by sending me out here. I've done things I'm not proud of, and I was hoping to get a new start out here, but, apparently, I need to atone for my sins of the past by fixing this before I can go on," Brett said. She was trying not to lie, because she knew only the truth would get her what she wanted from these people, but she couldn't tell them too much.

"So you're saying . . ." Rob began.

"I'm saying that even though I'm only nineteen, I know where this shit leads. I know what's going on. I saw one of my old bosses get her brains blown out," she continued, embellishing with what

Beth and Scott's gang thought was the truth. "And I don't want that to be me, or anyone I care about. I'm a bad kid from the wrong side of the tracks, trying to make good and hoping you'll help me do that." She squeezed Kathy's hand.

"Is there anything else?" Sally asked, evaluating the situation.

"Yeah," Brett said, grinning while she concocted a lie. "My dad was a media buyer for J. Walter Thompson in Detroit before he took to the bottle, so you should have pity on someone who grew up in that sort of environment."

"Oh you poor thing!" Sally cried.

# 17

Becky was walking to school because Scott hadn't gotten up on time to drive her. She figured since it was closing in on the end of the school year, she oughta try to get to class a bit more. And this way she had a chance to go to the fields behind the school and have a private joint. Sometimes it was nice to get stoned alone because it gave her a chance to think.

If she remembered right, the log she used to sit on when she was just a frosh was just ahead . . . Becky figured that it didn't really matter if she found that exact spot, not really. After all, what did anything matter?

About twenty feet away, Paul and Harry wandered through the

dew-covered grass, carefully peering about for interesting specimens to dissect in their favorite class, biology.

Harry looked at his watch. "We should get going, or else we'll be late to school," he said, pushing his glasses up his nose.

"Just a few more minutes," Paul said, going deeper into the trees toward the creek. "I'm sure if we go down by the creek, we'll find something really cool." He went into the trees.

Harry was leaning down to tie his shoe when he heard the terrified scream. It sent chills through his body. Then he heard Paul's frantic voice from the same direction, "Shit, Harry! Get over here!"


Brett squealed into the parking lot.

"Fuck!" she said emphatically as she pulled into an empty spot and looked at her watch. They would already be in fifth hour. She needed to get with Allie to tell her everything that had happened since yesterday morning and lay out everything they needed to do to be ready for tonight.

"What's the matter, honey?" Kathy asked.

"I need to get with Allie."

"She's in my fifth hour. I can tell her to meet you after school."

Brett reluctantly agreed.

"Brett?" Kathy said, stopping Brett from exiting the Jimmy. "I wish you'd tell me what is going on."

"I wish I could, too, babe," Brett said, looking into her deep brown eyes, "but . . ." she shrugged off the rest of her sentence.

"I can't believe my folks bought all that," she finally said, laying her head on Brett's shoulder.

"I think they don't really realize just how high the stakes are," Brett said, wrapping her arms around Kathy's slender frame and burying her face in the halo of Kathy's hair.

Kathy pulled back and looked into Brett's eyes. "Just who are you?"

"Someone who's far older than mere years can reveal," Brett answered truthfully with a resigned sigh.

~ ~ ~ ~ ~

Things were going better than he ever could have hoped; he was barely able to hide his smile as his students entered the classroom. He usually didn't mix business with pleasure, but this was special. He was thoroughly enjoying himself. He became increasingly excited when he remembered last night, the look of shock on the boy's face when he recognized the faculty member, the way the blood had gurgled up in the boy's throat as he lay dying. He remembered it as if it were happening again and relished each moment as he considered that last night had been a mere appetizer to tonight's main course.

He usually didn't let his partners know much, because he didn't want any evidence lying about when he left town, but he justified Brian's growing knowledge with the fact that Brian wouldn't be around to tell anybody his story when it was all done.

Almost snickering at his own ingenuity, he thought about the money he had at home, money that he had stashed there from his local bank account, which he had just all but cleared out. More money then he had ever made elsewhere. Money that was just the tip on the iceberg of what he would have when he sold tonight's videos of the drugged girls.

He had already given some of the drugs to Brian, and he himself had some tucked safely in his pant pocket. He reached down to finger the vial, his pleasure growing as he considered how he would later use it.

He was glad he had so carefully chosen the Roofies earlier. It had all of the effects he wanted, needed. It wouldn't knock the girls out; it would leave them active and able to react — and make them uninhibited and sexually aroused regardless of gender. Everything he needed.

Life was good.


When Brett walked into shop class, Carl Rogers glanced up.

"You're late," he said with a smirk as he assessed her physical condition.

"I had some problems," she said, laying her pass from the office on his desk.

"I can tell," he replied, still smirking. As she turned to join her friends, he continued. "Y'know, Jameson," he said, "you can't win all the fights."

She turned and met his eyes. "I know, but I sure as hell can try."

"My boys know how to take care of themselves and what belongs to them."

Brett stared at him. You bastard, she thought, I know you're at the bottom of this, and now all I've got to do is prove it. You'll show your true colors tonight.

She figured she'd get Allie to detain Brian that night, probably ask Madeline to take pictures of Allie and Brian while Brett used the time to break into Brian's bedroom. He was bound to have some sort of evidence that would implicate himself and probably Rogers as well.

Then, when Rogers was chaperoning the prom, she would search his house as well. She kicked herself for not thinking of searching Rogers's house earlier that day. If she did it now there was too much risk he'd get home before she was done. He had a sixth period prep, so he might head home after fifth hour.

Her final, alternate plan, in case all else went wrong, was to let Kathy and Allie play tonight's game — because she was sure tonight was the night Brian hoped to make the videos. She would watch until everyone involved was implicated to some extent. She wanted to nail the sons of bitches.

Not much of a plan, she admitted to herself, but it was all she had. She was gambling on the fact that all the boys involved were too amateurish to cover themselves. With last night's ruckus, she had lost valuable time. There was always tomorrow and next week, but she wasn't sure how much longer she could keep this charade going before it all came tumbling in on her. Plus, not even over her decayed carcass would anyone ever get away with doing anything like that to Allie or again to Kathy. Images of the video she had seen the day before flashed through her mind.

Beth's eyes were wide as she sat down. "Have you seen Scott?" she asked Brett.

"No, why?" Brett asked, wondering what was going on. The entire group was fixated on her.

"We haven't seen or heard from him all day," Jake said, his voice low, secretive.

"He did make it to the meeting last night, didn't he?" Steve asked.

"I dunno," Brett admitted, as the group huddled together to talk in whispered tones. "I didn't."

"Whaddya mean you didn't make it?" Steve yelled, furious. The rest of the class turned to look at them.

"Is there a problem?" Carl asked from the front of the room.

"No, no problem," Jerry replied. The group split up under Carl's baleful stare and quietly began working.

"Whaddya mean you didn't make it?" Steve asked a few moments later.

"I was unavoidably detained," Brett explained. Something wasn't being said.

"Fuck, man," Jake murmured. "Scott was like counting on you being there, man."

"You left him to the dogs so you could get laid?" Jerry asked, his eyes wide in wonder.

"I left him to the dogs because I was unconscious," Brett clarified. "Bri and his thugs beat the crap outta me."

"Shit," Steve said, looking up at the ceiling. "Shit, shit, shit."

"What's the matter?" Brett asked, her mind jumping to all the worst conclusions.

"What's the matter is he knew I was outta product but had sales to make today 'cuz of the prom —"

"And none of us has seen or heard from him since yesterday evening," Beth continued.

"He was countin' on you bein' there, man," Steve said, "and now he's disappeared."

"No, no, they couldn't," Brett began.

"Look, man," Jake said, cutting her off. "He's been pushin' all the wrong buttons with these dudes, gettin' 'em real pissed, and now he's gone."

Randi McMartin entered the classroom, looked around briefly, met Brett's eyes, and walked up to Carl's desk. They spoke briefly in hushed tones, and he nodded several times before Randi walked over to Brett.

"I need you to come with me," she said, looking down at where Brett was sitting.

"And what if I don't want to?" Brett asked, raising her eyebrow in a dare.

"Then I'd suggest we discuss it outside the classroom," Randi replied, her tone dark. Brett picked up her books and followed Randi into the corridor. Randi closed the door behind them.

"I have two plainclothes cops waiting outside," Randi began. "I suggest you come along peacefully."

"Are you arresting me?"

"No, I just want to talk with you."

"Then there's no way you can make me go with you."

"You're right," Randi said, nodding. "But I strongly suggest you do, because any cooperation you show to this investigation will be in your favor."

"And just what, specifically, is this investigation about?"

A few minutes later Brett was sitting in the Alma Police Department's interviewing room. She sat back in her chair, studying the bare walls, and lit a cigarette as she watched Randi briefly confer with a uniformed officer. When he left the room, Randi sat at the other end of the table and lit her own cigarette.

"What did you do between two P.M. yesterday and at seven A.M. today?"

Brett ran a hand through her short hair. "After school, I watched the cheerleaders and soccer team for a few minutes, then I drove Beth home and we talked briefly. You know what I did for the next several hours," she continued with a smirk, "because you were following me."

"Then what did you do?"

"I went to Kathy Moran's, hid my car in her garage, started to enter the house, but was delayed."

"How so?"

"I got the shit kicked outta me, so I spent the next several hours unconscious."

"Oh really? Who did it?"

"Some guys who don't like me much."

"Why didn't you go to the hospital?"

Brett shrugged. "Didn't want to."

"Tough guy, huh?" Randi clearly assessed Brett's bruises. "Not too tough, though, from the looks of you now."

Brett didn't say a word.

"So you woke up when?"

"I briefly came to a coupla times through the night, but didn't really fully regain consciousness until about eight A.M."

"Did you have any plans made for last night?"

"It's my turn now," Brett remarked with a grin. "You've got to answer a couple of questions before I'll say anything more. What is this investigation about?"

Randi regarded her, then seemed to reach a decision. "A body was found this morning in the woods."

"Whose body?" When Randi didn't immediately respond, Brett continued. "You've got my alibi — you and Kathy Moran, with whom I spent the night. A murder is something that quickly becomes common knowledge in a town this size."

"Scott Campbell," Randi replied, still staring at Brett. "His girlfriend, Becky, found his body this morning. She and two other students. Two boys."

Brett got up and paced. Randi leaned back in her chair and watched. Brett had guessed the body was Scott Campbell's, but she had needed verification. Brett knew she already had the upper hand. Randi probably figured she was talking with some green teenager, not an adult who couldn't count on all her fingers and toes the number of times the cops had pulled her in for questioning.

"You must have some clout," Brett said meditatively, "to get this sort of cooperation from another police department."

"They know I'm five steps ahead of them. They also know it's better to have me involved than anybody else." Brett knew Randi was convinced she knew Brett, but she didn't know how or from where. "We don't have the autopsy results yet, but Jake said that Scott was in class yesterday."

"I was supposed to meet some people with Scott last night," Brett replied, realizing she had to give in order to get. "He didn't tell me who or where. Just that I was supposed to meet him at midnight."

"And you missed the meeting?"

"And I missed the meeting," Brett verified. What she was giving Randi was only what Randi could easily discover herself. But the only reason she played this game was because she knew the clock was ticking. She glanced down at her watch.

"You gotta be somewhere?" Randi said, noting the gesture.

"I'm supposed to meet my sister after school."

"Ah, your 'sister,' " Randi mused. "Your other half." She stood and walked a bit closer to Brett before sitting on the edge of the table. "I'm not entirely convinced that you two are who you say you are, or that you two are even related."

"I think, therefore I am," Brett replied, sitting down in her chair and kicking her feet up on the table. She lit another cigarette and held the ashtray in her lap. She looked up at Randi. "We were born at Providence Hospital in Southfield," she said as she casually ran her hand through her hair.

"Then what about the fact that Madeline Jameson's only sibling is a single man who's living in Alaska?"

"We're the children of her bastard brother. He took his father's name when he was twenty-one."

"And what about Brett Higgins and Frankie Lorenzini?" Randi asked with a smirk.

"What about them?" Brett shot back.

"What did you do for them?"

"How do you know I ever even met them?"

"Besides your reaction to my question, Jake asked me about them and on a whim I called Frankie and asked about you. He had all sorts of wonderful things to say on the subject of Brett Jameson."

"Well, there you go," Brett replied with a wave of her hand as she leaned farther back in her chair. "You have proof that I am who I say I am."

"You haven't answered my question."

"What is it you're getting at, Randi?" Brett said, standing and facing her. "First you question who I am, then you tell me I've worked for some interesting people."

"What I'm getting at, whoever you are, is that I know you and your sister. If I can ever catch up with her, I'm sure I'll get it figured out. What I'm getting at is that I know somebody's on top of these kids — and nobody'd ever suspect Madeline Jameson. What I'm getting at is that maybe she pulled in some professional help."

"You live in one real screwed-up reality, Randi McMartin. You wouldn't know the truth if it fucked you up the ass!" Brett barked as she slammed out of the room.


Randi watched the door slam shut. She pounded the table. "Fuck!" She slammed her fist into the wall. "Fuck!" She grabbed the chair and tossed it across the room. "Fuck, fuck, fuck!" she screamed, pissed at herself for losing control, angry that she let some smart-ass kid get the better of her, enraged that she knew she was missing some crucial part of the puzzle that she knew was right under her nose.

The officer came back into the room. "Is everything all right in here?"

"Yeah, everything's all right," Randi growled as she pulled a handkerchief out of her pocket. She reached over and grabbed Brett's ashtray. "Be careful with this. Within an hour I need to know whose fingerprints are on it."

"I'm not sure —"

"Just do it!" she yelled. "I'll be back." She brusquely left the room.

She needed time alone. She knew she was missing something, something crucial. Nothing was fitting into place. Not only had she already failed monumentally, failed as soon as Scott Campbell had collapsed to the ground, dead, but she topped that off by losing it with Brett Jameson. She knew the son-of-a-bitch wasn't who he said he was, and she knew the two of them had met in Detroit. And she knew that, for whatever reason, he got under her skin.

She drove through town, replaying the interview in her head, wondering how she had gone from bargaining with a stupid teenager to losing her temper and her cool. She reanalyzed his every word and gesture. A vision of him running his hand through his hair flashed back at her. Who else had that gesture? That particular way?

Who else had those eyes? She knew the answer: Brett Higgins. She had studied the woman for far too long not to know that. But Brett Higgins was dead.

It could be Brett's younger brother, but that just didn't make any sense. And what would Allie be doing here with him, if that was indeed Allison Sullivan? None of it made much sense.

Randi thought back to that night. She herself had heard the shots, had seen the lightning, had seen them carrying the mutilated and burned corpse out of the building several hours later.

Randi visualized the barely intact hand falling off the stretcher, saw the flickering lights glinting off the stone. That was Brett's ring, all right, but who said Brett had been the one wearing it? They hadn't been able to get any other ID off of the corpse — its dentistry had been destroyed by Allie shooting it right in the mouth. The corpse had been pretty well destroyed and unidentifiable. But she knew what had happened and what Allie had done and who had been on that rooftop. Didn't she?

# 18

Kathy got out of gym class and went to wait for Brett at their prearranged spot. She was supposed to have brought Allie with her, but Allie had left school early to go shopping with Brian. Brian wanted her to have a new dress for the prom, and he wanted to pick it out for her. What a control freak.

Kathy figured Brian wanted to show off Allie. Plus, his male ego would've kicked him for letting her wear a dress she'd worn for any other man. Kathy knew a lot about how Brian thought these days, although she couldn't figure out where he got so much money. She knew he had never had a job. He said his folks gave it to him, but she didn't think they could afford to give him as much as he had.

She glanced down at her watch again. The seniors who didn't have a sixth-period class had already left the building, so the hallways were now almost empty. Most people who were going to prom had left to pick up their tuxes and dresses and get ready.

She saw a familiar face. "Beth!" she called out, hoping that her old friend would know where Brett was.

"Yeah, Kat?" Beth said, looking around her as she approached Kathy. Brett and Beth were the only two people who ever called Kathy by that particular nickname.

"Did Brett go to shop class today?" Kathy asked, even while she remembered the way Beth's eyes used to glimmer with excitement when something new or exciting was happening. If she had ever thought she might have made some wrong choices, she now realized that Beth most certainly had as well. A dark cloud shrouded her personality.

"Yeah, but he left early," Beth replied, still looking around. The guys would never let her live it down if they caught her talking with such a frou frou, even though Brett was now dating her.

"Why?" Kathy asked. "He was supposed to meet me and Allie here after class."

"Then where's Allie?" Beth said with a slight grin and a raised eyebrow as she glanced around. Kathy was definitely alone.

"She left to go shopping with Brian," Kathy said, glad to see the familiar smile light up Beth's face. She wondered why they had ever drifted apart.

"God, what a waste," Beth said before she thought. She was too busy noticing how deep the brown of Kathy's eyes were to do much thinking.

"Yeah, I know," Kathy admitted. "So why'd Brett leave?" she again asked. In some peculiar way, Beth reminded her a bit of Brett. She tried to brush the thought from her mind, but it lingered still, even as she remembered Brett's hands and tongue on and in her that morning.

"I don't really know," Beth replied, sitting next to Kathy on the bench. "Jake's aunt came and took him away."

"Jake's aunt?" Kathy repeated, noticing that Mr. Marin had stopped just down the hall from them to read a poster on the wall. She lowered her voice a bit. "Why?"

"I don't really know," Beth reluctantly admitted. "She and Brett don't get along."

195

"What aren't you telling me, Beth?" Kathy said, looking into Beth's eyes.

Beth sighed and put her head down in her hands. "She's a cop from Detroit."

"What's a Detroit cop doing in Alma?"

"It's a long story," Beth began, then she looked up at Kathy. "But I wouldn't expect to see Brett back real soon. Maybe I could give you a lift home?"

"Kathy Moran!" Mr. Marin cried, approaching them. "Just the girl I was looking for!" Both Beth and Kathy looked up in shock. "Brett Jameson," he clarified, "asked me to do a favor for him."

"Oh?" Kathy asked curiously.

"He had to leave, so he asked that I take you home."

"Brett asked that?" Beth said.

"He didn't know who else to ask, and we've become a bit friendly since he beat up those football players."

"Okay," Kathy said, standing. She turned and looked at Beth. "Thanks for the offer anyway."


Kathy gave directions to Mr. Marin as he drove her home.

"When we get there, I'll just wait outside while you run in and get ready . . ."

"That won't be necessary," Kathy responded.

"I'm sorry. I wasn't clear enough," Mr. Marin said. He looked over at Kathy and added with a wink, "I think Brett has a surprise for you, and I got talked into helping out."

"Really?" Kathy replied, curious, but Mr. Marin wouldn't give her any more clues. He was still formulating the story he would give her.

It took Kathy over an hour to get ready, but Mr. Marin was as good as his word in waiting for her. He had enjoyed the wait, the danger that Brett could have, at any time, shown up and revealed Marin's story as mere fiction. He also enjoyed the time alone, during which he could visualize how the rest of the evening would go.

He had worried about how he was going to get Kathy, how he might have needed to confront or fight Brett for her. But now that was all water and waste going down the toilet.

He struggled against an erection just thinking about it all.

"Madeline?" Brett said into the phone. "Can you come pick me up? I'm at the police station, and my car's at the school."

"What are you doing there?" Madeline asked, worried.

"Oh shit, not much. Randi brought me in to harass me."

"The Detroit cop?"

"It's a long story. But, also, Allie and Kathy are supposed to be waiting for me in the main hall by the library — can you grab them on your way here?"

"Allie left school just after third hour," Madeline replied. "She called to tell me she was going shopping with Brian Ewing."

"Fuck!" Brett said. "Okay, just get Kathy and get here as soon as you can."

Allie's head was spinning. Brian had talked her into the shopping expedition, and she agreed in part because she was so pissed at Brett for staying out all night. Brett had better have a damned good reason for it or else she was in more trouble than Jimmy Hoffa had ever been.

Perhaps she shouldn't have had that second glass of wine with lunch. Brian had taken her to a nice restaurant where he knew the waiter and, thus, had been allowed to order a bottle of wine. She could usually handle her alcohol, but maybe she was coming down with something.

Brian turned to her. "Allie, are you okay?" he asked, his voice filled with concern.

"Yeah, just a little lightheaded is all."

He smiled. "Ah, now I know your weak point is wine. Why don't you sit down and I'll get you a cola to drink?"

Allie reluctantly agreed. They had been shopping for several hours and still had not found a dress that Brian liked. They were in a mall in . . . somewhere. She wasn't quite sure where. Funny thing, that. She was usually so good with . . . She lost her trail of thought. She knew she was sitting in a food court, and she looked up and saw Brian approaching her with a cup of soda.

"Here you go," he said, handing it to her.

She had to be coming down with something. Even her Diet Pepsi didn't taste right.

Brett dodged out of the way when she saw Randi leaving the station in a huff. She had really gotten to that woman, she thought with a smirk. Although she was worried that Randi may still figure out her true identity, she figured she had some time before that happened. Enough time, she hoped. She cared too much for too many of the people involved.

She glanced down at her watch and hoped that Madeline was hurrying.

Kathy, carrying a purse and her makeup bag, climbed into Mr. Marin's car.

"I'm so sorry for taking so long, Mr. Marin."

"It's quite all right," he replied, pulling out of the driveway, still watching for Brett's car. "I ran to the store really quick myself," he lied, enjoying the fact that she was believing everything he was telling her.

Kathy used the vanity mirror to begin liberally applying makeup to her face in hopes of covering the bruises from the night before. She had been glad when she got home and her parents weren't there. Their already questionable opinion of Brett would've surely taken a dive when he did not arrive, in appropriate attire, to pick her up himself.

~ ~ ~ ~ ~

Brett saw Madeline's car pull up, and she raced to it from her hiding place.

"My god, Brett, what have you done now?" Madeline asked.

"Where's Kathy?" Brett asked, looking into the backseat.

"She wasn't there," Madeline began.

"Fuck!" Brett cried. "Fuck!"

"I believe she left with Mr. Marin," Madeline replied.

*"Mr. Marin?"*

"I don't know why. Brett, what's happened?"

"That's not important right now. What's important now is why Kathy left with Mr. Marin."

"I ran into your friend Beth when I was at the school. Since I hadn't seen Kathy, I asked if she had seen her, and that's how I found out she had left with Mr. Marin."

Brett leaned her head back against the headrest. Mr. Marin, she thought. Could it be . . .? She had to stop and think, reanalyze all her assumptions. Okay, she asked herself, what do I know for sure? Scott Campbell is dead. He and his gang were the bottom rung, the street people. Someone killed Scott, a someone she assumed to be Brian. She knew Brian was a rung above Scott.

All of this she based on her own knowledge, plus what had been said by others, like Beth. Scott himself had alluded to the fact that there were several rungs in this ladder.

She had assumed the top local man was Carl Rogers. Why? He was fairly new and he would've spent some time gaining both the trust of his football players and insights into the hierarchy of the school. He would have, then, started making his moves last fall, just when the shit started to hit the fan. Plus, she didn't like the man. He had known about last night and had sneered at her because of it. He was a misogynistic asshole. He was evil.

But if he was responsible, would he really make it that obvious? To have it all start so soon after he began at the school? Or would whoever was responsible wait until someone else started?

"Maybe Beth knows where they went?" Madeline meekly suggested, aware that Brett was deep in thought.

"What?" Brett asked, shaking her head as she looked at Madeline.

"I said, maybe Beth knows where they went."

"Maddy," Brett said. "I need you to do me a favor."


Randi looked around carefully before leaving Madeline's home with a bag filled with a hair brush, lipsticks , and other items that she had found in the room she supposed to be Allie's. She drove swiftly to the police station and quickly found the man she was looking for, who said they didn't have any information yet. She walked into the chief's office and picked up the phone.

A phone rang downstate in the office of Greg Morrow, Randi's immediate supervisor. He answered on the third ring.

"Greg Morrow," he said, his voice brusque.

"Greg, this is Randi. I need you to do me a favor," she began, her voice matching his in abruptness. "I have two sets of fingerprints here —"

"Randi, I thought you were on vacation."

"I am. But I need to know something."

"Whaddya need?"

"I want you to check these fingerprints against those of Allison Sullivan and Brett Higgins."

Greg sighed. "Randi, Brett Higgins is dead, has been dead for several years. Can't you just give it up already?"

"I know Brett is, but Allison Sullivan isn't, and I need to know if this is her," Randi countered. "Greg, this is important. We're dealing with murder."

Greg reluctantly agreed to postpone his weekend in order to personally supervise the identification and comparison of the fingerprints.

Randi ran through the department in Alma, dropping off the items she had recently acquired from the Jameson residence to be fingerprinted and arranging for the transmittal of the prints, via computer, to Detroit's criminal lab. Greg would have Brett's and Allie's prints on file, and because this was murder, which didn't happen very often in Alma, she had the full cooperation of the entire department.

Randi McMartin found a quiet corner and a cup of coffee. She kicked her feet up and began the wait, even though her body demanded action.


"Why don't we run in here?" Mr. Marin asked Kathy as he pulled into a fast-food restaurant. "I could use something to drink, and it looks like you could use a bathroom," he added, looking over at Kathy who was still struggling with her makeup kit and the small vanity mirror.

Kathy seemed thankful for the opportunity to properly finish her appearance.

Mr. Marin stood in line for the drinks while Kathy went to the restroom. When the drinks were ready, she hadn't come out yet. He stepped into a hidden corner.

When Kathy finally reappeared, Marin was grinning. He handed her the drink, and they went back to the car.


Beth's mother answered the door to Brett's knock. She reluctantly allowed Brett to wait in the living room as she retrieved her daughter.

"Hi," Beth said. "What's up?"

"Why'd Kathy leave with Mr. Marin?"

"He said you asked him to pick her up."

"Did he say where they were going?"

"I figured he was taking her to her place."

"Can I use your phone?" Brett asked, walking over and punching in Kathy's number. The phone rang four times, and then the answering machine picked up. Brett hung up without leaving a message.

"Fuck," Brett said. "I gotta go."

"What's the matter?" Beth said, grabbing her jacket as she followed Brett to the door.

"I'm not sure," Brett admitted as she went to her car. Beth followed.

"I'm coming with you."

"No."

"If I don't go with you, then I'll just follow you."

Brett briefly considered, knowing that she could lose Beth fairly easily, but also knowing it could be dangerous and waste valuable time. "Okay, but you've got to follow orders."

Beth agreed and they headed to the high school in the Jimmy.

Madeline Jameson knelt beside the bed, feeling under it for the boxes Brett said would be there. She felt one, pulled it out, then caught the other one and brought it out as well. She knelt, peering in at their contents.

Her mind wanted her to be surprised at what she found, but her heart told her she should've expected it.

Allie found herself standing in front of Brian wearing a dress. Her mind was fuzzy. She couldn't remember putting the dress on. He looked at her and smiled.

"That's it," he said.

Kathy rubbed at her temples.

"Headache?" Mr. Marin asked, glancing over at her.

"Yeah, it's been a long week."

He couldn't believe his luck. "As a high-school teacher," he said with a grin, "I've always found it important to keep some aspirin handy." He reached into his pocket and handed two tablets to Kathy, who took them without glancing at them.

Everything was going so smoothly. Even a fuckup like Brian couldn't screw this up. A couple more minutes of going in circles, and the pills and what was in her drink would start taking effect. Then he could go meet Brian and they could get on with the show.

He hoped Brian was drugging Allie with the proper doses. He knew how to deliver the Roofies, to ensure that this was the best night ever, but he wasn't so sure about Brian. Each girl was slightly different, so they needed to feed the Roofies to the girl slowly to find exactly how much would work correctly, how much they needed to give her to get the required reaction. The girls needed to be a little bit conscious and aware of what was happening during the filming to make a really good video. And he didn't need the girls tripping out on them or freaking.

"There's a call for you," the young officer said, pulling Randi out of her reverie. She had been thinking about the last time she had seen Allie back in Detroit. Allie had said she never wanted to see Randi again.

"Randi McMartin," Randi said, picking up the phone the cop had indicated.

"What the hell kind of stunt is this?" boomed Greg Morrow's voice.

"Whose prints are they?"

"You know damned well whose they are, Randi. You've got to get over all of that —"

"So they *are* Brett's and Allie's," Randi said. "Brett Higgins and Allison Sullivan."

"You know damned well they are. Randi, you need to take some extended —"

"Don't tell anybody about this," Randi said, hanging up the phone.

She was halfway out the door when she heard a phone ringing. She knew it was Greg; she knew he thought she was playing some sort of strange practical joke. But she also knew that she wasn't the one who was playing the joke, pulling the strings.

# 19

Fred Marin parked next to Brian's car in the motel parking lot. He led Kathy up to the room, where Brian immediately let them in.

Allie was sitting in a chair, holding a glass of wine and staring blankly forward.

"Brian?" Kathy said, squinting her eyes.

"Allie wanted us to double-date," Brian explained. "She thinks Brett and I will like each other once we get to know each other."

"Oh," Kathy said. She accepted the glass of wine Mr. Marin poured for her and took a sip.

Kathy knelt in front of Allie.

"You look really pretty tonight, Allie," Kathy said, looking up into Allie's glassy eyes.

"Thanks," Allie replied with a slight smile. "So do you." She reached down and ran a hand along Kathy's cheek.

"Just looking at them like that gives me a hard-on," Fred confided to Brian. "I'm glad I decided to come along for the filming."

"As if you don't want to have some fun yourself," Brian said.

Fred looked at the two girls. "I might decide to."

"So we're all set to go to Detroit?" Brian asked eagerly.

"Yeah," Fred said. "We're gonna have fun, tonight, my friend," he added, patting Brian on the back. "Real fun."

"Let's get this show on the road, then," Brian said. "It won't do to stay here very long. Somebody might recognize our cars once Allie and Kathy are missed."

Fred Marin agreed. He knew also that too many bodies turning up in Alma would be a very bad thing indeed.

Brett and Beth were standing by the Jimmy when Madeline pulled into the lot.

"Did you bring the boxes?" Brett said to Madeline as she climbed out of her car.

"Yes," Madeline said, pulling them out. "But I think we should go into the school for a moment," she added, looking down at them.

Brett acquiesced, and a few moments later they were sequestered in an empty classroom. Brett opened the boxes and readied herself as Beth stared in wide-eyed amazement. Brett strapped a Beretta to one calf and a knife to the other. She took off her jacket and put her shoulder holster on, checking the .357 to make sure it was loaded. She pocketed extra ammunition.

"Have you ever shot a gun?" she said, looking at Beth.

"Brett . . ." Madeline began.

"My dad used to take us hunting," Beth replied.

"It'll have to do," Brett said, handing her Allie's shoulder holster, gun, and a small Beretta for her calf. "The important thing is to get the .45 to Allie if you get the chance."

"To Allie?" Beth replied in amazement.

"Yeah, Allie."

"Brett, do you know what you're doing?" Madeline said, alarmed at the thought of Beth going out heavily armed.

"I'm punting, Madeline," Brett said forcefully, not allowing further questions. Beth decided now was not the time to question Allie's weapon experience.

As the three of them walked rapidly to the cars, Madeline asked, "Where are we going?"

"You're going home."

"No, we're coming with you," Leisa said, running up to walk alongside them.

Brett stopped and looked at Madeline and Leisa. Right now she just needed to quickly figure out where Fred and Brian had taken Kathy and Allie. If she was wrong about Fred, then there was nothing to worry about, but if she was right about him, then he wouldn't be home and there was something to worry about.

"Mr. Marin's house," Brett said, then looked at Leisa. "Do you know where he lives?"

"Yes, follow us," Leisa said. She led Madeline to her car and took the lead through the city of Alma to Fred's house.

Randi McMartin was in the left turn lane, ready to go north on Main, heading back to the Jameson residence to confront Brett and Allie. If they weren't there, she would scour the town looking for them. She looked up at the car across the street from her, the car turning left to go south on Main, and recognized the people in it. It was being driven by one of the faculty from Alma High, and in the front seat with him was the girl Randi had seen with Brett. When the car turned, Randi saw Allie and one of Jake's friends in the backseat. She made a quick decision and zipped, amidst a cacophony of horns and squealing tires, across the two lanes to her right to follow the car.

From her position carefully distanced behind the other car, she could barely make out Allie's golden halo of hair. She was certain it was her. She didn't know what to make of this, but instinct told her something was happening that wasn't good. She could only hope they would lead her to Brett.

"Did you hear that shit?" Fred Marin asked, glancing into the rearview mirror. "We're being followed — see if you can make out who the driver is."

"It's the cop," Brian replied when he glanced back.

"Fuck, we gotta deal with her," Fred replied, looking around for a good place to pull over. He saw a darkened factory on his right, so he pulled in and drove around the building, slowly at first, then racing ahead and around.

Randi slowed and pulled in, not sure if there was a back exit from the lot. She drove slowly but didn't see anybody or any exit near the back of the lot. She swore under her breath at the inefficiency of one person trying to follow another vehicle. She inched her car forward, knowing that at any moment the other car could race out the front of the lot and she wouldn't know anything because she couldn't see shit. She stopped the car and left the engine running as she got out and ran ahead to the corner of the building, using the building as cover for her and her car.

She pulled out her gun and crept forward along the side of the building.

"Drop it," said a man's voice behind her. She felt the cold steel of a gun against the back of her neck and started to raise her hands. "I said to drop it."

Randi dropped the gun, and he kicked it out of her reach. Keeping his own gun trained on her, he picked up her weapon then quickly frisked her, finding and removing her backup gun. "Now go slowly around the corner and keep your hands up." They went around the building to his car where Brian was watching the girls.

Keeping his gun on Randi, he handed Brian her gun and issued instructions to reorganize the car. When they were through, Fred had tied her hands securely with his tie and had positioned himself in the backseat between her and Allie, who sat limply behind the driver's seat. Kathy was slumped against the window in the front passenger seat.

Randi briefly wondered what was going on, until she looked into Allie's eyes. That was when she realized both girls were drugged.

Great going, McMartin, she silently swore to herself. You were so worried about what Brett Higgins was up to with Allie and Madeline that you never noticed anybody else.

Once they were inside Fred's house, Brett told everyone to spread out and search the place. They were looking for anything that might tell them where Fred had taken the girls.

"You never told me your friends had such interesting talents," Leisa said to Madeline about Brett's lock-picking abilities.

"Get to work," Brett ordered, glancing around to see where would be the most likely spot for Fred to keep any information about tonight's activities. It had been a very warm day and Fred didn't have the air conditioning on, but Brett turned cold when she turned on the light in what was obviously Fred's bedroom.

The walls were covered with pictures of Allie and Kathy — pictures of all sizes, from all angles, taken at various times throughout the day and night. There was even a picture of Kathy that Brett recognized from one of the videos. Apparently Fred had digitized and printed it for his wall. Kathy wasn't wearing anything in the picture, and all her private parts were exposed.

Brett wanted to rip the room apart, piece by piece. She wanted to destroy it, destroy any evidence of this sick and disgusting man and his obsession and perversion. And she wanted to kill him.

But first she had to track him down.

Brett went to the desk in the bedroom and started sorting through the papers there, then flipped on the computer, knowing it would take a few moments to boot up. Her mind was racing. There were four of them now, so they could split up and search the town and the surrounding areas. In a town this size, it shouldn't take them long at all.

But what if Marin had left town?

"Brett, Brett!" Leisa called, running back into the room. She stopped dead in the doorway, seeing the shrine to Allie and Kathy.

"What've you got?"

"This," Leisa said, her hand shaking when she presented Brett with a piece of paper that was lightly shaded with a pencil so that three numbers stood out in white, all with area code 313.

"He had a pad of paper next to the phone, so I shaded it with a pencil and" — she studied the walls — "and I thought Carl was an evil bastard," Leisa said, standing next to Brett and taking the room in.

Brett took the paper and studied the number. Something in the back of her mind scratched at her. "Shit," she said glancing at her watch as she realized just where they were headed. "C'mon everyone!" she yelled, gathering them in the front room where she quickly drew Madeline and Leisa a map. "You two try to keep up with me, but mostly keep an eye out for any cops. We don't have time to get pulled over."

"How do you know where they're headed?" Leisa asked.

"I just do, and they've got a lead on us, so we gotta get a move on." Brett rushed to her car with Beth right behind her. Madeline and Leisa jumped into theirs.

"Brett, what's going on?" Beth asked as soon as they were on the road. Brett was going as fast as she dared.

"I don't even want to think about it."

"Well, what is it?" Beth replied. "At least tell me who the good guys and the bad guys are."

"Fred and Brian are the bad guys."

Beth considered this for a moment, then, "Are you a cop?"

"Hell no!" Brett said.

"Then why did you leave with Randi this afternoon?"

"Beth, she pulled me in for questioning. Scott Campbell's been killed," Brett replied. Brett didn't know what Randi McMartin would say, and she didn't know what Allie might say. She figured Brian and Fred had somehow carried through a plan to drug the girls, as Brian had done with Kathy in the past, and were now off to film the rapes. Brett decided her best bet was for honesty, to tell Beth all that she knew. It was best that she tell her, instead of having her find out some other way.

"Beth," Brett began, "I guess the best way to explain it all is to begin by saying that my name isn't really Brett Jameson. My real name is Brett Higgins."

~ ~ ~ ~ ~

Fred kept the gun painfully jabbed into Randi's side, and Brian had an extra gun in his lap in the front. Fred didn't like giving Brian a gun, but that seemed to be the only solution at the moment; he wanted some sort of backup.

He liked towns like Alma, large enough to not worry about strangers, but small enough to not have a very good police department. He had a bank account in a different country, under a different name, with almost 300 grand in it. Of course, he'd soon be adding to it all the money he had made here, and all of the money he'd make off the videos they'd shoot tonight.

This was going to be special. He'd have video accounts to help him relive the night over and over. He'd have the knowledge that he'd done something spectacular, something he could share, in part, with a few close friends. For a lot of money. Never before had he found such a ready accomplice as Brian Ewing, and he'd be sure to tell that to Brian, right before he killed him. He already knew how he'd get the gun from Brian. He'd simply pick it up when Brian was playing with the girls. After all, the movies they were going to sell couldn't have his own face in them. The ones they'd sell would have the girls, Brian, and some guy who was a friend of the man with the video equipment.

He'd kill all four of them — Randi, Allie, Kathy, and Brian — capturing it on film of course, and then go on a nice vacation. He smiled at the thought of the blood, oh so much blood, over and over again; after all, there were four people to dispose of now.

He was glad he'd tracked down better equipment with which to make tonight's movie, and in fact the man who would handle the distribution would also be the one there to do the filming. A man after his own heart, Tom had heartily approved the creation of a real snuff film. These were going to be extraordinary movies.

"Shit," Beth said, when Brett concluded her story a few minutes later. "And I thought some of the movies they made these days were fucked up."

"I hope I can trust you to not repeat any of this," Brett said, glancing over.

"Yeah, you can," Beth said, looking down. "Brett, what you said a coupla days ago . . . I . . . What did you mean?"

"That I think I know what you're goin' through," Brett said.

"You could tell?" Beth said in amazement.

"You have a lot to learn, kid," Brett said.

"So where are we going?"

"Detroit. The numbers Leisa got from that pad I recognized from a few years back. A man named Jack O'Rourke occasionally makes homemade videos of some of the girls who work at his topless bars. He has a small studio setup in an almost abandoned building in Detroit. I'd guess that's where Fred's taking them. He probably knows he can get even more money if the movies look a bit better than the ones I saw."

Brett glanced in the rearview mirror to make sure Madeline and Leisa were keeping up as she switched roads going through Lansing. Once she got to I-96 it'd be almost a straight shot to the studio, and it had just better be the right place, she silently prayed to herself.

"What is Brett's story? How come she can pick locks, and how did she know those phone numbers?" Leisa said as she cut through traffic, trying to keep up with Brett.

"She is a criminal. Reformed, of course."

"And Allie?"

"She used to be a police detective."

"Ah, of course. Maddy, you never cease to amaze me."

"Yes, I know, dear."

"Uh-oh," Leisa said, pumping the brakes. A cop flipped on his lights and came out of hiding right behind Brett.

"No, dear, not the brake. The gas, put the pedal to the metal." Madeline reached over and tapped Leisa's knee. "Do it now. We must make sure the officer pulls us over so he does not detain Brett."

"Oh no," Leisa said, quickly racing up behind the cop and cutting him off by pulling between him and Brett. "I'm gonna be in so much trouble."

Following the excellent directions written on his pad of paper, Fred easily located the building. Two men were waiting for them.

"I'm Tom and this is Dick," the larger and beefier of the men said. He had obviously identified the group, which wasn't very difficult because of the way they looked — two girls in prom dresses were a bit of a giveaway.

They moved inside. Dick threw Allie over his shoulder, Tom covered Randi with Brian's gun, and Brian carried Kathy. They went up three flights of stairs to the top floor of the building, where Tom unlocked a room that was secured with a heavy padlock.

Inside was the set for a bedroom with some other furnishings scattered about. It was low rent, and the different furnishing would allow for the set to be quickly and easily changed to different scenes, including an office and a classroom.

"I know who these two are and him," Tom said, "but what about her?" He indicated Randi.

"She's some dyke cop who was following us," Fred replied. "Who's your friend?"

"Dick is an actor. He's done these sorts of things before. Dick, watch everybody for a minute." He pulled Fred aside so that nobody else could overhear them. "You can do the girls, but you don't want us to sell that movie, y'see?"

"Yeah, I do. Don't need to implicate myself."

"Ya got that right. We can film it for ya, though — give ya somethin' to remember the night by."

Fred grinned his reply. He definitely wanted to remember this night.

Tom looked at the girls. "Ya sure weren't lying when you said these babes were hot."

"Don't I know it. Young, sexy, and beautiful. What more can we want?"

"Okay, so we start with a basic bedroom scene with Brian and the girls, then we do Dick in a classroom setting, then you can have some fun with them. We leave 'em all alive till the end, 'cause we don't want them to know what's coming. Don't need nobody gettin' scared on us, y'know?" He turned to look at the girls again. "I think I'll want to enjoy some of that sweet pussy too, though."

Fred turned to the set while Tom set up the cameras.

The girls were on the bed, looking simply luscious as they held each other. Brian was standing a few feet away, watching them. Brian sat down on the bed and began touching them through their clothes.

"Let's get this show on the road," Tom called. "Brian, you're up first — and I see you're ready for it." Brian already had a hard-on. "Just remember, you two," he said to Dick and Brian, "if the girls want to touch each other, y'know, finger each other, suck each other, anything like that, let them do it. Guys love girls doin' each other, y'know?"

"Yeah, I know," Brian said, advancing on the bed. Kathy and Allie were numbly holding each other. "Let's get you a little more comfortable," he said, sliding behind Allie and unzipping her dress. "I'm gonna stick it to you good, you know," he whispered, pushing the dress down so that the only thing she wore above the waist was her lacy, strapless bra. He pushed the dress down farther and looked at Kathy. "Don't she look hot?" he asked her, taking Kathy's hand and placing it on Allie's breast, guiding the thumb to caress the exposed, soft flesh at the top of Allie's breast.

Kathy was a natural. While she caressed Allie's breasts, seemingly hypnotized by them, Brian unzipped her dress and took it off her completely, getting upset when he realized that Kathy had on a garter belt and stockings. She had never worn them for him, so apparently she got them just for her hot date with Brett. Well, he'd really show that son-of-a-bitch tonight — he'd be the one fucking both girls. He laid Allie back and pulled off her dress. He knew she'd be wearing a garter belt and stockings too — the ones they had bought for her earlier.

He stood up, pulled his shirt off, and threw it on the ground. He was rock hard, probably harder than he'd ever been before. Not only did seeing the two girls touch each other turn him on, but also the idea of putting the screw to Brett Jameson. Both Allie and Kathy were incredibly hot, and he'd always wanted two girls at the same time. And having an audience was a turn-on, especially knowing how closely Tom and Dick were paying attention to him with their cameras. The thought of other guys watching the tape, seeing his big, hard dick and wishing they could be him was every kinky fantasy he'd ever had rolled into one.

"Here I come, girls," he said, "your Prince Charming in the flesh." He dropped his trousers and climbed into bed with them.


Horrified, Randi watched helplessly as she struggled futilely against the bonds that held her hands and legs tight.


"That's Fred's car, isn't it?" Brett said, pulling up a few spots over from it, beside the building with the wrought-iron fence around it.

Brett pulled her gun and headed into the building, fearful of what she would walk in on. She was surprised that the front door was unlocked. She motioned for silence to Beth, who had also pulled her gun, which she held with a shaking hand, and went into the darkened building.

She quickly looked over the first floor, then moved up to the second floor.

As soon as she hit the third floor she saw the door with the padlock hanging next to it. Bingo.

"Are you sure you're ready?" she whispered to Beth, who nodded. "You know this might — we might die."

Beth gulped. "I know."

Brett yanked open the door and jumped into the entrance. A darkened flight of stairs led to the next floor.

~ ~ ~ ~ ~

Fred looked at Tom. "Did you hear something?"

"Nah, man, just chill. Nobody knows about this joint," Tom said from behind the camera. "Now be quiet."

At Tom's urging Brian had taken off his jockey shorts and was now in bed with the two girls, trying to get them to caress him and lick him. Even drugged, though, Allie was focusing on Kathy, leaning in to kiss her. Kathy appeared surprised at first, but then got into it, meeting Allie's tongue with her own.

The guys were surprised by that, but now there wasn't a soft dick around the set.

"Get them completely naked," Tom whispered to Brian.

Brian placed Kathy's hand on his dick and reached to unclasp her bra.

Brett signaled silence to Beth and led the way up the dimly lit stairs. A few shafts of late sun sneaked in through the walls and from the open door gave them their only light.

Brett stealthily climbed the stairs, the only sound her breathing in her ears.

"I don't know what the fuck's happening," Tom murmured to Fred, "but we're gonna hafta let those girls suck each other's cunts." Fred didn't reply because he didn't need to. Both girls were now totally naked as Brian touched them all over, but they still had eyes only for each other. They were touching each other in far more intimate ways then Brian was.

He glanced over to see that Randi was still securely bound. He briefly wondered what her story was, because although she was obviously a dyke, she didn't seem to get turned on by this, just angrier by the moment. He thought she was going to blow up.

Dick was rubbing himself through the material of his jeans. Fred returned his interest to the young girls on the bed.

~ ~ ~ ~ ~

Brett stopped at the top of the staircase and lightly grasped the doorknob. She looked behind her to see that Beth, her face ashen and her body trembling, was right there.

Not much noise was coming from beyond the door, but Brett knew this had to be the place.

Taking her .357 in both hands, she stepped back, looked at Beth, and gave a ferocious kick right next to the doorknob. She hit the deck while shooting at the big, beefy man behind the camera who had his gun already drawn when Brett's shot spun him around and knocked him down.

A bullet whizzed by her, imbedding itself in the floor by her ear. Several more shots went over her head as Beth returned the fire from her position behind Brett. Beth's mark went down, and she finished unloading into him. Brett rolled to her feet just as Fred grabbed his gun and yanked Randi to her feet, using her as a human shield.

"Watch out!" Beth yelled, and Brett turned just in time to slam a second shot into the first, big cameraman, stopping him from his attempt to grab his gun again. Her first shot had winged him, but this time she was sure he was down for good.

Brian tried to use Allie as a shield, but her body was so limp she fell to the floor, leaving his flaccidity exposed, with pee running down his leg. He grabbed for the bedspread, but there was none.

Just as Fred fired at Brett, Brian jumped for the gun Dick had dropped when Beth shot him. Fortunately both Fred and Brian were terrible shots — incredibly wide at every attempt. "Hold it right there, asshole," Beth said, pointing her gun at Brian, but watching Fred out of the side of her eye.

Both men tried another shot, and Brett shot Brian's arm before diving out of the way. Brian screamed out in pain and dropped to the floor.

"Nice shot," Beth said appreciatively.

"Look, just take the girls and get outta here," Fred said with sweat dripping down his face.

"Beth, get them," Brett said, keeping her gun trained on Fred. Beth went over to the bedroom set, picked up Brian's gun and kicked him in the groin for good measure. Beth grabbed Brian's shirt, wrapped it around Kathy, and tried to push Allie into her dress. She gathered up Kathy and Allie as best she could, halfway dragging them across the room. Brett respected that Beth was obviously a good deal stronger than she looked.

"Take them to the car. I'll be right out," Brett said.

"But —"

"Do as I say."

Beth got the girls out of the room.

Brett and Fred stared at each other, he with his gun to Randi's head, and she with hers trained on him. "Okay, now you," Fred said, "or else this cop gets it."

Brett inched toward the door, even as Fred did likewise toward the door behind him.

"You got what you came for," Fred assured her. "And I'll let the cop go as soon as I'm safe."

Brett backed out the door. Why should she risk her neck for some cop who hated her guts?

She started down the steps. She knew Fred would end up killing Randi. She would die, but Brett would get out of the building and catch him when he tried to escape. He would pay for what he'd tried to do to Allie. And for what had already been done to Kathy.

Brett walked out into the fading daylight, and then it flashed through her mind. She remembered the winter night when she basically told Frankie to kill a man.

"Daniel McMartin," she whispered. She had probably helped the stupid cop's brother get killed. She had ordered him killed in fact.

Randi probably thought Brett was evil. As evil as Brett had at first thought Carl was, and now Fred.

But Brett wasn't the same woman anymore, and she could not leave Randi to die at the hands of that motherfuckin' pervert by a shot that was as good as one in the back.

She took the stairs two at a time and burst back into the room. Fred had vanished through the other door. Brett ran across the room, avoiding the blood on the floor and reloading her .357, chambering a round, as she ran, while looking about to ensure Fred was not hidden in the room. Brian still writhed moaning on the floor. She kicked his ribs as she ran past.

The other door only led to a set of steps that went up. The idiot had trapped himself on the roof. She sprinted up the narrow stairs, her anger building with each step.

Fred was on the edge of the building, looking about frantically for an escape route that did not exist. "You said you were leaving!" he whined.

"I lied. Let the cop go."

"You know, I always knew Brian was a witless toad," Fred said, still looking around even as he held his gun tightly to Randi's head. "Not ready for anything more real than his little toys. Wanting to, but not able, to run with the big boys."

"Brett Higgins," Randi said coldly, even though she was standing on the edge of a precipice and Brett was the only savior in sight. "You're supposed to be dead."

"Shut up, bitch," Fred said, twisting Randi's neck so she winced with pain. "Brett Higgins was a woman, or are you so screwed up sexually you can't tell one from the other?"

"You see, Fred," Brett said, trying to think of a way to warn Randi when she was going to shoot. "I'm a bad guy, and the cop you've got over there thought she'd killed me years ago."

"Then why don't you just kill us both?" Fred replied.

The setting sun burned on Brett's skin. She had to concentrate, focus. One wrong move and Randi would buy the farm. Brett had no question that if he had the chance, Fred would kill Randi. He wouldn't think to try to take out Brett first if Brett did anything. She had nothing to lose. His aim was bad, anyway.

"I could kill you," Brett said, catching Randi's eye. "I could kill you one," she tapped her foot once, "two," she tapped her foot again, "and bang! You'd be dead." Fred jerked and Randi nodded her head imperceptibly to say she caught the signal. Now, Brett just had to hope Fred hadn't. She also had to hope Fred wouldn't be able to pull his trigger in the microsecond he had between the time Brett pulled the trigger and the time he died. Her aim had to be the truest it'd ever been. Hopefully all those hours at the firing range hadn't been wasted.

"You little faggot chicken-shit," Fred sneered. "Why don't you just do it then?"

"As you well know," Brett said, an idea entering her head. "Both Kathy and Allie can attest to the fact that I ain't no faggot." She tapped her foot once and met Randi's eyes. "But only Allie and Randi know that I am really a lesbian." Twice. "I *am* Brett Higgins." Fred gripped Randi tightly to his chest, his face a glistening mask of sweat, but in the moment she had, Randi used all her strength to break his grip on her left arm so she could hit his gun hand and pull her head down.

Brett pulled the trigger. Fred's jaw dropped in amazement as her bullet ripped his head open. She leapt forward as the force from the shot sent him, with Randi still in his clutches backward, off the side of the building.

Brett lunged forward to the edge of the building. Randi, her hands still bound, held a desperate but tenuous grip on the edge of the frieze that encircled the building.

Randi was just out of Brett's reach. Her eyes darted from Brett's toward the ground. Brett knew that she was her only option, that there was nothing else Randi could do or hope for. The only thing between Randi and death was the woman she had tried to kill years before.

Brett, who was already hanging dangerously off the side of the building, tried to grab Randi. But Brett couldn't stretch those last few inches and have any chance of saving herself, let alone Randi.

Randi's hands began to slip off the stone. Her arms were flexed; she was putting herself and her strength to the limit trying to hang on. Just beyond Randi, Brett could see Fred's mangled corpse impaled on a spire of the wrought-iron fence.

Neither could bridge the gap between them.

"I've got you," Beth screamed as she grabbed Brett's ankles. Brett let go of the building, putting her trust in Beth's strength. As Brett grabbed Randi's wrist, she felt them all slip down even farther. Beth might be strong, but the weight of two full-grown women was too much. Beth slid farther toward the edge, holding on to Brett's ankles with all her strength, bracing her legs against the side of the building, using tension to keep them all from sliding off the roof to the pavement below.

Randi grabbed Brett's arms with both hands, her nails biting painfully into Brett's skin.

"Fuck!" Brett screamed as they slipped again. Beth's grip was slipping, and Brett felt a tingling through her body. It was difficult to breathe.

Brett had no grip on the building. If Beth let go, Brett would die with Randi.

Suddenly Brett felt more hands on her legs and ankles. She tightened her grip on Randi, knowing that Randi's strength was waning. Sweat dripped from her face and her heart beat frantically. She'd never been so scared before. She could hear gasps from whoever was helping Beth as they combined their weight and strength to pull both Brett and Randi up.

As her knees inched up over the edge, the stone scraped painfully up her leg. Every inch was agonizing. Her eyes held Randi's, whose grip on her arms was weakening. "I have you," she said, trying desperately to hang on. She hoped her eyes conveyed more confidence than she actually felt.

Randi grunted her reply, and the hands on Brett's ankles edged her back onto the roof of the building. Once Brett's knees were planted on firm ground, she used her last ounce of strength to hoist Randi over the top. Randi fell into her arms.

"Sorry, Randi, you're not my type," Brett said with a laugh to break the tension as Randi lay across her, panting. She looked up to find that Leisa and Madeline had finally caught up with them. "Too bad girls, you missed all the real excitement."

# 20

"I can't believe I never heard of you two being involved with Jack O'Rourke and sending him to prison — not even Greg knew!" Randi said, pacing Brett and Allie's hotel room where they had again taken up residence. Allie had spent Friday night in the hospital and then yesterday in the hotel recuperating from her ordeal.

"They wanted to protect us," Allie said, referring to how the D.A.'s office had kept it quiet so that they could more quickly and easily try O'Rourke and get him to prison.

Randi and Allie were alone in the room. Brett had agreed to be gone that afternoon so that Allie and Randi could have it out in privacy. Randi looked across the room at Allie. "And now you two are moving back down here?"

"Yes. We are."

"You're a damned good detective, Allie. I could probably get you

221

on the team," Randi said, referring to the organized crime team she was on. This would mean Allie could have full-time status as a detective.

Allie's eyes lit up. "That would be wonderful." She ran forward and hugged her. "Thank you."

"Thank you for figuring out what was going on up in Alma. I was really worried about my nephew."

"It wasn't me that figured it out, and you know that."

"But I don't like Brett. I never have and I never will. She's scum, and I don't see why you stay with her."

"I'm telling you again — she never killed your brother," Allie replied, facing off with her. She knew Brett hadn't killed Daniel. Brett had told Frankie to kill him. And Allie knew that at that point Daniel was a drug addict out of control. He was also a rapist, a thief, and a murderer. And if he had lived, he would've killed somebody Brett cared about. Allie could tell Randi that Brett hadn't killed Daniel because she hadn't. Frankie had.

"It doesn't matter; she's still a criminal."

"Why the hell can't you understand that she could've just let Fred kill you?"

"So she did one good thing in her entire life!"

"Not only did she go back after you, but she also practically jumped off a goddamned building after you!"

"Knowing what you know, how can you go on with her?" Randi interrupted, stopping and facing Allie.

Allie shook her head in frustration. Randi was just too damn stubborn. "She's reformed. She risked her life for you. If Leisa and Madeline hadn't gotten there when they did, she would've gone down with you."

"I know that. I was there, remember?"

"Is that the only way you'll have anything to do with her — if she's risking her life to save yours?"

"Allie . . ."

"Randi," Allie said, laying her arms on Randi's shoulders. "You said you loved me once . . ."

"I still do, Allie," Randi replied, looking deep into Allie's eyes.

Allie suddenly realized just how alone Randi was.

Randi looked deep into the blue pools of Allie's eyes as her hands slowly came to rest on Allie's hips. The woman she loved was totally in love with the woman she hated. Life was hell. "What are you trying to do, Allie?"

"I'm trying to make sure that you're okay with the fact that we're moving back here."

"As all right as I'll ever be."

# 21

Brett found Kathy at home alone. Kathy greeted her with a hug and a kiss on the cheek when she opened the door. Brett pulled back from her and looked deep into her Bambi brown eyes.

"Brett, I wasn't sure if I was ever going to see you again," Kathy said, joy lighting up her eyes. "I can't say enough about all that you did." The newspapers still had not caught on to the fact that Brett was really a woman.

Kathy felt so good in Brett's arms, so right. But Brett knew what she had to do. She couldn't let Kathy find out and then have to deal with it on her own. The easy thing to do would've been to just disappear forever from Kathy's life and not confront any of these issues. But of course the easiest thing would've been for Brett herself to have gotten involved with drugs all those many years ago, just like her cousin Marie had.

"Come on, we need to sit down," Brett said, leading Kathy into the living room where they sat on the couch that they had lain on about a week ago, making out. Kathy wrapped Brett's arms around her, cuddling in close. "How are you doing?" Brett asked.

Kathy shrugged, sighed, and pulled away. "As good as I can be, considering . . ." Brett had convinced the police not to let anyone know about the earlier videos because she didn't want Kathy to know the full extent of what had happened. "I barely remember a thing about Friday," she said. "But I do know that Brian had probably done it to me before."

Brett turned on the couch so that she could face Kathy, who was staring straight ahead. She cupped Kathy's face in her hands. "You probably shouldn't think too much about it." Scenes from those awful videos rushed through her mind. All the videos were now in Brett's custody, including the tapes from Friday, just in case any of the legal suits required them.

"They did do it before, didn't they? Tell me." Her eyes focused on Brett's.

"Yeah. They did."

Kathy shivered. "I don't understand . . ."

"Brian will be spending quite a while in prison. Fortunately, he recently turned eighteen so he can be tried as an adult. His future, his life, is destroyed. He'll pay. Fred was an evil man who has now been put out of his misery."

Kathy shook her head and looked at Brett. "What I still don't get is just who you are. The papers said very little about it."

"Allie and I are old friends of Madeline's. Allie used to be a cop, a detective."

"And you?"

"I was what most would consider a criminal."

Kathy smiled. She didn't believe Brett's easy explanation.

Brett couldn't look at her. "I'm a thirty-three-year-old ex-criminal. You can do much better."

"Thirty-three?" Kathy exclaimed in shock. "But you, you look nineteen! that means you're almost twice as old as I am." A tear ran down her cheek. Brett ached to wipe it off. "And what do you mean a 'criminal'?" Her brown eyes looked deep into Brett's.

"I've done some things I'm not really proud of."

Kathy looked away for a moment. "I don't care," she said finally. "I still want you. I can't help myself."

"My real name is Brett Higgins."

"Are you really Allie's brother?"

"No." She didn't want to say it. She didn't want to explain who she really was. But she had to tell Kathy that she was really a woman.

Kathy pulled away from Brett. "You're acting strange. What's going on?"

Brett turned to face her. "I'm so sorry, hon."

Kathy looked as if Brett had slapped her. "Oh god. You're her boyfriend, aren't you?"

"Almost." Brett took a deep breath. Kathy's face dropped. "But not quite." Kathy's eyes lit up with a glimmer of hope. "I'm her girlfriend."

"What? I don't get it."

"We're lesbian lovers."

"I . . . I don't understand . . ."

"I'm a woman. I'm a lesbian, and Allie is my lover."

"No, no," Kathy said, turning away. "You're lying. I don't know why, but you're lying."

"Kathy," Brett went to gather her into her arms, but Kathy pulled away and turned on her.

"How could you?" Kathy screamed, slapping Brett's face.

"I didn't mean to hurt you," Brett said, running her hand over her own cheek, feeling the sting.

"Bastard!" Kathy yelled, again slapping her before turning away. Brett grabbed her by the shoulders and turned Kathy to face her. "Prick!" Kathy screamed as she kneed Brett in the groin, which didn't have the desired effect but was painful nonetheless. Kathy collapsed into a corner. "Leave me alone."

"I didn't want to hurt you."

"Why?" Kathy was crying openly now.

"I couldn't pass as a teenaged girl, but I could as a teenaged boy."

"You made love to me!"

Oh no, Brett thought to herself. She wasn't going to let this dissolve into *Desert Hearts*, with who did what to whom and why. "What was I supposed to do? You would've been suspicious otherwise!"

"It could've stopped at a kiss, Brett," Kathy replied. "Whoever the fuck you really are."

Brett painfully knew that what Kathy said was the truth. "If I didn't do the things I had done, my cover would've been blown."

"Why me?" Kathy asked, wiping at the tears that had finally stopped.

"I needed you to get to Brian. You clued me in to a lot of things. We couldn't've done it without you, y'know."

"We — you and Allie," Kathy replied.

"Me and Allie."

"You have no idea what you've done to me," Kathy said, her face an expressionless mask except for the tears that had started flowing again.

"Yes, I do," Brett said, slowly moving toward Kathy. "And I wish to God I could undo it."

"You used me."

Brett knew what she had to say to Kathy, knew why she had really needed to see her. "I fell in love with you." She looked deep into Kathy's brown eyes, losing herself for a moment. "I shouldn't've done the things I did, but there's nothing I can do about it now." She looked away from the hurt in Kathy's eyes. "Just know that I love you, and didn't mean to hurt you."

The silence stretched out until Kathy gently touched Brett's face. Brett looked once again into her eyes. "Do you really?" Kathy asked.

Brett reached over and wiped the tears from Kathy's cheeks. She held Kathy's face and looked into her eyes before she spoke. "If it weren't for Allie, I would be here trying to talk you into running away with me," Brett said truthfully. "But, again, if it weren't for Allie, I'd have probably ended up dead on some street in Detroit."

Kathy leaned in to Brett's arms. Brett held her, running her hands through her hair and down her back. Enjoying the silky feel of the strands playing through her fingers. Enjoying the softness of Kathy's breasts pressed against her own. Brett felt a sigh run through Kathy's entire being.

"I'm gay, aren't I?" Kathy whispered, her face still buried in Brett's neck.

"Only you know the answer to that," Brett said, pulling back to once again study Kathy's lovely face while thinking about how, in the videos, when she was drugged, Kathy was interested in Allie and how Brian was merely an annoying distraction.

"I'm scared," Kathy said.

"Someday, Kat, you'll meet the right person for you, but I can't tell you if that person is going to be a man or a woman. All I know is that you deserve to be happy. But the only way you'll find that happiness is if you put all this behind you and look for it."

Kathy leaned forward to brush her lips over Brett's. Brett knew she shouldn't be doing this, she knew the age difference, she knew she should think of Allie, and that Kathy was confused, but all that didn't matter as she melted into the kiss and enjoyed Kathy's body pressed against her own.

Brett slipped her tongue into Kathy's mouth, gasping at the heat between them.

"I wish I didn't like Allie so much," Kathy finally murmured.

Brett kissed the top of Kathy's head.

"I think deep down inside, I'm not really surprised to find out you're a woman." She pulled up Brett's shirt a bit to place her hand on her waist.

"Kathy," Brett murmured, trying to move her hand.

"No, don't . . . Brett. I need to see what you really look like. You look young for thirty-three."

"Grecian Formula works wonders."

Kathy ran her fingers over Brett's shoulders, down her arms, squeezing her muscles. She ran her fingers down the front of Brett's chest, over her breasts. "Isn't that uncomfortable?" she asked, fingering the Ace bandage. Brett had worn it one final time so Kathy wouldn't figure out prematurely what she needed to tell her.

"I'm not too fond of it."

"Take it off," Kathy ordered, unbuttoning Brett's shirt.

Brett took hold of Kathy's hands. "Kathy, I can't."

"Yes, you can." Something in her face was different. Two weeks ago she had been a girl, and now she was a woman. She had an understanding and a wisdom in her eyes now. It was strange the things that caused change in people. "Brett, I know that after today we'll never see each other again. I understand you'll leave here today and go back to Allie. But I need this. I need to make love with you as a woman. I need to see you, and have you love me, and me love you, as the two women we really are."

Brett stood, took Kathy's hand, and led her to the bedroom.

She pulled Kathy into her arms, pressing their bodies together, feeling Kathy with her body, her lips and her hands. Kathy's body was perfect, the body of a perfect eighteen-year-old. She started to pull Kathy's shirt off.

"Oh no, you don't," Kathy said, stopping Brett's hands. "I let you do it last time, but this time I need to know you, Brett, know you as the woman you are." She pulled off Brett's shirt and T-shirt, leaving her wearing only the Ace bandage and a gold chain.

Kathy started to unravel the bandage. "No," Brett said, holding Kathy's hands and looking directly into her eyes. She pulled Kathy into her arms, and they kissed with their eyes open. Looking into Kathy's eyes when they kissed sent a bolt of lightning through Brett.

Kathy took off Brett's Ace bandage, let it drop to the ground, and fondled Brett's breasts until her nipples were rock hard. "You really are a woman," she said without amazement.

Brett pulled off Kathy's shirt and bra and brought her hands to Kathy's softness, moaning at the feeling of the extended nipples against her palms while their tongues danced in each other's mouths.

Kathy pulled away from Brett and gasped. "I want . . . I need to be inside you," she said. "Will you let me be inside you?"

Even as she was shocked at the words, as the words sent a thrill through her, Brett placed Kathy's hand on her crotch.

Kathy looked at Brett, feeling the bulk at the crux of her legs. "Socks?" she said, confused.

"Mr. Softie," Brett replied with a grin.

Kathy unbuckled Brett's belt, unsnapped and unzipped her jeans, reached into her boxers under Mr. Softie and felt curly hair. She went down deeper and slid her fingers against Brett's wetness and gasped.

Tingles shot through Brett's body, and she pushed her hips against Kathy while her knees became weak. Kathy slid a finger into Brett.

"Oh god," Brett murmured, breaking their kiss. She suddenly

realized that somehow they had switched positions so that she was now the one pressed against the wall.

She gently pulled Kathy's fingers from her, picked her up and laid her on the bed, all the while wanting to feel Kathy's fingers inside her again. She went to take off Kathy's jeans, but Kathy stopped her.

"No, only if you take yours off," Kathy said, pushing Brett away and standing.

Brett reached down and pulled off her jeans, underwear, and socks, as did Kathy. She then pulled Kathy against her, their naked bodies pressed tightly together, and kissed her deeply.

It normally would have stunned Brett when Kathy suddenly and forcefully pushed her onto the bed, except that she wanted Kathy too much.

Kathy knelt on the bed looking down at Brett's naked body. "Oh god, you are so beautiful. I never would've believed your body looked like this."

Brett sat up and grabbed Kathy, but Kathy said, "No," and seized Brett's wrists, pushing her back onto the bed. Brett could've overpowered her, but instead she leaned forward to nibble at Kathy's breasts, which hung tantalizingly close to her mouth.

"Oh no, you don't," Kathy said, again kneeling upright and looking down at Brett's naked body. Brett lay there, under her scrutiny, wanting her. She didn't normally let women, even Allie, look at her like that, or make love to her, but she wanted to feel Kathy inside of her again, wanted Kathy to make her come, wanted to give herself to Kathy, such as Kathy had already given herself to Brett.

"I never knew it could be like this, I never knew anything could be so soft . . ." Kathy said, running her hands over Brett's body, examining her, feeling her, from the muscles of her arms, to the softness of her breasts, to the hardness of her nipples and the tautness of her stomach. She ran her hands all over Brett, increasingly more bold till she went below Brett's stomach to run her fingers through the damp patch of hair between Brett's legs. Brett was squirming.

Kathy moved farther down on the bed so that she could kneel between Brett's legs, opening her up to look at her. Brett took a deep breath, not believing she was letting Kathy do that. But Kathy was making Brett incredibly hot. Letting Kathy so unabashedly examine her made her unbelievably wet, and she wanted Kathy to fulfill the promise that it all gave.

Brett crossed her arms behind her head and opened her legs a bit farther, giving Kathy access. Kathy held Brett open and ran her thumbs up and down her clit.

"So wet . . ." Kathy said to herself. "Oh god . . ." She eased two fingers into Brett, still looking directly into Brett's eyes, which sent another bolt of lightning through Brett. She was looking into this woman's eyes, looking at this woman who possessed her, feeling the odd sensation of those fingers inside her.

"I want to do to you what you did to me," Kathy said, lowering her head and stretching out on the bed so that she could taste Brett. When her warm, wet, soft tongue touched Brett, Brett could've melted. Kathy ran her tongue up and down Brett, and it was as if she was listening to Brett's every movement and noise, because she knew just what Brett wanted, what Brett needed, to take her there.

Brett always felt a little guilty when she let a woman give her such pleasure, as if she couldn't understand that another woman could derive as much pleasure from making love to her as Brett could from making love to the other woman. And if the truth were told, she also didn't think she deserved it. But for this moment, she let herself enjoy what Kathy was doing to her, which sent shivers through her, making her melt, putting her on edge . . . Every fiber of her being felt the sensation accumulating between her legs, right where Kathy licked and thrust . . .

She started shivering and shaking, and then she was writhing across the bed, her body out of control, reaching the peak, hitting it, filled wholly and totally with the greatest ecstasy.

"Aaahhhh," Brett breathed, reaching down to pull Kathy's head away from her. Kathy resisted, until Brett finally had to cover herself to keep Kathy and her tongue away.

"Are you sure?" Kathy asked, with a glimmer of mischief in her eyes.

Brett could only gulp for air. "Get up here," she gasped, pulling Kathy into her arms. Brett was used, spent, wasted, but as soon as she felt Kathy's soft breasts against her, the silk of her skin, the smell of her intoxicating scent, she began to come back to life.

Then she remembered that this was her last chance, ever, with this incredible young woman. Her last chance to show her how exquisite it was to love a woman and be loved in return.

Brett's hands began to roam Kathy's body with a purpose, with this realization in mind.

"I'm not done with you, you know," Brett said, sitting up and pushing Kathy onto her back, holding her there.

Beth pulled up, parked, and then stood behind the rock on which Kathy sat. Hands deep in her pockets, she looked at the graceful back and spoke softly. "You didn't make it to graduation."

Kathy shook her head without turning around. "I just couldn't."

Beth sat next to her on the rock. There was a somewhat awkward pause, so Kathy said, "How's your sister doing?"

"As good as she can, I guess. Finding Scott like that really messed her up, but at least now she's in rehab and has been clean for a coupla weeks." Kathy nodded her reply, so Beth forced herself to speak again. "Remember when we were young? We were going to grow up to do great things, and be lifelong friends as well."

Kathy still refused to look at her. "In this world, dreams rarely come true," she said somberly.

"Some of yours did. You grew up to be captain of the cheerleading squad. You went with the captain of the football team," Beth replied. She had lived through this moment, or one similar, ever since that fateful night. She had just come from home, where she had gone after commencement, and then Brett called to ask her to talk with, and help, Kathy. That was the only way Beth had been able to screw up the courage to speak to Kathy.

"How did you know where to find me?" Kathy asked, still staring straight ahead.

"Brett," Beth replied.

"How's she doin'?" Kathy asked. Beth could've sworn she heard Kat choke back a tear.

"She's okay. She asked me to talk with you. She's worried about you, you know." When Kathy still did not answer, Beth took her hand. "Kat, what really happened with you and Brett?"

"I fell in love with her," Kat said after a moment's pause. "With *her*."

Beth knelt in front of her and took her into her arms, holding her as she cried against Beth's shoulder. Her heart went out to Kat. She wanted, hoped, and prayed, to make it better.

After what seemed an eternity, Kathy stopped crying, but she did not move from Beth's arms. "Beth," she murmured, her breath tickling Beth's neck, "back when we pledged our eternal friendship, and I wanted to be captain of the cheerleaders, and date the captain of the football team, what did you dream?"

Beth shrugged. "Not much."

"C'mon," Kathy said, sitting up and looking into Beth's hazel eyes. "What did you want?"

Beth considered the question as she looked deep into Kathy's beautiful brown eyes. "I wanted to grow up to marry you," she said truthfully as she leaned forward for love's first kiss.

# 22

The phone rang just as Brett was tossing the rest of her clothes into a duffel bag. She was glad to be leaving the hotel finally. She and Allie had found a bungalow in Royal Oak and were moving right away. Royal Oak was a queer neighborhood along the Woodward corridor.

"Hello?" she answered the phone.

"Brett. It's Randi. Is Allie there?" Brett and Randi were barely on speaking terms.

"Yeah, just a sec, I'll get her." Brett covered the receiver and yelled, "Allie! It's that cop again!" Allie and Randi had been talking quite a bit lately, and Brett had a sinking feeling that she knew what it was about — a position for Allie on the special organized crime team that Randi was on.

Allie entered from the bathroom wearing only two towels — one around her body and one on her head.

"Hey, Randi, what's up?" Allie asked as soon as Brett gave her the phone. Brett stood behind her and kissed her damp skin between the shoulder blades. "Um," Allie said into the phone, twitching a bit at the brush of Brett's lips. She turned around and gave Brett the eye.

Brett returned her look with one of her very best innocent puppy looks. Allie still shooed her away.

"That's wonderful, Randi!" Allie said into the phone.

Brett picked up the paper and flipped through the local news, stopping at an article about another dead dancer being found in a Dumpster in Detroit. She read the details closely. She was going back in business with Frankie, so she'd have her own stable of dancers to look after.

"Guess what, sweetie?" Allie said a few moments later, sitting next to Brett on the bed. "Randi got me a spot on the organized crime team! Isn't that wonderful?" She had taken the towel off her head and was now covered with only the one towel.

Brett hated the idea of Allie being a cop. Hated the idea of Allie working with Randi, being in danger, taking risks, and being on a team that was far too concerned with the areas in which she, Brett, earned her living.

But she couldn't say that to Allie, because being on the team was what Allie had always wanted to do. Just as Brett had hated being away from her own work, so had Allie.

So Brett looked deep into Allie's blue eyes, smiled, and said, "Yes, dear, that's wonderful."

After all, she loved the woman enough to do anything for her.

# Visit
# Bella Books
## at

# www.bellabooks.com